Chance

Peter Dudgeon

For Emma and Lucy.

Chapter One

October 2nd 2014

With no strangers to kill, I killed time instead; surveying suburbia through wooden slats. The playing cards, which only twenty minutes ago had been virginal and eager to fall into my palm, had become warm and sticky from shuffling. I heard myself sigh, as I slipped the pack into my jacket pocket.

I splayed the blind with my fingers. It was strange to see the sun again. It sent a low, triangular beam across the bonnet. In the middle of the sun shard, was a wasp. When humans feel sunshine they slow down, relax. Not that wasp. He relished his illuminated orgy; back arched, tail thrusting and pumping at the metallic paint. Eventually, he slowed, lost grip and rolled down the bonnet, drunk from stinging.

And it struck me. He wasn't concerned about his victim, about how much it felt the prick and the poison. He just loved the act itself. I empathise. Does that make me different? Does that make me weird? I guess so.

I'm not like the others. I'm different in many ways, the most fundamental of which is this: I'm not afraid of death. They are, they're terrified. Actually, that's not quite true. It's not death they're afraid of. It's the not knowing.

You see it in their faces as the hearse drives by. Look carefully. They're not thinking about the slow failing agony of cancer or the stabbing hand of heart failure. No.

They think, "I don't know when, or how it will happen to me." And at the epicentre of their self-pity is the scariest possibility, that beyond death could be nothing but a dark, stretching void. Is it a possibility or a certainty? It's the not knowing which scares them. Or rather, the knowing that they will never find out until, of course, the reaper comes.

Whereas I, on the other hand, love the unknown. Each time I do it, one of them could kill me, could send me into the void, or to a better life. Or I might survive, and they might die. I love the not knowing, of leaving it to chance.

Chapter Two

Cassie Janus approached the gates of Manor Forest primary school. She was late. She paused before the gate, peering around the hedge to make sure Rachel wasn't there waiting to swing the gate back at her. Or something worse.

She was in luck, Rachel and the rest of the kids must have already gone inside. She hurried through the gate and along the path, wishing she hadn't brought so many books, the straps of her rucksack cutting into her collar bones.

Cassie's primary school was much like any other. There were two hundred and sixteen pupils spread over seven academic years. First year pupils were still falling for 'fingers on lips.' The older kid's playtime bravado masked the looming fear of going to secondary school, of being the new kids once again.

For normal kids the fun of first friendships, of playing Tig and learning Hopscotch overwhelmed the fleeting pain of naive playground bitching. And for Cassie? 'The happiest days of your life,' her mother had once said. A hollow platitude when you're young, especially when you're Cassie Janus.

Cassie struggled through the entrance to the school. The door's strong hinge trapped her overflowing bag, as though trying to slow the progress of a tortoise by grabbing its shell. She finally got free, and looked along the corridor, the main thoroughfare leading to the classrooms.

Rachel stood at the far end, leaning against a long line of coat-pegs. Her two loyal friends, Maria and Tanya, flanked her.

Everyone knew which coat-peg was Rachel's, not just from the name card, but from the red devil horns she'd penned above the 'a' and the 'e' of her name on the card's laminated surface. It was a signature she'd scrawled and scratched on concealed walls, bench legs and bike racks. Cassie couldn't understand why a teacher hadn't asked her to scrub the devil horns off the laminate. Were they as scared of Rachel as Cassie was?

She hung up her coat. Mercifully, her peg was at the nearest end, a good ten yards from where Rachel stood. Cassie's adversary had broad shoulders and thick forearms, for a girl of her age. Thick Auburn hair and a perpetually rouge complexion reflected Rachel's temper, which frequently erupted.

What was Rachel hanging around for? Classes were just starting.

Waiting for me? She gulped.

There was no other route. She had to pass Rachel to get to class. She hurried, her left arm brushing the wall as she walked.

"Anus!" Cassie kept her eyes on the floor, ignoring Rachel. "Don't blank me, Anus." Rachel stepped away from the pegs, towards Cassie. Maria and Tanya shadowed her.

She had to say something, "My name is Janus. Cassie Ja-nus. Get it?" Cassie's weak tone and avoiding gaze sapped the strength from her words.

"Yeah I get it ... Anus. God you're such a freak. You think you're so clever, don't you. Actually, you're not an anus; you're an arse, a smart arse. At home time, I'm going to give you something to figure out."

Cassie was determined not to cry. She looked up at Rachel, feeling short and weak. Cassie hadn't felt the weight of Rachel's fist before, but others had, and it was only a matter of time. She tried to envisage winning a fight against Rachel but couldn't picture it. She was so thin and pale that some kids called her spaghetti-legs. Her feet were growing out of proportion with the rest of her body. Some shoes gave her a clown-like appearance. She tripped frequently. Cassie coming out on top in a fight with Rachel? Nobody was going to make that bet.

"Just leave me alone. My mum will be waiting to pick me up after school so don't even think of starting anything." She took an arced path along the corridor, putting distance between herself and her tormentors. Rachel closed in and shoved Cassie as she passed. Cassie ricocheted off the wall. The plaster slapped painfully against her shoulder and she involuntarily emitted a 'humph.' Rachel and her friends giggled as Cassie lost her battle to remain upright, falling to her knees and tearing her thick black tights in the process.

She got back to her feet and hurried away, making sure they couldn't see the tear forming in the corner of her eye. She was less upset by the pain in her knees and shoulder than by the thought she'd ruined clothes her mother couldn't afford to replace. Once around the corner, using the sleeve of her dirty cardigan, she wiped tears away from each cheek, before walking into class.

On days like today, I just feel like blurting it out. I'd love to tell Rachel what her stepdad's going to do, just to see the look on her stupid face. That would shut her up.

But Cassie knew she wouldn't tell. She was smart enough to figure the consequences; normal people can't see through the eyes of others and how else could she know? More than wanting to be free of Rachel, more than wanting her mother to get better, more than anything in the world, she wanted to be normal.

"Cassie, you're late, sit down."

"Sorry Miss."

Chapter Three

Alfred Tucker leant against the prison wall rolling a cigarette, the yellow tinge of his wrinkled fingers a seasoned smoker's souvenir. An unusually warm summer had given way to short days and dark, bitter nights. Alfred cupped his hand around the cigarette, protecting it from the wind. He successfully lit up on his third attempt.

The street was intermittently illuminated by streetlights, one either side of the prison gates. Despite his desire to get as far away from that place as possible, Alfred stood beneath the weak incandescence, smoking and contemplating what would happen now. He turned up the collar of his denim jacket.

The probation service had organised a halfway house. Alfred pulled out its business card from his pocket. He tilted the card at various angles, catching sufficient light for his ageing eyes to discern the address.

135 Archers street, yeah I remember where that is. Half an hour to get there, I reckon. If I walk quickly it might keep me warm. Jesus, look at the state of the traffic. Doesn't anybody walk nowadays?

As he walked he indulged in a bad habit. It was one he'd formed and tried to break during his eighteen years in prison: reflecting on the events leading to his conviction.

What if things had worked out differently?

He recalled a vivid image of Emma's face on their wedding day. As he raised her veil, the warmth of her broad smile and the reciprocated desire behind those deep brown eyes, which made them sparkle, overwhelmed him. He had never before felt love and desire with such intensity as in that moment and doubted he ever would again.

During his eighteen-year sentence, he'd spent immeasurable time apportioning blame for Emma's infidelity. Work had been all consuming and, with a baby on the way, money had become tight. He'd grafted through long, hard shifts and the time they spent together had become scarce. She'd been distant for months before Alfred finally asked her what was wrong. All he could get out of her was, "I'm just tired."

Consumed by bitterness, throughout his early years in prison, he'd laid the blame for her affair squarely on Emma's shoulders, but age and endless opportunities for reflection led him to feel partly, if not wholly, responsible.

Oh God, what if I'd just stopped to think for a moment before acting?

The 'What if?' game was seductive.

What if I hadn't rowed with my supervisor that night? What if I had completed the night shift as planned? Would her affair have run its course without me being any the wiser?

Asking himself these questions was a pointless exercise. He *had* left work early, he *had* found them and he *had* beaten that man into a coma from which there was no return. Still, now he was a free man, the 'What if?' game didn't feel like the torture it had been in the confines of his cell.

Time to start over. He looked down at the suede holdall by his side. It was light, easy to carry. Having few possessions, he wondered why he didn't feel impoverished. Owning little brought an unexpected feeling of liberation: he had little to lose.

Alfred paused at the intersection of Nile Street and Rochester Avenue. The foolproof route would be along Nile Street, but turning left down Rochester Avenue would cut ten minutes off the walk (if he remembered correctly, a big if.) Rochester Avenue was winding, ill-lit and strangely foreboding but the prospect of cutting short the walk and getting out of the cold was irresistible.

Rochester Avenue it is.

He was making swift progress when the loud and assured voice of a man made him stop and turn his head, "Excuse me. Could I get a light?" The words were spoken from a narrow alley to his left. Alfred took a step towards the voice. His eyes adjusted to the dark and he saw the silhouette of a figure standing between an industrial bin and a pile of black bin bags. A fox, foraging in one of the bags, turned its head towards Alfred then scurried off into the distance.

"Sure," Alfred rummaged in his inside pocket for his lighter. The alleyway shielded the wind and silence hovered, until his lighter broke it, with a burst of raking clicks. The gas ignited as he struck the flint for a fourth time.

The flame, briefly illuminating the alleyway, was subsumed by the Taser's blue haze. The pain, which shot from the top of Alfred's skull to the base of his spine, gave way to a numb floating feeling as his legs buckled beneath him. Alfred lost his fight to remain conscious a moment after realising that he was being dragged down the dark alley, a noose rhythmically tightening and loosening around his ankles with each concerted effort.

Chapter Four

Cassie, who was normally attentive, stared out of the classroom window, hardly registering the swirling leaves rising and falling in the cruel October wind. Would her prayers be answered, would her mother meet her after school? Being met at the gates had started out as normality, drifted into exception and was now a rare event, particularly since Mummy had sold their old Mini. Not having a car didn't concern Cassie, walking with her mum was great, even when Mummy got tempted by passing taxis and hailed one, halfway home.

Would Mummy come to meet her today? She doubted it. Any other day, it wouldn't matter so much. The usual end of day pattern was this: wait until all the other mums and dads had come and gone, until the other kids had skipped or ridden home, full of stories about their day at school. And Fifteen minutes after school closing time she'd know that Mummy had got sidetracked again and Cassie would walk home on her own. Again.

It wasn't so bad, a forty-five minute walk, that's all. She didn't even mind when it rained. The rain meant the walk past the park would be okay. Rachel didn't hang out at the park when the weather was bad. Cassie looked up at the clock: two forty-five. Three quarters of an hour of English and then she would find out for sure whether her mum would be there to save her from Rachel.

Time, please pass slowly.

Nine-year-olds, you had to love them, but they could try your patience, especially when thirty of them have no interest in what you're teaching. Today was more challenging than most. Miss Hilary April, Cassie's teacher for most of her lessons, was wilting; constantly attempting to regain her pupils' attention had sapped her energy.

Hilary relied on Cassie answering questions, when all others were silent, but half an hour into the lesson, Cassie hadn't uttered a word. Hilary walked up to the side of Cassie's desk and crouched down, the way only primary school teachers can, knees together, with perfect poise.

Cassie's dark fringe was usually curtained either side of her face to disguise a long overdue cut. Today it hung over her eyes, covering the top half of her pupils. "Cassie, are you okay?"

"Yes miss."

"Are you sure?"

"Yes Miss, Just focussing. I thought I was going to fit again, so I'm concentrating."

"I think you better see the nurse."

"No, Miss it's okay, I can feel it going away, I just need to sit quietly."

Cassie had only suffered a seizure once in Miss April's class and it scared the life out of her and her pupils. The first aid certificate hanging above Hilary's desk proved irrelevant as she entirely forgot what she was supposed to do. She'd watched Cassie twitching on the floor helplessly, involuntarily kicking Alex's chair (Alex was Cassie's class neighbour.) Alex had whimpered and then cried. Blood had trickled from the corner of Cassie's mouth as one of the kids spoke up, "Miss should I get the nurse?"

The intense memory lingered. Fragments of that day crept back, distracting Hilary as she tried to teach. She caught herself frequently glancing in Cassie's direction, having to restart conversations. "Sorry, Hun, what was your question again?" A freckle-laden boy with tight ginger curls said, "I *said* ... can ... I ... go ... to the toilet ... Miss."

"Yes Eddie, of course, I'm sorry."

As they mercifully drifted towards home time, Hilary decided to set the class a short task, to read the first chapter of 'Diary of a Wimpy Kid'. Ten blissful minutes of peace to spend working out what to cook for tea, whether to pop round to Mum's to pick up those flapjacks and wheel her bin out; mundane distractions from distressing flashbacks of Cassie's seizure.

Of course, Cassie was first to finish reading. Hilary watched as Cassie stared out of the window. She was meticulously pinching the elastic pale skin of each knuckle, swapping hands when she ran out of fingers.

Cassie, what the hell are you thinking about? Your eyes are so vacant. What planet are you on? Stay with us Cassie.

Hilary couldn't wait for the others to finish; the home-time bell was approaching. "Okay, let's stop there. What did we think? Err, Cassie could you start?"

Cassie shook her head and looked towards her teacher, finally back on earth.

"I think the characters are weak and the descriptions are lazy."

Sometimes I can't believe she's only a kid. She thinks with a depth that's rare in adults, rarer still in a nine-year-old.

"That's an interesting view Cassie."

The bell rang and a shuffling hubbub grew.

"We'll talk about it tomorrow. Right, you can leave when you're ready."

As Cassie reached the classroom door, she turned for a moment, looking at Miss April. She opened her mouth, in freeze-frame, then closed it and walked out.

Chapter Five

"What's that?"

"What's what?"

"Look up there, on the side of the escalator."

"I don't see anything."

"Fran, are you blind?"

"Oh, that. So somebody's dropped a piece of card. You really must be bored. Just a quick look round Harvey Nichols, then we'll get a coffee, I promise."

"It's a playing card. Don't you think that's bizarre?"

"Dacia, you do get amazed by the most mundane things."

"Don't you find stuff like that weird? Here we are, entering a department store in Knightsbridge, a place where you could spend years and never see anyone playing cards ... and there's a random playing card on the side of an escalator. It's a sign. I'm picking it up."

Francesca shook her head and laughed. "You are *so* random."

Dacia let out a long sigh as she dropped her Next shopping bags on the white wicker chair beside her. "So what are you drinking?"

"Vanilla latte. Bring lots of sugar."

As Francesca disappeared inside to buy coffee, Dacia watched people around her. More than anything, she noticed women and their clothes. So many of her clients were wealthy and, as she cut their hair, she always noticed their shoes, their jackets.

One day, I'll have a pair of Jimmy Choo shoes. Maybe I'll have saved up enough by next year.

A woman, sitting three tables away, drew Dacia's attention. Her legs were crossed and she was reading. She was so engrossed in Hello magazine that she didn't notice Dacia staring.

My God, she's beautiful. If those are hair extensions, I can't tell from here. Look at her DKNY watch. How much did that cost? Two hundred? With that suit she looks like a businesswoman. How much do you earn?

Dacia stared down at the fake Armani watch she'd bought from a market stall in Croydon and shrugged her shoulders, trying to stop herself feeling envious and failing miserably. Looking up again, she noticed a thickset man sitting at a table. In contrast to the woman she'd been spying on, he did nothing to damage her self esteem; Grey V-necked T-shirt, faded jeans, Casio digital watch, Converse trainers and a Targus rucksack. Entirely unremarkable, except ... did he look up at her and smile? She looked away. Some smiles aren't friendly - something about the eyes.

Creep.

She stopped people-watching and pulled a compact and lipstick from her handbag. Studying the compact's mirror, as she reapplied lipstick, she concluded that today, like most days, she looked good. Tired perhaps, but her highlights were fresh, her eyebrows recently threaded, her skin clear and her fake tan was subtle, evenly applied. Tired? Yes, but hot, nevertheless.

As she reached to put the lipstick back in her bag, the Jack of Diamonds looked up at her. A trick of her imagination made her feel like the knave was winking at her. She smiled, pulled him out of the bag and sat, rolling the card through her fingers. It was a trick she'd learned after watching her father do it repeatedly.

Two hours later, Dacia had lost all patience for shopping and was glad to be on her way home. She just wished the damn bus would hurry up.

"Shall we meet up tonight?" Clearly, spending the whole morning together hadn't been enough for Francesca. Dacia smiled.

"Yeah, come round to mine. Mum and Dad are away this weekend. I've got the place to myself."

"Perfect." The bus approached.

Francesca planted a firm but brief kiss on Dacia's lips and squeezed her hand.

Dacia climbed on board, paid the driver and sat at the front on the top deck. The bus soon passed Francesca, who was walking away from the bus stop, shopping bags swinging and bouncing against her legs.

Dacia waved and Francesca lifted a bag-laden arm to wave back.

As Dacia used the Yale key to unlock the front door, she reflected on how many years she'd been letting herself in. A 'latch key kid', was the expression her mother had used in humour. Dacia couldn't see the joke.

The empty house, floored with tile and wood, reverberated the slightest of sounds. In a moment Dacia would turn on the radio for company but, first, she would light up. She dropped her shopping bags, resting her handbag on the frosted glass telephone table.

She found the packet easily, popping her last cigarette between her lips. The packet usually housed her lighter too, so why was it paper-light? She stared down into its emptiness.

Where the hell's my lighter gone?

It was only a minor setback, but this didn't stop Dacia shaking her head and tutting. She was rummaging in her handbag when a sound disturbed her. She thought it had drifted from the back of the house: perhaps a door slamming or a chair falling in the kitchen. Her cigarette fell from her mouth to the floor.

"Hello? Is anyone there?" Momentary silence.

She heard a faint grunt, like a throat being cleared.

The solitude of an empty house had always unnerved her. That human sound, the sound of trespass, escalated unease into blinding white terror. She swallowed hard. Her tremor-inflicted fingers searched her handbag again, this time for her mobile phone. Its battery was dead. The phone fell from her fingers, back into the bag. The house phone was in the dining room, to the left of the kitchen.

Silent, accelerating steps carried Dacia towards the dining room. Her laboured breaths drowned out the shallow buzz of distant household appliances. She was careful to open the study door quietly. She peered inside, scanning the room.

Everything was where it should be. Her father's writing desk beneath the window was on the far wall. The phone sat, seemingly un-tampered, on a corner of the desk. To her left was the fireplace. A brass stand, on the fake marble plinth, offered her the wrought iron poker.

I'm calling the police. Then I'm grabbing you.

She stepped in and closed the door behind her. She was on the phone in an instant. Holding the receiver with her right hand, she used her left to dial the numbers, shaking fingers making the task painfully difficult.

He opened the dining room door as quietly as Dacia had moments earlier.

With the phone to her ear, the dial tone sounded harsh, urgent and strangely angry. Her finger hit nine on the keypad. Another nine. Then a large hand, a cloth cupped in its palm, covered her mouth and nose. She felt the pressure of his chest on the back of her head. A hand hitched up her skirt. His finger slid inside the lace of her stocking before moving towards the inside of her thigh. As consciousness slipped away, she heard a whisper that was distant, as though a voice from a dream.

"It's okay Sweetheart, I've got you."

Chapter Six

As Cassie walked down the corridor, to collect her coat, her chest became tight. She had to stop. She reached up to the bank of coats, holding onto an empty hook. Her breathing had become short and rapid. She looked down at her hand. It had turned a waxy white-yellow.

Don't fit, don't fit, not now.

She felt detached from her surroundings and yet perceived with immense clarity.

Mummy's at home, asleep on the couch. She's had him round and they've been sucking in that stuff again, it's made her forget and she felt okay, then they did the thing grown-ups do, the thing they call sex which has nothing to do with whether you're a boy or a girl. He left and she lay on the couch to rest her eyes. That was an hour ago, and she's still there.

Rachel is waiting for me outside with her friends. They'll chase me down on their bikes. I won't be able to outrun them. They'll knock me down hard and my face will hit the gravel. I'll crunch grit between my teeth, not realising until I'm home that the split in my nose is full of dirt. It will bleed so much. The scar will be deep, dominating my face.

The colour returned to her cheeks and the sounds of excited kids, zipping up jackets and chatting became clear again. She was relieved to find herself upright, still gripping the hook, having narrowly escaped a seizure. Aaron, the only person in the whole school she could genuinely call a friend, moved towards her. He'd threaded one arm through the sleeve of his winter coat and was struggling with the other. "Cassie you okay? You're not going to fit are you?"

"No, but I need you to do me a favour."

"Okay, what?"

"I need to borrow your bike."

"Cassie, it's Wednesday, you know I've got to get back on my own tonight. I can't walk all that way."

Cassie knew Aaron would struggle with the walk. He deliberately avoided all forms of exercise. The weekly enforced fifteen-minute bike ride was a chore, but was infinitely better than walking.

"I know, but I'm in trouble, big trouble. Just this once, can you meet me at the back with your bike?"

"Okay, okay. But what sort of trouble?"

"I'll tell you later. I've got to hurry. Thanks."

The playground out the back of the school was deserted. Cassie stood on the Hopscotch grid, shifting her weight from one foot to the other and back again, rubbing her arms to keep warm.

Come on Aaron, where are you?

Aaron appeared from around the school's brick wall, wheeling his bike. It was a stunt BMX, with six-inch red-flecked metallic bars protruding from the centre of each wheel. Another expensive present Cassie could only dream of receiving.

Her face dropped when she remembered the bike had just one gear; not great for a rapid escape. She masked her disappointment by smiling as he slid the handle into her palm.

"Take care of it. Mum will go ape if I get it scratched." Aaron had always described his mum as a worrier.

"I will ... take care of it, that is."

Cassie leant over the bike frame, landing her lips on the side of Aaron's cheek, with a louder smack than she'd intended. It was the first time she'd kissed a boy, and from the flush spreading across his cheeks, she presumed it was his first time too. Aaron opened his mouth, but no words came.

Mainly to rescue him from the silence, Cassie said, "You better start moving. Your mum'll panic if you're late."

"You're not wrong. Why don't they just let us bring our phones? I could have called her."

That's alright if you have a phone and a mother who answers.

"Remember. No scratches Janus."

"Pinkie promise." Cassie straddled the bike, as Aaron jogged off in the opposite direction to join the throng at the front of the school - heading out the way they were supposed to.

Cassie sped away through the school's side gate. Crowds of kids were appearing from her right, having bottlenecked then spilled from the main gate. She turned left, behind an ivy-covered wire fence.

Cassie pumped her legs furiously, glancing over her shoulder every few seconds to make sure she wasn't being followed. Her tightening thigh muscles burned. The cold air made her lungs hurt and a vague taste of blood crept into her throat.

Surely when I grow up this fear will go away; it must be just a kid thing, like crying when you hurt yourself.

As these thoughts took over, she sped along the path. The Co-op shop was a blur of blue and white in her peripheral view. She approached a tight right-hand bend and should have slowed down, given the hedge obscuring her view. Cassie leant to her right, her wheels banking round the corner. Her coat sleeve clipped the hedge's dying leaves and thorn-ridden branches. An oncoming woman was pushing a pram in Cassie's direction. She saw the woman and her baby too late and leant left, overcompensating, losing control. Her snaking front tyre slid onto the road.

There was a screech of tyre rubber. A Mitsubishi pickup's bonnet hit Cassie's bike, sideways on. Her rag-doll body rolled up the windscreen, the wiper arm taking a chunk of cloth and flesh from her hip. The mighty "Eeeeeek" of the pickup's brakes drowned out her scream.

Chapter Seven

The woman, who Cassie had narrowly missed as she careered into the road, watched the pickup slam into Aaron's bike. Her right hand drifted up over her gaping mouth as she stood on the pavement, unable to process what she'd witnessed. The sound of bike frame on bull bars had been so nauseous; the skin across her abdomen had tightened, crawled.

Her sleeping baby woke and began to cry. The intensity of the collision, only moments old, had slowed down time. She felt sure she'd witnessed that poor girl take three full turns as she'd rolled up the windscreen.

Cassie hovered on the edge of consciousness. A vague, distant notion of falling came then drew away as she rolled down the bonnet towards the road. A strange mixture of pain and weightlessness gave way to a floating sensation. And, for a few moments, she was no longer herself.

My man arms reach out. One arm's holding a half used roll of silvery, metallic tape, the other pinching and stretching the tape's end, drawing it out. And beyond the tape, a girl on a bed. She's naked. Naked and still.

I drop the tape. It dangles from my left hand. My free hand takes her wrist. It's warm, she's alive. I'm positioning it against the rail of the bed head, then I'm wrapping tape. Slowly, neatly. The taped must be perfectly placed, aligned as neatly as it was on the roll. It will take time. I feel calm. Serene. Taking in the moment in. Savouring it.

The intense jolt of Cassie's body finally hitting the concrete broke her trance-like state. She became momentarily aware of her surroundings. Grassy weeds sprouted from where the road met the curb, jutting up her nostril, tickling. She felt a hand on her back and a woman's voice, at first gentle, "Oh sweetheart, help is on its way, you'll be okay," then purposeful and angry, "The least you can do is phone an ambulance ... NOW!"

Consciousness drifted away.

Cassie came to. A bizarre, semiconscious thought surprised her: *I thought the roof would be white but it's grey, metallic.*

She sat up, bending at the waist to a stiff ninety degrees. A blanket came loose, bunching in her lap. A paramedic in green uniform sat next to the stretcher, fiddling with a temporary drip, cursing at a speed bump.

Cassie's stomach thrust forward, her spine in a violent arch. She grabbed at the paramedic's wrist, gripping it tightly, her fingers trapping a plastic tube against the woman's skin.

Cassie felt her eyes rolling upwards. She was about to go under again and there was nothing she could do to stop it. She fell back against the stretcher. Her last conscious notion was of something around her neck, preventing her head from hitting the pillow. She slipped away again.

"I need help, she's convulsing, I need."

... help... Oh please sweet Jesus help me. Make him go away. The flash is blinding. He'll leave when he's done won't he? Of course he will. If I can get this gag off, I can talk to him, I'll reason with him. It's so tight. Please put the camera down ... why would you take pictures of this?

A momento.

You're sick.

Oh my God, what's he holding now? I think I'm going to be sick against this gag. Sweet Jesus, don't choke.

Darkness.

Chapter Eight

Leanne Janus's eyes crept open but her surroundings stubbornly refused to come into focus. She was in the front room of her one bedroom apartment, lying on a dark green sofa, the type that folds out to make a bed.

Her tight black jeans were still undone and barely reached her hipbone, which pushed against taut skin betraying how dangerously underweight she'd become. Equally exposed were her ribs. Her blouse was open and her black bra lay in the middle of the beige carpet.

Snippets of their drink and drug induced afternoon sex drifted in, unformed and disconnected. The swirling patterns of the Artex ceiling span in random directions and she closed her eyes to shut them out.

Don't be sick.

As she rubbed her temples, eyes shut tight, snippets became scenes, scenes became a narrative. Alcohol has the unnerving ability to edit a story. She hoped important moments hadn't been left on the cutting room floor.

Daniel had visited. He'd needed someone to talk to. Until recently he'd been unemployed. His friend Brian had taken a risk on him, offering him a job on his market stall. It was only on Wednesday and Saturday mornings but some income was better than none and he could get away with continuing to claim job seekers allowance. *'I've been friends with him since we were five years old, you know, through thick and thin. I can't believe he accused me of stealing, I still can't believe it.'*

Daniel losing his new job had felt like a big deal and, as commiseration provided a perfect excuse for escapism, they'd spent the early part of the afternoon putting the world to rights over Jack Daniels. The whiskey had been complemented by Leanne's marijuana stash, now entirely depleted. Almost as though it had been some distant recurring dream, she remembered them having sex. It had been a long time since she'd used the phrase 'making love.'

Nausea overcame her and she quickly got to her feet. There was no time to get to the bathroom. The kitchen sink would have to do. As she stood, arms holding onto the sides of the sink, her back convulsing, Leanne caught sight of her phone on the worktop. Three missed calls.

Shit, what time is it? Four o'clock, oh fuck, Cassie.

She wiped her mouth and, suddenly feeling sober, dialled her voicemail. Leanne closed her eyes.

I bet she's had another seizure. The school will have looked after her. It'll be okay.

The first message delivered the brutal news.

'Miss Janus, I'm calling from the accident and emergency department of Croydon University Hospital. Your daughter has been admitted following a road traffic accident. She's in a stable condition, but please come into the hospital as soon as you get this message.' Leanne didn't get to hear the subsequent voicemails. She grabbed her coat, went to call a cab, then decided that, with a stop only fifty yards away, the bus would be quicker.

She leant her head against the bus window, momentarily closing her eyes. The noise of the diesel engine reverberated through the cold surface, compounding her headache and she sat up again.

What would my mother say about me drinking and smoking pot in the afternoon?

What does that matter? I doubt if I'll ever see her again.

It *did* matter though. Nothing would please Leanne more than finally proving she could cope. She knew she could be better. At seventeen, a bright future had laid out in front of her; she'd been on track to get straight 'A's in her A levels.

Her dad had encouraged her to aim for a place at Oxford or Cambridge, Manchester Business school at a push. Leanne suspected her mother was looking forward to, once again, living alone with Leanne's dad. Leanne had had to listen to her mother's raptures about all the exotic breaks that would be possible, when her mum and dad were no longer shackled to school term times.

Then, shortly before Leanne's eighteenth birthday, her father left her mother for a paediatric nurse, thirteen years his junior. Leanne had rarely seen him since, and Cassie barely knew she had a granddad.

Leanne's relationship with her mother had never been warm but after her dad left, it deteriorated almost as rapidly as her grades. Her mother made it clear that Leanne was to take a large share of the blame for her father leaving. Eventually, they could no longer stand living together and Leanne moved out.

She sofa surfed for six months before falling pregnant. The council had stepped in, providing the flat where she still lived, two months before Cassie's birth.

I can be better. We'll get through this together, me and Cassie. Just got to straighten myself out. I will straighten myself out.

Chapter Nine

The bleeping, though mechanical and cold, rang home the warm news that Cassie hadn't anticipated: she was still alive. The intense terror she'd felt in her dream-like state was a distant memory; a faint echo.

Her left hand felt unusually warm. Unable to turn her head, she swivelled her pupils to establish who was comforting her. A nurse sat on a chair next to Cassie's bed, smiling at her, gently holding her hand and stroking her forehead.

Cassie became aware of a familiar voice and her mother came into focus, far beyond the nurse's shoulder, in the corridor of the hospital. She raised and lowered her arms towards another lady who looked calm, as though they were talking about the weather. Cassie didn't have the energy to listen and retreated into sleep.

"What do you mean, make an assessment?"

"Really it's nothing to be alarmed about. It's just that, given what her teacher and her friends have said, we have to understand if any issues need to be addressed. We wouldn't be focussing on you, we'll be talking to her teachers and her friends as well. Sometimes things are going on with childre-"

"I know what's going on Miss, Miss?"

"Mrs Robinson, please call me Laura."

"Mrs Robinson, what's going on is that she's different. She has epilepsy and suffers seizures from time-to-time, and you know what kids are like, they home in on anyone that doesn't fit their mould. Well fuck their, mould. If I find out that any of them had anything to do with this. I-"

"Miss Janus, please take a deep breath. Please don't say anything you'll regret. You're understandably upset. Come on, let me get you a coffee, your daughter needs her rest, please come next door."

Leanne leant one arm across her stomach, the other propped her weary head. "Don't tell me what she needs." Her voice had become weak; no potency in the protest. Mrs Robinson took Leanne by the arm and gently encouraged her away from the ward.

Chapter Ten

Laura felt burdened. Her workbag was hitched over her left shoulder; she felt the weight of the file it contained: the Cassie Janus file. Her right hand was on the back of Leanne's elbow, encouraging her along the corridor.

She'd passed the restaurant (canteen if we're honest) twenty minutes earlier, on her way in. It would have been perfect for their conversation, but was too far away. She scanned left and right for a room they might temporarily commandeer. Croydon hospital was like many others - a rabbit warren of purposeful spaces with dotted clusters of padded chairs. She saw, halfway along the corridor and to their right, five such chairs lined against the wall - no room for a cluster. Beyond the empty chairs, an elderly woman made slow progress towards them, with the aid of a stick. She wore a gown; the type that helpfully (if you're a consultant) and unhelpfully (if you're a patient) fastens up the back.

Laura watched, part of her wondered what this lady's story was - was that a look of deep reflection or was she just lost, confused - another part willed the woman to make her way past the chairs, so she could talk to Leanne in private.

"Let's take a seat over there." Laura gestured with her bag-laden arm. Leanne pulled hers away and headed for the seats.

Laura was in luck; the elderly lady had no intention of sitting down. She resisted the urge to ask if the woman was okay, if she needed help - she had enough on her plate. Laura offered only a kind smile instead, which the woman looked straight through.

Leanne sat in the first chair they came to. Laura dumped her bag on the next seat, claiming her place.

"Can I get you a drink?" There was a vending machine at a T-junction at the end of the corridor.

Leanne leant forward, taking out a Blackberry from her jean's back pocket, "Sure, why not. Coffee, white, two sugars."

Laura moved to collect her purse; no hint of an offer to pay from Leanne. She was elbow-deep in her bag's silky lining, when she finally laid her hand on it. *Why do purses always make their way to the bottom?*

Just past the row of seats, there was a red and white 'no mobiles' sign. Laura glanced over her shoulder at Leanne, who was now double-thumbing her phone's keys - probably texting. Not wise to point out the sign. This was going to be hard enough without riling her at the offset.

What can I say to start the conversation?

Feeding the machine with coins gave Laura valuable thinking time.

Croydon children's services had assigned Laura to Cassie's case. The police had contacted them, concerned about their inability to reach Miss Janus. Leanne was well known to the service, though this was the first time Laura had dealt with her case. Now ... how to share this in a way that doesn't feel like a threat, or an accusation of neglect. If there was anything more dangerous than criticising a mother's parenting, she hadn't experienced it.

Laura smiled subtly, as she handed the drink to Leanne. You had to get that first smile just right. You can't grin. This woman's kid's in the hospital. But you can't look sullen, either. Sullen can be interpreted as under-confident, of not having a way forward.

The coffee was dire (the forty pence, beige cup, powdered milk variety) but Miss Janus sipped frequently. Laura drank hers with a hidden grimace, desperate for them to have *something* in common - rank coffee was the only 'something' at the moment.

In a way, the chairs' position - facing the corridor's wall - made the conversation difficult; eye contact often helped. Sometimes though, not facing someone can take the heat out of a conversation. It also made their silence more comfortable.

Leanne surprised Laura by making the first move.

"I *do* love her, you know."

"No one doubts that."

"What *do* they doubt?"

Laura, choose your words carefully.

"Just whether you've had the sort of family help many people take for granted. We're here to support families like yours, Miss Janus."

"You can call me Leanne."

"And please, call me Laura."

Laura took a risk and reached over their armrests, gently laying her hand on Leanne's wrist.

"Nobody at the school is saying very much-"

Leanne pulled her wrist away, "You've been to the school?"

"Yes, it was on the way. Miss April, Cassie's teacher ... do you know her?"

"I met her teacher once, I think. Red hair, freckles."

"That's her."

"Miss April suggested I call Aaron hall."

"Who's he?"

"Claims to be friends with Cassie. I called his mother on Miss April's suggestion."

"I doubt they're good friends, I would know about it."

"You're probably right. According to Aaron's mother, it was Aaron's bike Cassie was riding when ... at the time it happened."

"Oh."

From behind a double door along the corridor, there was a heaving sound and a splat, followed by a consoling tone.

Leanne grimaced, "God, I hate hospitals."

Laura was keen to get the conversation back on track.

"He says she was scared of someone at school and asked to borrow his bike, to get home quickly."

Leanne sat back. Her coffee cup was empty. She squashed it between her thumb and forefinger.

"Figures. That'll be why she took such an odd route home. She was trying to avoid someone."

For the first time, Leanne turned, fixing her eyes on Laura.

"I wish to God she would stop bottling things up."

Laura detected alcohol on Leanne's breath. Leanne looked away and Laura felt as though her thoughts had been read. *Best not to mention that, not yet.*

"It's really common that kids don't tell their parents what's going on. It's no reflection on you. We could arrange for Cassie to speak to someone."

"A therapist?"

"A suitably qualified person."

"No, not a chance. No one's messing with her head. She just needs to get home, get well and the school need to clamp down on whoever's bothering her. If you want to help, find out what's going on there."

"I intend to. I'll have to come and see you again though, just to see how you're both coming along. I can update you on what I've found out."

Leanne turned to Laura and took a deep breath, puffed out her chest and opened her mouth to speak. Laura braced herself for an onslaught but a loud, rapid clunking and the voice of a nurse approaching from behind Leanne disturbed their conversation.

"Miss Janus, Cassie's awake. She's weak, but she can talk. Would you like to speak with her?" Leanne closed her mouth and got up to follow the nurse. She handed her empty cup back to Laura.

"We'll be in touch. I hope she's back on her feet soon." Leanne ignored her, turning her back and following the nurse.

Chapter Eleven

"Dacia!" Francesca, tunnelling her view with cupped hands, looked through the living room window. She saw nothing untoward and knocked on the front door for the fifth time. She shouted through the letterbox. "DACIA!"

Trying to phone Dacia's mobile was proving futile. Nevertheless, she tried again; straight to voicemail. Francesca contemplated calling Dacia's parents but didn't want to alarm them over something that was probably nothing.

She's probably gone out.

But she always answers her phone ... and she said she would be in!

Francesca remembered that Dacia's parents left a spare key to the front door beneath a fake rock along a rose bed in the front garden. She hurriedly prised the object from a deep, worm infested recess in the soil, breaking off two false nails as she dug. She slid open the rock-box, dropping the key into her palm. Francesca unlocked the front door and stepped inside, wiping mud from her shoes onto the doormat. She started down the hall, each clunking step on wood feeling like an intrusion.

"Dacia, are you okay?" She opened the door to each downstairs room, leaning into each, checking for Dacia's presence, calling her name repeatedly. The pitch of her voice became higher with each holler. As she leant into the kitchen she saw the back door ajar and growing concern turned into blind panic. She retreated, back into the hall, then turned and ran towards the stairs, ahead and to her left. With her left hand she reached up to the wooden acorn atop the bannister. Using it as a pivot, she swung onto the bottom step. As she ran up the stairs, her urgent steps produced rapid, rhythmical thuds, like a woodpecker attacking a tree.

Please God let there be nothing wrong. Dacia, I love you. Francesca, get a grip. Don't let your imagination run away with you. You always think the worst. She'll be okay, you'll see. She'll just be in a deep sleep. She'll have accidentally left the back door open. Probably went out for a cigarette and forgot to lock it. The catch isn't great, it's easy to leave the door ajar and be none the wiser. The wind probably got up and blew it open.

When I get upstairs I'll find her sound asleep and I'll leave a note, so I don't disturb her. Dacia, I'm sure you're fine. When you wake we'll have a great evening together I promise. Please be okay.

She checked Dacia's bedroom first. The hot pink curtains were tied back. The bed was still made. Dacia's favourite childhood teddy bear, propped up against plump white pillows, stared back at Francesca with solemn eyes.

Obvious, benign explanations were vanishing as quickly as she could create them and terrible, unthinkable scenarios took over.

In the bathroom, everything was where it should have been. She looked for signs that Dacia had been there recently. There was no mist on the mirror, or condensation on the double-glazing. The plush towels, hung over the bath, were so dry they were rough to the touch.

Finding nothing in the spare bedroom either (it needed only a cursory glance), she barely dared to open the door to Dacia's parents' room, feeling like an intruder. Surely, under the circumstances, she would be forgiven.

Francesca's mind refused to absorb the scene in front of her, in a bid to preserve sanity. It was a picture, held at arms length, not reality. It *couldn't* be reality.

Dacia had been left without the slightest dignity. Her arms and legs were secured tightly to the posts of her parents' bed with silver Duck tape. The chest of drawers that stood opposite the bed, spewed tan coloured tights and numerous white panties out of its ransacked drawers. The drawers jutted out at irregular angles as though the chest had been shaken in an earth tremor.

One of the tights had clearly been taken from the drawer, stretched, and used to wedge Dacia's jaws open. Her eyes were wide, lifeless and yet full of glassy fear, gazing towards the ceiling. The rest of the room was undisturbed. The clothes Dacia had worn earlier that day were laid out neatly next to the bed. The line started with stockings then suspenders, then a red pencil skirt, then her ivory top. All were folded into evenly distributed squares. Her handbag completed the line. The Jack of Diamonds poked out over the clasp.

Francesca couldn't acknowledge that Dacia was dead. Dacia's pale skin and the blue tinge, ringing the base of her neck, filled Francesca's stomach with a knowing dread, but her mind refused the painful truth.

In a rational state, Francesca would have retreated and called the police. Instead, from a position that didn't feel like the inside of her own mind, she went about freeing Dacia's body.

First she would free Dacia's arms. The bed was king sized. Dacia was only five foot three and her arms were stretched upwards like the wings of a fallen eagle. Francesca watched herself desperately tug and peel at the tape around Dacia's wrists. She finally loosened both before moving down the bed, to free her splayed legs. The act of reaching for each corner brought Francesca's hands, her neck and her cheek in and out of contact with the unnatural coolness of Dacia's skin. She shook as much from fear as from the cold.

The last time I touched her she was warm. She'll never be warm again.

Her tears fell on Dacia's stomach. She brushed them away with the back of her hand, leaving a salty sheen. She ached to see that stomach rise and fall again. So pale, so still. She reached behind Dacia's head to undo the tight knot keeping her lips apart. She brought Dacia's knees together and rolled her onto her side before gently stroking her eyelids shut. She held Dacia's lifeless body, sobbing as she rocked back and forth. It was a few minutes before a sour thought brought her back to her senses.

What if the person who did this is still in the house?

Francesca laid Dacia's body on the bed, folding her arms across her chest. She grabbed her mobile, dialling nine nine nine as quickly as her quivering fingers would allow.

Chapter Twelve

Leanne had overestimated her tolerance for boredom. She'd been in the hospital, by Cassie's bedside, since nine in the morning. It was shortly after eleven and she was restless. She'd spent an hour hunched forward on a deep cushioned seat, having dragged it forward, close to Cassie's bed. She occasionally stroked the back of Cassie's fingers.

A nurse called Miss Branagan, checked on them periodically. An hour earlier, Leanne had overheard her on the phone at the nurse's station, confirming that there were two paediatric recovery beds occupied, three beds free. Leanne guessed this meant that kids were on their way but, so far, none had materialised.

The ward was quiet apart from the infrequent yet regular beep coming from the machine beyond Cassie's bed. Leanne hadn't the first clue what the machine was monitoring but felt assured; Miss Branagan occasionally checked the screen and nodded gently. Nurse Branagan was a squat, stocky woman with commanding forearms. She was quiet and pleasant, smiling at Leanne each time she passed.

A small television on a folding grey arm jutted out over Cassie's bed. Leanne got up and turned it on. She fooled herself into thinking that this was for Cassie's benefit.

The sound of the TV might bring her round.

Jeremy Kyle's opening titles greeted her. A scrolling banner at the bottom of the screen promised imminent live paternity tests. Jeremy introduced a young woman, sitting centre stage, with half her head shaved, the other half peroxide blonde and backcombed. She began talking about her boyfriend as though he was 'the one.' Her angelic description didn't match the man who appeared screen right. His guttural, spitting accusations of infidelity started the moment he walked on set.

Leanne watched the ensuing chaos, occasionally smiling. At the commercial break she got up to go to the toilet. When she returned, turning the corner past the nurses station, she was irritated by the scene coming into view.

The television had been switched off and swung well out of the way. Nurse Branagan sat in Leanne's chair, with her left hand holding Cassie's. Her right was turned, it's back gently stroked Cassie's forehead. The nurse was whispering something. As Leanne approached she felt a knot of jealousy, mixed with guilt, twist in her stomach. *She* should have been there as Cassie woke.

"Nurse Branagan, I've got this." Leanne sat on the long flat chair arm and reached towards Cassie's face. The nurse pulled her hand from Cassie's forehead, in response. Leanne smiled at Cassie and said, "It's okay sweetheart, I'm here." Cassie's eyes merely flickered into slits, not really seeing.

Leanne looked down and saw white patches on the nurse's otherwise ruddy hand where Cassie was squeezing. The nurse saw Leanne's territorial glance.

"Your mummy's here Cassie." It took some effort but nurse Branagan broke Cassie's grip and transferred Cassie's hand into Leanne's. Cassie's fingers became limp, impotent in her mother's hand. The nurse emptied the chair and left them alone. Leanne took the seat, surprised at how warm it felt.

Dry saliva tried to keep Cassie's white lips sealed but she managed to open her mouth, "Water."

There was a glass of water on the bedside table. Leanne picked it up and held the rim to Cassie's lips, wary of giving her more than she could cope with.

"Here sweetheart."

Cassie took several sips then rested her head back again. Leanne noticed tears surfacing in Cassie's eyes.

Just leaning forward is hurting her. She must be in so much pain.

Cassie looked away from Leanne, turning her head just a few degrees to the right, as far as the neck brace would allow.

Why won't she look at me?

Leanne couldn't think of anything better to say and so asked the obvious, stroking Cassie's forehead as she spoke, "How are you feeling?"

"I ache."

"Where does it hurt?"

"All over. My hip's the worst"

"The doctors say there's nothing that won't heal quickly, with you being so young. The neck brace is just a precaution and they hope to take it off in a few days. A week and you'll be up and about. In six weeks they reckon you'll be more or less back to your normal self."

To Leanne, six weeks was nothing. She'd forgotten that, as a child, six weeks was the length of a seemingly endless summer holiday. They sat in silence until Leanne couldn't resist quizzing Cassie about the accident.

"Cassie, how come you were on that boy's bike?"

"I was trying to get away."

"From who?"

"Rachel Atkinson." Leanne looked into her lap, plunging into a desperate attempt to recollect. She used to be friendly with a few of the other mums, but couldn't remember a kid called Rachel. Nothing was coming. She shook her head and looked up.

"Should I know her?"

"No."

"Who is she?"

"Just another girl in my year."

"Has she been bothering you?"

And that *did* make Cassie turn, the fraction she could, in Leanne's direction. Her pupils swept to the corner of her eye, towards Leanne. This gave Cassie a look that didn't suit her, a look verging on malice.

"Bothering me? She was going to *attack* me."

"How do you know?"

"She told me she was going to, straight after school."

"Oh Cassie, it was probably just a bluff. I bet she was just trying to rattle you."

Cassie's eyes closed and she continued talking with them shut.

"She *would* have attacked me, her and her friends."

"What makes you so sure?"

"They hurt me earlier that day, they don't bluff." Her eyelids pinched out a tear, which ran along her cheek, settling in her ear. Leanne moved to wipe Cassie's face, but felt resistance in her flinching cheek. "Oh Cassie I'm so sorry. Did you tell your teacher?" Leanne squeezed her hand, but Cassie was either unable or unwilling to squeeze back. Perhaps both.

"No, that only makes it worse."

"Anyway, sweetheart, if you'd met me at the gates, I would have stopped them." With the mechanical certainty of a camera shutter, Cassie's eyes flicked open.

Leanne had pleaded with herself not to lie to her daughter. Cassie always had a way of seeing through her lies. But Leanne couldn't help herself. She knew that Cassie hadn't waited around to see if she would turn up and so couldn't possibly know it wasn't true. Surely it was better to have Cassie think Mummy had been there for her. Yes, telling a white lie was the right thing to do.

Cassie made a concerted wincing effort to tilt her head towards her mum. The look on her face scared Leanne. Her eyes were loveless wells. In that moment, Cassie could have been someone else's child. The girl looking at Leanne surely wasn't the person she'd carried inside her for nine long months.

"You *didn't* come to school for me." She left a pause, intensifying that sideways stare. Leanne felt like Cassie was trying to pierce the wall of her soul.

"Cassie, that's not true."

"Don't make it worse." Cassie centred her head, looking upwards at the ceiling.

She can't know that I wasn't on my way to school. Nobody knows where I was when I picked up that voicemail. But she knows, *somehow she knows.*

"Cassie, you've just come round. You're probably confused."

There was a long pause during which the faint hum of equipment and tension became mingled and confused.

"Mummy I need to rest. Can I be left alone?" She closed her eyes and breathed deeply. Leanne stayed with her for a few minutes, holding Cassie's listless fingers. She watched her chest rise and fall, her breath slowing and deepening. She was sure that Cassie didn't hear her say, "Sure, my darling, you rest up," before slipping her hand away.

Cassie heard every word and also the clip of her mother's footsteps gradually growing quieter. She was grateful to be alone.

Chapter Thirteen

During the three days she'd been in the hospital, Cassie had done little more than sleep. She'd suffered two broken ribs, a fractured shoulder blade and had broken the radius in her right arm. Strangely she considered herself lucky. They were all clean breaks and, with young bones, would heal quickly.

Thankfully a numbness, which had spread over her feet the day after the accident, had retreated. She'd even managed a giggle when the doctor brushed a finger up the sole of each foot. Her mother, standing behind the consultant at the time, hadn't been able to hide her relief. Cassie suspected that, for Mummy, the prospect of looking after a disabled child was unbearable. Her mum struggled to 'look after' Cassie as it was.

Getting rid of the neck-brace had been the biggest relief. As they'd removed it, a stiff throbbing had spread around the base of her neck. She didn't care. The feeling of free movement was a powerful anaesthetic.

So far Leanne had resisted the urge to question her daughter again about what had happened on the day of the accident and Cassie was grateful for it. Occasionally Cassie's thoughts turned to her premonition: seeing what Rachel had intended to do to her and then back towards the sickening moment when the car struck Aaron's bike. Cassie was gradually learning to push these thoughts away.

What she failed to banish was the nightmare that had gripped her in the ambulance. It felt so real. And now it vividly returned as she lay on her own in the ward. It started with her mind flattening the meringue peaks of the cream Artex ceiling, into an unfamiliar crisp white plane. Then ...

I can't speak. I can't move. I'm tugging, shoulders flexing and moving nowhere. He's bent over, past the bed. I hear unzipping. Has he got a bag down there?

He's standing up now. He's so tall, and that mask; black cloth with neat eyeholes. There's nothing in the eyes. No emotion, like he's concentrating. Studying. I don't want to cry but can't stop the tears.

He's holding up a camera, it looks heavy, professional. He's holding it so still. A flash, too bright in the semi dark (he must have closed the curtains before I came to).

He rests the camera in the gap between my ankles. Then bends again. What's he getting this time? Oh God, he can't use that. It's too big. I've got to free my legs, to kick out. My hips are burning with the effort of squirming; I'm weakening when I need to be strong. He can't use that on me. Can't.

It's so difficult to do, with the rough nylon wedge in my mouth, but I swallow hard.

Cassie squeezed her eyes shut so tightly that deep lines fanned out across her temples, "Go away, go away."

"Well that's charming. It hardly looks like you're fighting off visitors."

Aaron's voice dispelled her vision the way detergent dispels grease, completely and without effort. Cassie was relieved.

She opened her eyes again and saw Aaron standing in front of her bed, wearing jeans and a jumper, which boasted the vague shape of an embroidered motorbike. She could only imagine his Gran must have knitted it. She smiled, knowing he had zero interest in motorbikes.

"I must have been waking up. I talk in my sleep."

He walked towards her bed, extending his arm to offer Cassie his Rubik's cube. "Here, you can borrow this. You must be bored out of your brain by now." Three days in a hospital bed for most nine-year-olds would have felt like an eternity but, as Cassie's mother kept pointing out to the doctors, she was coping well.

"Thanks. Though I may have to wait a while, I think I'll need two good arms to do that." Aaron blushed at his stupidity. "It's not so bad though. There's a TV and I've got my books." She looked over at a pile of six paperbacks that, in truth, she'd barely managed to pick up; her shoulder ached immensely. 'Harry Potter and the Order of the Phoenix' was the top book. All the others were flat, stacked neatly, but this one's first third was scrunched - a casualty of the crash. It had been in her rucksack when she'd careered into the pickup.

"Harry Potter ... again. How many more times are you going to read them Cassie? You should read proper books like I do."

Aaron used the term 'proper books' in an attempt to make her smile. He knew that she viewed the subject of his reading with a mixture of bewilderment and disgust.

Ever since visiting the London Dungeons he'd been obsessed with finding out as much as he could about Jack the Ripper. He had described ad nauseam to Cassie, the tour's climax which was a scene played out by actors.

Around thirty tourists were shepherded into a mocked-up nineteenth century pub and told to sit at tables, or lean against walls, to hear a Cockney barmaid tell the story of Jack the ripper.

As the barmaid, in her white frilly-necked saloon dress, relayed the tale, the lights would momentarily go out, plunging the room into darkness. Each time the lights flashed back up she'd changed position, facing some unfortunate tourist who received her cold stare, menacingly close, before reconvening her monologue.

Aaron's mother screamed louder than anyone else in the room, having become unexpectedly confronted by the barmaid. Aaron could only smile, eyes wide with wonder at the terror this actress evoked. His mother was secretly a little upset that her son took delight in her discomfort.

What Aaron would later describe as 'the best part' came at the end of the scene when the lights went out again. It became clear that the barmaid had been replaced by none other than the ripper himself, dressed in a black cloak, repeatedly swinging a kitchen knife in a slashing arc, lit by nothing but strobe lights which resembled the illumination of lightening, offering brief glimpses of his homicidal grin. As Aaron's mother buried her head in her hands, to avoid the horrific spectacle, all Aaron could say was, "cooooool … "

Since then Aaron had become preoccupied with reading about the ripper and, recently, about other serial killers. His mother found his interest mildly disturbing, surely just a phase that would pass.

"Aaron, do you feel normal?"

"What do you mean?"

"Well, like at school. They keep getting at me, like I'm weird or something. Mummy keeps telling me it's good to be different and I guess she's right. Harry Potter's different from other kids, but different in a good way. Everything that's different about me is bad. I throw fits all the time, my clothes are different. Nobody but the teachers seem to like me-"

"I like you."

She smiled in an attempt to appreciate his gesture.

"Thanks Aaron, but do you know what I mean?"

"You think too much. Some kids are mean, that's all. You're not weird. Now, *I'm* weird. Mum says that if she sees me reading about murderers again, she's going to take my Xbox off me, and I don't even play on my Xbox, how weird is that?"

"Okay, maybe you *are* weird." She giggled weakly. "I don't know how you can get to sleep after reading that stuff."

"Doesn't it interest you?" Aaron paused dramatically, squinting his eyes and turning his head, giving her a sinister stare, "People leading secret lives, planning their next … eeeeevil deeeeed."

Cassie normally laughed at Aaron's silly impressions but couldn't managed a smile.

"What's up?" Cassie looked away and they sat in silence for far too long. Aaron shuffled his chair so his knees touched Cassie's bedcovers, and said, under his breath, "Come on. What's up?"

"Aaron, I think there might be something wrong with me." She kept her volume below the detection of their mothers who stood chatting in the corridor.

"I know things."

"All right Cassie, you don't have to show off. Everyone knows you're the cleverest in our year."

"I don't mean stuff like that. Please be serious, just this once Aaron. I mean things I shouldn't know."

"Like what?"

Cassie stopped talking, looked at the wall and considered not continuing at all.

"Remember last summer, when I warned you about the wasps nest hanging from that willow tree?"

"Yeah, what about it?"

She paused and took a deep breath, contemplating how to explain; just one chance to make him believe.

"I lied Aaron."

"Lied?"

"I hadn't seen it earlier. Well I had, but not in the way you think."

"Cassie, you're not making sense."

"The night before, I had a seizure. I hadn't had one in months and then suddenly it came, a really big one. As everything went black I dreamt of that street. You were riding your bike on the pavement, and didn't see the nest until it was too late. They stung your face and neck. Your throat swelled and you were gasping for breath."

Cassie turned her head to one side and closed her eyes, as the memory came back stronger. She knew that talking about it might make her go under again, but she couldn't bear to keep her secret a moment longer.

"Cassie, chill out. It was just a bad dream. I get them all the time."

"No Aaron it *wasn't* a dream."

"Or just a weird sense of deja vu. I've heard that happens a lot with epileptics. No one really knows why but-"

"It wasn't deja vu and it wasn't a dream. You aren't listening. That *would* have happened, if I hadn't warned you."

"You can't know that."

"I shouldn't know that ..." her voice became distant, disconnected from her thoughts. She looked beyond him, through the window towards the grey sky, "... but I do."

"I think your head's gone squiffy from that medicine they've been giving you."

Cassie's lips wavered. She turned to face him and grabbed his wrist as tightly as she could manage, using her good arm. "You've got to believe me Aaron. You've got to. I've never told anyone because I know people will think I'm mad. Promise not to tell, Aaron, promise."

"Alright, alright, I believe you and I won't tell."

Cassie's grip loosened on his wrist and she relaxed back into her bed. The pain came in a wave, stronger than ever and a groan was accompanied by a clicking sound in the back of her throat.

"Cassie, Cassie, are you okay?"

"Aaron. Fetch someone. Please."

"Miss Janus, Mum, I think something's wrong with Cassie!"

Chapter Fourteen

Laura Robinson landed her bag and keys unceremoniously on the kitchen worktop. She quickly closed the back door behind her to retain some heat in their Victorian semi. Winter was definitely on its way, a season she hated. Closing the door did more than keep out the cold, though, it put a full stop at the end of her working day; an audible prompt to leave guilt behind (until tomorrow). Guilt of never being able to do enough for the families on her caseload - she hadn't even had time to follow up on Cassie Janus and her flakey mother.

Unusually Malcolm had finished work before her and was busy preparing meatballs with linguine. In a smooth well-practiced rhythm, he grabbed her handbag, hung it in the wardrobe and placed her car key on the 'keep calm and drink wine,' key holder near the back door.

"Malcolm, please don't clean up after me." He pretended hurt, batting his eyes at her. His attempt to look like a pitiful puppy made her smile.

"I'm sorry. I didn't mean to snap. It was just a long day."

"Come here." He reached out and planted his large hands on her waist, landing a kiss firmly on her lips. "Let's chill out, eat and drink wine".

"Sounds good to me."

She poured them both a glass of Merlot and grabbed a red chequered tea towel from the oven handle. He was the type of cook that washed dishes as he went along and Laura was happy to dry up as she sipped Merlot. Wine had miraculous powers, transforming chores into pastimes.

On days like today, she chastised herself for her ingratitude. Malcolm and Laura's relationship was two years old; married for seven months. Before their relationship she'd been mostly single for the best part of ten years, the first five of which were spent avoiding men entirely. The scars of her first serious relationship had taken those long five years to fade.

Her marriage to Roger had been a disaster. She was twenty-one when they met. He was walking perfection at first. She would often look at pictures of the two of them taken at her friend's engagement party, him with his sharp three-piece grey suit, her in a black cocktail dress (getting back in that dress was a life-long unfulfilled ambition). He was so handsome, not in a typically macho chiselled-jawed way though. He had a soft but strong upright demeanour, a grace when he walked and danced.

Roger's father was a hedge fund manager for J.P. Morgan and the money flowed effortlessly downhill into Roger's pockets. They got married at twenty-three and honeymooned in the Bahamas.

Looking back, she should have spotted the signs. He wouldn't say, "I want you," he would say, "I'm *going* to *have* you." He didn't say, "I want to be with you forever." He said, "I *will* be with you forever." At the time she read this as his deep passion; he wanted to be with her *so* much. She wished she could go back, grab her younger self by the shoulders, and shake some sense into her.

Doubts started on the first night of their honeymoon. He'd had three too many beers and decided to get an early night. It was just past nine o'clock. Laura wasn't ready to go to bed, so she kissed him goodnight and sat at the palm-covered beach bar, enjoying the warmth of the night air and trying to dismiss thoughts that she'd seen anger in Roger's eyes as they'd parted.

A man approached her at the bar. He explained that he was with his fiancée. As it transpired, she had also overestimated her ability to handle strong rum in the sunshine, and was sleeping it off. He was polite, at a loose end.

They chatted for maybe half an hour until a fist thudded against his cheekbone, knocking him off his stool. Roger shook the pain from his knuckles and grabbed Laura's arm. She remembered the twisting Chinese burn of pain as he dragged her to their apartment, ignoring her angry complaints that dwindled to ineffectual pleading.

Once inside their room he yelled at her, "You're *my* wife. No one else's. Look what your flirting has brought me too. Don't you understand that I love you so much I can't see you with another man. Perhaps I just love you more than you love me."

Laura remembered protesting that this wasn't true, as though punching someone else out of jealousy was somehow a sign of deep love. Every time she looked back on that night, she winced at her own stupidity.

In the morning he woke, apologetic. That's when he confessed. He was plagued by early childhood memories of his father abusing his mother. His mother disappeared when he was six. His father said that she'd left him for another man. He remembered the police being round a lot at the time; too much.

Roger cried as he spoke, telling Laura she was the only one he'd confided in. He said he wanted to see a counsellor and thanked her, in advance, for her support. She sat on the bed with his head against her chest, stroking his thick black hair, feeling his tears drop into her lap. She decided to stay with him. She would heal him.

At first he was true to his word about the counselling. Monthly sessions drifted to bimonthly, eventually settling on quarterly until fifteen months after their honeymoon, he'd stopped them altogether. Laura didn't mind, the sessions had done their job; his temper hadn't flared as badly as it had in the Bahamas. Sure, she avoided spending time with her friends and family so as not to anger him. But who doesn't make sacrifices for their marriage, particularly when their partner loves them so much. Right?

Roger left the junior position his father had secured for him at Morgan Stanley. He confessed to having a trust fund worth over two million pounds. He didn't need to prove anything in that job anymore and it was a distraction from his recovery, from their marriage. He suggested a move to Devon, to a beach-home, in a blissful location overlooking the sea. He wanted to focus on their relationship.

Laura's mother had told her that move was a mistake, but who listens to their mother? Laura had been studying social sciences at University at the time. Suspending her studies hadn't been an issue, she was permitted to finish the course through distance learning. It would take an extra year, but she wasn't in a rush. It was hardly like they were relying on her career.

Within a month of the move, she knew her mother was right. Roger had too much time on his hands, too much time to think. He had no patience for her studies, and so she set the alarm on her phone early each morning, burying it beneath her pillow so it wouldn't wake him. She'd creep downstairs, and put her head in her books for two hours before he woke. It was the morning on which she started a module on domestic violence that the veil of their marriage fell from her eyes and she could see clearly.

She remembered reading it, a table with 'Inner Thoughts and feelings' and 'Partner's Behaviour,' as column headings. Under the latter column was listed: Blame you for their own behaviour (check) ... Ignore or put down your accomplishments (check) .... Control where you go or what you do (check) ... acts excessively jealous (check) keeps you from seeing your friends and family (why did we move here ... oh my God ... check) ... limit your access to money, the phone, or the car (only one car, I ask him for money when I need it ... check). Constantly check up on you ... (che...)

"What are you doing?" He stood, in crumpled checked pyjamas, looking down at her sprawling books. She slammed the book shut.

"Nothing." In that moment, she knew she would leave. It was just a case of when. Two months later, whilst he was working out in their gym, she packed a few clothes, some makeup and two hundred pounds in cash. She hid it in their garage, and set her alarm for two thirty a.m.

She begged a room at an old friend's house (a girlfriend still living with her mother whom Roger had never met). Laura got a message to her own mum saying she was okay, but asking her not to say she'd called, if Roger got in touch.

He never did. His radio silence initially felt like a miracle. She never imagined he'd let her go that easily. She never looked him up, resisting the occasional temptation to Google his name. At first the narrative she told herself, that he might have committed suicide, was a scary one, a guilty one. Then, over the years, it became a comfortable and likely explanation. He *wouldn't* have let go that easily. 'I'll never let you go,' were his words, repeated often. She believed him.

Her painful memories were interrupted by Malcolm's voice.

"Are you okay? You seem miles away."

"Honestly, I'm fine."

There were no more pots to dry. As he dished up their linguine, she reflected on her relationship with Malcolm, how patient he'd been with her. He understood her hesitance, her cautiousness when it came to trust. He never took this as rejection. Slowly, she'd learned to love again. But this time it wasn't deranged jealousy masquerading as love. This was real.

A short while later they sat opposite each other at their small dining room table, Laura occasionally complimenting him on a genuinely fantastic meal, Malcolm smiling in return.

Ordinarily, they finished their meal in time to watch the seven O'clock news, but they were running late. Laura used the nearby remote to turn on the flat screen television, which hung on the kitchen wall. She flicked over to the news.

"Really Laura, you know I don't like the TV on while we're eating."

"I know, but we've almost finished our dessert." He briefly looked at her, sighed, and carried on scooping Crème Brule. The television stayed on.

The first story reported the murder of a young woman found in a house on Coney Hill Road, East Croydon. Laura had missed the commentary from the presenter in the studio, who'd handed over to the crew at the scene. The reporter stood outside a house, which had been cordoned off with black metallic stakes plunged into garden soil. The stakes were wrapped in narrow, yellow plastic tape, which repetitively stated: 'Police Line, Do Not Cross'. The tape flapped in gusty winds, as did the reporter's hair, which she frequently removed from her eye line, the wind promptly landing it back across her face. She was doing an admirable job of not letting this faze her.

"Thanks Richard, I'm standing outside the house on Coney Hill Road. The young victim, whose name has not been released, is thought to have been found in a first floor bedroom. Although police are not yet in a position to confirm or deny, reports of foul play are circulating. It's believed the house belongs to the victim's parents, though this is, again, unconfirmed at this point. The police are due to issue a statement within the hour and we will, of course, have more for you the moment we have it." The screen split into two and the presenter came into view.

"Anna, are there any further indications that this might have been murder?"

"Well, nobody's using that word at the moment, and again these are unconfirmed reports, but we've heard she may have been found tied, and in a state of undress. As I say, too early to confirm and I think we have to be careful about speculating at this point."

It struck Laura that they hadn't been 'careful' at all and that they'd unnecessarily put a whole host of pictures in the minds of viewers without proper evidence. This annoyed Laura greatly, with her own department having been the victim of unhelpful media attention when twin girls were beaten to death by their parents. The blame was laid squarely at the door of children's services, unjustly, in Laura's view.

She knew that Malcolm hated talking about work in the evenings, but she guessed this was in his jurisdiction and felt compelled to dig.

"Malcolm, do you know the people working on this?"

"Laura, please can't we just forget about work tonight?"

"I guess." Her conciliatory words were not matched by the hunch of her shoulders.

"Okay, look, I'll tell you what I know, which isn't much. The reports of her being found naked and restrained are correct. Her girlfriend found her in her parents' room. It appears someone broke into the house and attacked her. That's all I know. We've got a couple of people assigned to it, but if they don't find a suspect quickly, the team will grow. It wouldn't surprise me in the least if I end up joining them."

"It amazes me how anyone thinks they can get away with this, in this day and age, given what the forensics people seem to be able to do with DNA."

"From what I can gather they won't be short of DNA samples, but that only helps if the suspect's DNA's registered."

"I guess. Look, sorry for asking, let's forget about work, go into the lounge and watch a trashy movie."

"Amen to that."

A faint clunk accompanied Laura turning off the TV.

Chapter Fifteen

"Oh sweetie, do cover your mouth when you yawn. Don't they teach you young people manners any more?" Amanda put her free hand over her mouth and, though she waited a moment before replying, her words struggled to form in her gaping jaws. In her other hand, she held a Blackberry and was sending a text message to her partner.

"Swaarry. Ah. Sorry I'm just so tired."

"Nonsense, tonight we're celebrating and I won't have tired girls. Where is that useless boyfriend of yours anyway?"

"With his mates."

"Well leave him to it. This baby won't be the last one opened tonight." He held aloft the bottle of Bollinger with his right hand and gently caressed it with the back of his left, dragging his skin across it with theatrical sexuality. His flamboyance was starting to draw attention from other passengers but Peter Eccleston didn't care. In fact, he loved the attention.

Yes both these girls whom I employ are young enough to be my daughter and yes I do intend to get them horrendously drunk and no, I shan't be making advances on them, but if it happens the other way round, to hell with it. You only live once. And today a play, two years in the making, is being commissioned and will be performed at some of the most prestigious theatres in London and damn it if I'm not going to live to the max tonight. Just anyone try and stop me.

They sat in the cafe bar at the table nearest to the kiosk where overpriced drinks and snacks were on sale. After distributing the rest of the champagne between the three transparent plastic cups, he stood up and took a few unsteady paces towards the kiosk. He wasn't sure whether it was the champagne or the motion of the carriage, or both, that caused him to sway and frankly, he couldn't have cared less. The short plump lady with thick black glasses standing behind the bar, looked miserable though sounded incongruently chipper as he approached. "Yes sir, what can I get for you?"

"Yes, thank you young lady," he perused the drinks menu whilst unfastening the brass buttons on his navy blazer, "I'll have two bottles of your champagne, they are those ridiculously small ones aren't they?"

Not wanting to confirm his view, though still wishing to be polite, she held up a bottle for him to see.

"Thought so, yes, two please. And looking at this I don't suppose you have any olives back there?"

"Sorry sir, you suppose correctly. But we do have roasted nuts."

The champagne had loosened his tongue and he almost conveyed how ghastly nuts and champagne would be and then stopped himself sounding impossibly pretentious. "Just the champagne will be fine."

He sat back down and drank the quarter cup of champagne he had left. Noticing that all their cups were empty, he moved to refill them. Samantha, a young woman with unnaturally blonde hair who had been working with him for three months, placed her hand over the cup, "Honestly you're going to get me drunk."

"Indeed my dear," he said, lifting her hand easily out of the way. With their drinks charged, he held his aloft.

"A toast." They both mirrored his gesture, raising their cups dutifully.

"To becoming the toast of the West End."

"Hear hear." The silent meeting of their cups dulled what should have been a fine moment.

As Peter rested back in his chair his hand brushed the side of Amanda's skirt. He apologised and pulled his hand closer to his side. His fingers came to rest on something protruding from the crack between the seat cushions. It was a deck of playing cards.

"Well look what we have here. Sam, how long have we got left on the train?"

"About thirty minutes."

"Splendid. We're going to play gin rummy and I won't take no for an answer."

As Samantha and Amanda looked at each other, an onlooker might have felt their glances were without meaning. This couldn't have been further from the truth. They knew exactly what was running through each other's minds.

Can't he just leave us in peace to check Facebook?

Remembering who paid their wages, they put on a brave face, "Yes, let's!"

As the train pulled leisurely into Kings Cross, two minutes ahead of schedule, Peter was in no hurry to exit the carriage. He clapped and rubbed his hands, overly elated to have won the game. Samantha and Amanda were keen to get home, both rapidly zipping jackets and hitching handbags over their shoulders.

"So, where to now ladies?"

They looked at each other, wondering who would make their excuses first. Samantha was bravest, "Sorry Peter, but I'm shattered, I can't stay out tonight. Perhaps we could do something this weekend instead." Peter's smile inverted then returned.

"Saturday ... yes, that's a great idea. Let's all go out for drinks and a meal, I know a fabulous Lebanese place in Covent Garden. The owner's as camp as Christmas, but a real sweetie, and the food is fantastic. Saturday it is."

Samantha, who had only offered Saturday as a stalling tactic, smiled and said her goodbyes. She kissed Peter on the cheek and hugged Amanda before moving briskly along the carriage, joining the escaping queue. "And what about you Amanda my darling, I suppose you are also taking a rain check?"

"Afraid so. My boyfriend's been texting again. He's still out and wants to meet up." In the most dramatic voice he could muster, whilst holding the back of his hand to his forehead in a grandiose gesture, he said, "I know when I have been cast aside for a younger fellow, feel no ill for it."

Amanda giggled, "You are so silly," and landed a loud smacking kiss on the side of his cheek so firmly that she left a lipstick mark, which, in rubbing off for him, made Peter sorrier she was leaving.

Alone now, Peter listened again to the announcement: 'We're now at Kings Cross where this service terminates. Please take a moment to ensure you have all of your personal belongings with you and do mind the gap as you alight.' He looked out of the window at rushed executives. Most had sombre faces, a few had glossy black or matt slate monoliths to their ears with shiny silver apples at the centre. No harm in letting the crowds die down. It surprised him how quickly the platform turned from bustling throng to ghostly emptiness.

He sighed, threw back half a cup of champagne and rubbed his lips with his palm. As he stood up to leave the carriage, he was amazed to see he wasn't alone. There was one remaining passenger: a stocky man whose face, covered by a hooded top, he couldn't see.

God this country is going to hell. I remember the day when nobody covered their face in public, when it would be rude to do so. Changing times, and not for the better.

Deciding not to contend with the tube, Peter hailed a cab outside the station. He knew the journey to Primrose Hill would be slow, it always was in the city traffic, but he couldn't face the tube. It was always full of people, devoid of life. Much better to engage in some banter with a Cockney driver on the way back. Spending the rest of the night in his apartment was a lonely prospect.

As it turned out the taxi driver wasn't a Cockney, he was Iranian, which was about as much conversation as Peter could get out of him. He ended up spending the journey absentmindedly shuffling the playing cards he'd unconsciously shoved in his Blazer pocket, staring out of the window as he did so.

The wing mirrors were out of sight from his position in the back seat. The motorcyclist, who followed them through heavy traffic, went unnoticed.

It wasn't until Peter fished in his wallet to pay the taxi driver that he realised how drunk he'd become. In the dim street light, all the coins looked the same and he ended up handing over two twenty pound notes.

"Keep the change."

"Thank you. Goodnight sir."

As the taxi drove off, he began fumbling in his jacket pockets for the keys to his flat. He mumbled under his breath, "Got to be here somewhere," finally yanking them from his inside pocket. He saw three keyholes, not the usual one, and covered one eye with his palm to help locate the real one. In his inebriated state, he failed to notice that the key didn't turn the usual three hundred and sixty degrees required to unlock it.

Peter closed the front door behind him and dropped his keys onto the mahogany telephone table. They slid off the shiny bevelled edge onto the floor and he dismissed the issue with the wave of his arm. He abandoned his original plan to make himself a coffee and decided to go straight to bed.

Peter used his hands to steady himself as he climbed the stairs towards his bedroom. He threw his jacket onto the bed and unfastened his cuffs on the way to the en-suite bathroom.

You should have learnt by your age Peter.

He ran the cold water and lowered his face towards it. The splashing cleared his head a little but what brought him to a state of stone cold sobriety was the mirrored reflection of a man standing behind him, a black hood covering his face. Cold eyes studied him through neat circular holes.

Chapter Sixteen

Cassie was only vaguely aware of Aaron running out to get help. The prospect of a fit wasn't her biggest fear. Seizures were foreboding but familiar, predictable.

It was the prospect of untold visions that terrified her. Seizures didn't always conjure these visions, and sometimes she saw things without fully slipping into a fit. But mostly the two came hand in hand; scary on their own, terrifying together.

Cassie could barely remember a time without this curse. Her first fit happened when she was four years old. She didn't know for *certain* that it was her first fit, but her mother assured her this was the case. The story had been told and retold, embellished each time.

Cassie had been with her mother, crossing the road towards Aldi's overflow car park in the cold winter rain. She weakly recalled her mother being cross with her for dawdling. Apparently, they were halfway across the road when Cassie tripped in her oversized red Wellingtons.

When her mum tried to pick her up by her arm, Cassie's body was shaking. Her mother's favourite description of this was, 'It was like holding up a writhing snake by its tail.' This apparently excused her accidentally dropping Cassie onto the crossing, in fright. An approaching car broke sharply. Following cars slipped along the surface water, clipping each other's bumpers. Cassie remembered none of that, of course.

But her mind was permanently etched with the vision, which accompanied the fit.

She recalled it vividly as a doctor rushed into Cassie's ward (his presence part of some numb, blurry version of reality). Miss Brody was their American neighbour who had come to the United Kingdom to be with, what her mother described as, her 'Internet husband.' Miss Brody's idyllic picture of what her life would be like with him evaporated seven weeks after they moved in together. He'd found someone else, so the rumour went. Another online lover, was the speculative gossip.

When Cassie's head had hit the road's damp gravel, she'd seen Miss Brody endlessly pacing the length of the house, moaning and sobbing. She'd witnessed this as if it were a film on fast forward, speeding towards an ending entirely in-keeping with this woman's misery: Miss Brody tied a rope around the banister of their staircase, shaped a noose with the other end, and slipped it over her neck. Despite her significant frame, she leapt like an Olympic hurdler, over the bannister. The sound of her spine snapping and the sight of the skin stretched over her elongated neck, had kept Cassie awake for days.

Like that vision, the memory of those sleepless nights never left her. Katie, Cassie's doll (her only companion), would sit next to Cassie's pillow, leaning against the wall. Sometimes Cassie would cuddle Katie as she drifted towards sleep, grateful for the softness of Katie's checked shift dress. But, the first night after her vision, Cassie couldn't bring herself to touch Katie, who looked at her with bent neck and ever-open eyes. Cassie stared back in the semi-dark, unable to shift the thought that perhaps Katie could see Mrs Brody too. Maybe that's why Katie couldn't close her eyes and couldn't sleep. And even if Katie *could* close them, the dark cave, which closed eyes transported her to at night, might be filled with the same bright clear images which haunted Cassie.

That night, before sleep had finally taken her, Cassie had pulled a black biro from her junk draw, pinned Katie's eyelids down and scribbled on them. She'd pressed so hard that Katie's right eyelid refused to open again, no matter how much Cassie flipped it with her thumb.

Each afternoon, after preschool, for the entire week that followed, Cassie had looked out of her window into Miss Brody's house, whilst holding Katie's hand - the doll's legs splayed limply on the floor. She frequently saw Miss Brody moving about *(pacing)*, relieved she was still alive.

On the Friday afternoon, Cassie had secretly stared out of her bedroom window again. There were no signs of Miss Brody until she saw paramedics wheel a stretcher up ramps and into the back of an ambulance. Through her own ghostly double reflection in the glazing, she'd regarded the stretchered figure. It was covered in what looked like tin foil and strapped tightly over the knees, across the waist and chest. The straps made prominent a bosom that Cassie guessed could only have belonged to Miss Brody.

Since then Cassie hadn't seen anything as disturbing as Miss Brody's suicide. Until this year, of course. This year something bad was happening and she couldn't figure out what. The images were so muddy and confusing. Cassie knew a man was doing things to people, hurting them. She felt their fear. They understood some of what he was doing (in a way that Cassie could not) but they didn't know why. It was all so bewildering. So disturbing.

She was aware of the doctor touching her arm, then last remaining part of her conscious mind prayed she wouldn't see anything as terrifying as a bound girl, or God forbid, someone doing what Miss Brody did.

Face down on the bed. How the hell did I get here? The last thing I remember was being in the bathroom and ... that man ... that mask.

Jesus, my face is completely numb. Pull your tongue back in your mouth for God sake. Oh my lord I can't. Sounds like someone unzipping. Who the hell is he? Where the hell is he? If I could only turn onto my back to see what's happening.

65

What's that stretching sensation at the top of my arms? I can't see my hands. Are they tied behind my back? Oh God I'm so numb. Anaesthetised? Wearing off? I want to shout out but I can't move my mouth, my face, my tongue. What's that scraping in my nails. Aaargh, sweet Jesus Christ, the pain in my hand. Please, I don't mind being numb again, just make the pain stop.

Is that the click of a shutter? What's just landed next to my head on the pillow? Sweet Jesus it's a fingernail. My fingernail.

Darkness.

I'm walking downstairs. I don't know the house, but I'm sure I can find the kitchen. I get to the sink and carefully shift cans of upholstery cleaner, tins of shoe polish and fly spray. The wasp on a can reminds me of my wasp. I smile. I'm looking for detergent and find it. Great, liquitabs. That's perfect; I can just make a small hole, and squeeze out what I need.

I'm walking back up the stairs. My breathing is slow, deep, pulse steady. I'm back in the bedroom. I see the man, naked, face down, arms tied to slats halfway down the bed. His legs are taped to the ends of the bed. I see him, but I don't pay him much attention. The immediate job is the stain. The blood's okay, that gives effect, but there's other stuff. I must have frightened him too much. That's okay. I like surprises.

I bite the plastic of the sachet. I do it quickly to avoid getting any in my mouth. Ugh, I did get some, the taste pools water in the well of my mouth. Must swallow it, not spit it out. That's better.

Now, to clean this up. I'm humming a tune I don't recognise.

Chapter Seventeen

Laura stood outside the room in which Hilary April was winding up her final class of the morning. As she waited, she looked at a wall display she imagined the class inside had created. It was made up of pictures painted on white A4 sheets, backed with slightly larger cards of various colours giving each the rough appearance of being framed. The display was entitled, "My earliest memory." Most of the pictures were of a single person, sometimes men, usually women, whom Laura imagined were the children's parents. A few were comparatively abstract, depicting swings and toys.

One picture she felt had a special depth and beauty. It depicted an outreached child's arm, holding hands with that of a teddy bear. The picture was so strikingly different from the rest that Laura leaned closer, looking for the scrawled name of the artist. Perhaps it was Cassie? Written in blue ink on the bottom right hand corner: Aaron Hall.

A pang of maternal disappointment startled her, and she took a step back.

Where the hell did that come from?

Laura couldn't have children. The last boyfriend she'd had, before Malcolm, was obsessed with having kids. He'd startled her by mentioning it on their first date. Whilst their relationship only lasted six weeks (he had this annoying habit of biting his nails over dinner) it had got Laura thinking.

Not many more fertile years left, and I don't even know if I can have kids, even if 'Mr Right' or at least 'Mr Good Enough' does exist.

She'd taken an afternoon off work and was tested. And that was the end of it. She'd briefly toyed with the idea of IVF but that was a commitment she had neither the energy nor the funds for. It was hard enough for her to commit to sharing a bed, let alone a child. She'd mostly managed to banish thoughts of infertility.

Laura had become determined not to dwell on the issue. She remembered a saying, or a prayer, perhaps from Sunday school: find the grace to accept the things you cannot change. It became a mantra, her last reflection before sleep.

She avoided TV shows that extolled the wonders of motherhood and her work was a constant reminder that parenthood, and childhood for that matter, had many downsides. She'd almost persuaded herself that she was lucky, in a way. It simplified her relationships and choices of partner. If a prospective soulmate wanted kids, that was a clear non-starter.

Malcolm never wanted children. He was too busy with work to be a proper father (his words, not hers). At first she suspected he said this to placate her but, over time, she'd come to believe him.

Pupils, bursting through the classroom door, broke her thoughts. She heard Miss April from inside the room, "It's not a race. Walk!" As the children passed, she offered each a smile. One or two smiled back. The others ran off without noticing her. Laura knocked on the side of the open door, "Hello again, may I come in?"

Hilary glanced at Laura then looked away, preoccupied with hurriedly collecting text books. "Mrs Robinson, Hi. Look ... I'm really sorry, but I don't have time to talk at the minute. I've got to prepare for the next class *and* I need to grab a bite to eat. I'm sorry but could we do this some other time?"

"I understand. Let me help you gather these books, then why don't we walk together to buy a sandwich. I don't need long and we can walk and talk." Laura wasn't going to take 'later' for an answer and they both knew it.

"Okay, I know a place nearby." They walked down a busy corridor, each occasionally sidestepping kids who weren't looking where they were going. One knocked Hilary off balance, "Slow Down!" Miss April looked weary, perhaps fed up of being the nag.

"Look, Miss April."

"You can call me Hilary."

"Hilary, I'll get straight to the point, I know you're busy. Since we last spoke, I've taken on Cassie Janus's case, for the foreseeable future at least, and I just wanted to gain your view on a couple of things."

"Okay, how can I help?"

"From speaking to her mother, it looks like Cassie's accusing a girl - Rachel Atkinson - of bullying her on the day of her accident. I wondered if you'd had any dealings with Rachel and whether she'd given you any cause for concern.

I also wanted to talk to you about Cassie and her family situation. I'll be paying a visit to their house later in the week and I'd appreciate a second opinion about Miss Janus's ability to ... well about how much support we might have to give the family."

"Mrs Robinson, I'll tell you what I know but I'm not sure how much help it's going to be. If I was being frank, and probably a little unprofessional, I'd tell you that Rachel Atkinson is turning out to be a nasty piece of work, which isn't a surprise given the environment she's growing up in."

"Have you been to her house?"

"No ... but I met her mother once at a parents' evening and that was enough. I've been doing this job for almost ten years and that's the first time someone's been abusive and sworn at me."

Hilary paused, and Laura wasn't sure if that was her last word on the subject. Then, perhaps feeling guilty for letting her harassed impatience colour her account, she added, "Then again, maybe I just caught her on a bad day. Perhaps I shouldn't speculate about Rachel's home life."

Some people feel a sting of conscience when they bitch about people behind their back. Laura guessed Hilary was one of those people. Giving Rachel's family the benefit of the doubt sounded like Hilary easing that sting. Laura didn't buy it.

"Best to be on the safe side, though. If you plan to visit them at home, I suggest making sure someone knows where you're going."

"Standard protocol."

"Of course. I don't mean to tell you your job."

Laura felt her tone might have been unintentionally officious.

"That's okay, it's sound advice. And what about Rachel's relationship with Cassie?"

"I've not heard about them falling out, but it wouldn't surprise me if Rachel was hassling Cassie. There have been plenty of complaints from other parents and Cassie's ... different, you know ... an easy target. I think we've given Rachel Atkinson one too many chances, but hey, I'm not in charge of school policy."

"Thank you, that's very helpful. What's your view of Cassie and her family?" They'd reached the outside of a corner shop, a short walk from the school gates. Hilary stopped and turned towards Laura.

"Let's nip in, grab a sandwich, and talk as we walk back. My assessment of Cassie's situation is nowhere near as straight forward."

Hilary was through the queue first and waited for Laura outside. She leant on the circular steel rail of a disabled ramp. The flimsy carrier bag dangled from her folded arms - her wrist through its handle.

"Sorry to keep you."

"It's okay."

On the way back to school, Hilary's pace slowed and Laura sensed her relaxing. "So what is it you want to know about Cassie?"

"Honestly anything that could help us determine how much attention we should pay to her family circumstances."

"And by 'attention' I am taking it you mean whether you should consider removing her?"

"Not anything that drastic I'm sure … for the time being at least. But I'm almost certain Miss Janus will paint a rosy picture when I visit. I'll try to get Cassie to open up to me, but I suspect she's old enough to want to protect her mother. I wondered if you had any concerns worth following up on?"

"Mrs Robinson, I'm sure you'll draw your own conclusions when you go round there, but my assessment is this: Cassie pretty much looks after herself. She's not the only child who has to walk home alone, but she does hang round longer than anyone else. I imagine from one day to the next she doesn't know for sure if anyone *will* pick her up - of course she never admits as much."

"You've spoken with Cassie about this?"

"Once."

"Recently?"

"No, it was about six months ago." Hilary paused, opened, closed then scrunched her mouth as though a truth was resisting escape.

"Look, I don't like talking about this, but it might come out when you start speaking to Cassie, so you might as well hear it from me. I would prefer you keep what I'm about to tell you to yourself."

"Of course."

They'd reached the classroom and sat at either side of Miss April's desk, opening triangular sandwich packets. Hilary's was a BLT. She used her well-manicured nails to extract thick slices of tomato, dropping them into the bin next to her desk.

She grabbed a tissue from a box on the desk, wiping mayonnaise from her fingertips as she spoke.

"Cassie came to me, saying she'd had a really bad dream she couldn't talk to anyone else about. She'd dreamt that a man I knew was ... was looking at pictures of ... at pictures he shouldn't be and that the dream was 'ever so real.' That was strange enough, but then she went on, begging me to look for a memory stick tucked under the water tank in my loft. She said, 'Stop him, please I don't want to dream of it any more.'" Laura had stopped eating and listened intently. Hilary paused again, looked down and took a deep breath before continuing.

"I didn't handle it well and dismissed what she'd said. I just put it down to a silly dream. I felt so invaded by what she'd said ... I immediately blamed it on her unsettled home life. That's when I asked her about how come she hangs back at school so often. She was reluctant to talk but *did* say she couldn't always remember whether her mummy was due to pick her up that day. I knew it was a lie - she's far too bright to regularly forget something like that."

"Can I ask, did you ever tell your partner about Cassie's dream?"

Hilary looked down at her scarcely touched sandwich. She sighed, dropped the sandwich packet onto her desk and brushed her hands over the bin.

"Oh what the hell, I'm surprised no one has told you yet, it was the number one topic of conversation around here for long enough. What she said just got me a little curious. I cursed my own stupidity as I climbed into the loft to check out what she'd said. I slipped my hand into a small gap under the water tank, and there it was. I can't tell you how weird that moment was. I remember it resting on my palm. I stared at it for ages. "

"Were there images?"

"Yes, I saw one, the police said there were thousands."

"So you reported him?"

"Of course, in an instant. Who wouldn't? You think you know someone ..." Hilary's eyes lost focus and her head turned towards the window. Laura resisted the urge to speak.

Hilary finally continued, "Anyway, I don't know how Cassie knew what she knew and I'm not going to get into a debate about that. All I will say is that Cassie Janus is a bright girl, with levels of perception beyond that of anyone I've ever met.

Her mother struggles to cope, sure, but does that put Cassie in any danger? Probably not. I get the impression she can look after herself. These days she even seems relaxed about her epilepsy. If I were you, my only concern would be whether Miss Janus leaves her alone in the house. I've no proof of this, but Cassie's never mentioned grandparents or family friends. I'm guessing her mum doesn't have much of a support network. Look, Mrs Robinson, I really do have to prepare for my class now, would you excuse me?"

"Of course. Thank you for your time. Please don't worry about what you've told me, I can assure you it will remain between us."

"I would appreciate it. You know ... Oh it doesn't matter."

"No, go on, please."

"Look, I don't know what you believe in, Mrs Robinson, and for that matter, some days, neither do I. But now and again I toy with certain ideas. I'm pretty certain that there's no afterlife and that there's no re-incarnation. But there *is* something about Cassie that makes me doubt myself.

The way she speaks, it's her vocabulary. A kid of her age should talk with a naivety, an innocence. Cassie talks with anything but ... and those eyes of hers. I don't know, it's maybe that she's just seen too much, but she's one of those kids who seem like they've been here before, you know the type?"

Hilary turned her back on Laura, and began scrubbing away at a whiteboard with a sponge-tipped board rubber, attacking faint black marks that weren't budging. She continued talking as she worked, "Oh look, I'm just trying to say that Cassie's a special kid and I wish you luck with her." Hilary took a large (first) bite of her sandwich, having to rip a protruding, stiff piece of bacon from her teeth.

"Look ... sincerely ... thank you, not just for your time ... but for your honesty too." Laura stood up to leave. She hovered by the doorway.

Hilary carried on scrubbing and replied without looking up, through half-chewed food, "You're welcome."

Chapter Eighteen

"Cassie, there's someone here to see you."

The size of their flat meant Leanne didn't have to raise her voice greatly, for Cassie to hear her from the bedroom.

"Who is it Mum?"

"It's that boy ... Aaron, that's your name isn't it honey? Yeah Aaron."

"Can you send him in?" There was no reply but Cassie heard approaching footsteps outside her bedroom door.

She was grateful for the visit. During the last few days, Cassie and her mother had barely spoken, exchanging perfunctory words, avoiding the subject on both of their minds: why Leanne had not been there to pick Cassie up from school, and why she chose to lie about it.

With each passing day Cassie's arm and shoulder blade were hurting less, but she had no desire to venture out of the house and doubted her mum would have let her if she'd asked. So for the past three days she'd stayed in, mostly reading.

Since arriving home, she'd had only one brief seizure and the accompanying dream was unsettling but nothing like the disturbing visions, which had plagued her since the accident. She was thankful for it.

Aaron poked his plump, ruddy cheeks around the corner of her bedroom door and smiled, "Can I come in?"

"Yep." Cassie sat up in bed. Aaron placed himself on the edge of the duvet, nestled into the lump made by Cassie's upturned feet, placing a small rucksack on the floor as he did so. She closed her book with a thump and placed it on the bedside table.

"Old Potter beaten off the evil minions of old what's 'is face yet?"

"Not quite." She smiled, having grown that thick skin which most people develop at some point in their youth.

"Aaron, thanks for coming, I've been going out of my mind, stuck in here like this."

"Now ... what sort of person would leave his best friend to get better, without the advantage of a hand held computer to wile away the hours?"

Aaron reached into his rucksack. He pulled out a metallic burgundy Nintendo DS. It was deeply scratched and one hinge was cracked. He handed it to Cassie.

"It's a little battered, but it still works okay."

"I can't take this, you use it all the time."

"Don't get me wrong Janus, it's not for keeps, just for a week or two. By the time I get it back, it'll be a novelty again."

"Thanks."

"There's a Harry Potter game in there as well, so you don't get Hogwarts withdrawal."

Cassie ignored his gentle mocking and, with some effort, sat forward to offer him a weak hug, which he gently returned. When she let him go, she saw his cheeks had flushed. He was a naturally red faced child who turned crimson when embarrassed. Cassie couldn't resist, "Aaron, is it too warm in here?"

"Very funny ... have you been managing to get any sleep with that sling on?"

"Not much. It's my shoulder, it wrecks during the night."

"Bet you've not even cried once though, have you?"

Cassie considered a moment, "No ... guess that's a bit strange?"

"Only for a girl." She would have thumped his arm for that comment, if she'd been fit. "Mind you, I think *I'd* have blubbered like a baby if I'd broken my arm. Still on painkillers?"

"Yep, for about another week I guess."

"Still sending you squiffy?" Cassie stared at him for a moment, inferring doubt. How could he be so dismissive? She'd confided in him.

"You said you believed me." Her voice moved up half an octave and she shuffled back, more upright, so her toe mound no longer touched him.

"No, I do Cassie, it's just..."

"Just what?"

"There are some things you said that don't add up."

"Like what?"

"Well ... if you can *really* tell the future why wouldn't you prevent a load of bad things happening to people? And why wouldn't you just get your mum to place bets on horses for you? You could both get filthy rich."

"Aaron, it just doesn't work like that."

"How does it work?"

"I'm not sure I want to tell you any more. I don't think you'll believe me."

"No, please Cassie, I want to know. I don't mean to not believe you, I just want to understand."

"I don't see *everything* and I can't *make* myself see things. They come to me, almost every time when I fit and sometimes when I'm close to one and it goes away. And I never see things that are just facts. It's always something emotional, usually something bad."

"But millions of things go on in the world that are bad, what makes you not see something from ... I don't know ... China or somewhere?"

"Aaron. Quiet."

"What?"

"Just be quiet for a minute. I know that will be difficult," she offered him a teasing smile, "but be totally quiet and tell me what you can hear."

Aaron looked up at the peeling wallpaper on Cassie's bedroom ceiling, trying to concentrate on sounds. After a moment Cassie enquired, "Well?"

"A dog barking, your clock ticking and a door slamming in the kitchen."

"Yep, you heard the dog that was far away because it was loud and you heard the clock ticking because it was close, even though it was quiet. What I see is like that. If someone next door feels really sad and I mean *really* sad, I see what's happening to them and sometimes, what *will* happen.

So it usually has to be close to me; if someone in China is sad, I don't feel it at all. But if fifty thousand people are sad because of say, an earthquake, I might see something because their feelings, when they are all together like that, are so loud. I knew about the Tsunami in Japan thirty minutes before it happened, I couldn't exactly see it, I felt like I was being washed away, surrounded by ... by bodies. I don't know *when* something's going to happen, apart from, now and again, I'll see a clock or a watch. Then I'll know the time, even the date sometimes."

Aaron looked down at Cassie's duvet.

"Look Aaron. I know you don't believe me and in a way I don't blame you. But ... you know what ... you're my friend and *should* know me well enough to know that I don't lie. And if you need proof, I'll give it to you." Aaron looked up at her.

"How?"

"Are you free this afternoon?"

"Yes, why?"

"I want you to go down to the playing field, and hide just behind the grass mound, near the swings. Take your phone with you and call me at three thirty. I'll make sure I have our phone next to my bed. You'll be able to see the clock tower from there. Use the time on the tower, not your phone, just in case."

"Why? In case of what?"

"I don't want to tell you now. But would you do it for me?"

Aaron held his palms up as if checking for rain. "Sure, why not."

"It will only take thirty minutes, then you can come back here or go home, it's up to you. But Aaron, make sure you stay out of sight. You might remember, just in view of the mound, there's a line of trees and beyond that line, a dark trench that used to be a shallow stream before it was dammed, where trees now hang over. Stay out of sight of those trees."

"I know it, but why Cassie?"

"Just trust me. Call me at three thirty and stay out of sight."

Chapter Nineteen

The bright autumn sun had done little to dry out the grass. As Aaron lay on his front at a sloping angle with his stomach pressed against the ground, he felt dew seeping through his jeans.

All I need is a pair of binoculars and I'll look like a solider scoping an enemy base. Cassie Janus, what have you got me into?

All was quiet on the field; it was rare to see kids playing there this time of year. As Cassie had described, Aaron could see the clock tower of a distant church. If he concentrated, he could read the time: three twenty-five. He pulled his iPhone out of his pocket (noting its time - the church's clock was three minutes slow) and brought Cassie's number up on the display, preparing to call her quickly, when the time came. He only had 21% charge and cursed his luck.

Still it should be enough to make the call.

After half a ring, Cassie picked up.

"Aaron?"

Aaron kept his voice low, covert, "Yes it's me."

"What's the time, I mean the time on the clock tower?"

"Three twenty-five, maybe twenty-six now."

"Good, not too far out. We've not missed it. You're early, it won't happen for another few minutes. Have you got enough charge on your phone to stay on the line for around fifteen minutes?"

Aaron looked at his charge and was dubious, but liked to be optimistic, "Should be okay. Stop worrying. Anyway, what is it you think I'm going to see?"

"Not 'think' ... know. Rachel Atkinson and her friends, Maria Richardson and Tanya Reynolds will shortly walk down the gravel track next to the snooker hall and onto the field. They'll have someone with them. She's a new girl at the school. Her name is Sophie, I don't know her second name."

"I can just about make out the track from ... wait, I see them."

"Stay very still and quiet. It won't happen if they think anyone else is there." Aaron's breath was visible against the cold air. He felt exposed.

"What, what will happen?"

"Aaron, Sophie is trying to make friends. She's not worked out yet who she can trust and who she can't. Her mother pulled her out of her last school because of people picking on her. She met Tanya yesterday, who asked her to come and meet her friends. Tanya suggested they could play on the swings. Sophie didn't realise that Rachel would be there. She's walking into a trap."

Aaron could see a girl he didn't recognise, and presumed it was Sophie, pointing towards the swings that were positioned on the side of the field, not far from Aaron. He lowered his voice still further, to a whisper.

"Cassie, I have to move. I think they're coming over here."

"Aaron no! Stay put. Trust me, they won't come over to the swings." Aaron watched as Tanya appeared to say something to Sophie and gestured towards the other side of the field, towards the tree line Cassie had described. The group changed direction, heading towards the trees.

"You're right. They all seem happy enough though."

"They're pretending. They want her to think that they're her friends."

"Cassie, look I know I like reading about weird stuff, but this is starting to get too creepy for words. Do I need to go and get help?"

"No Aaron."

"So nothing bad's going to happen to her?"

"It will. But don't do anything."

"Why Cassie?"

"Because then you'll believe."

"Cassie, I already do. Come on, tell me what will happen if I do nothing." The three girls slipped behind the line of trees and disappeared out of sight.

"They'll disappear any moment and within five minutes you will see Sophie running out, probably holding her hand and crying. Within a week or so it will have stopped hurting, I'm sure."

"What will they have done to her?"

"It's a made up initiation. They'll tell her that everyone who makes it into their circle of friends has passed the match test."

"What's that?"

"They light a match and hold it under her palm. If she can stand the pain until the match burns out, she's in their gang. If she can't, she's out. She's so desperate to fit in that she will hold it as long as she can, but they know it's impossible."

"My God, Cassie, I've got to stop them."

"Too late, it's already happening." There was a young, distant scream, quickly building to a crescendo. Sophie burst through the line of the trees, all arms and legs, uncoordinated like a straw man. She was still too far away to know for sure, but Aaron thought she was crying; the hidden ordeal had reddened her complexion.

Laughter echoed across the field.

"Cassie I'm hanging up."

"Aaro..." Click.

Aaron turned onto his back, still positioned out of sight behind the grassed mound. He felt shame for not believing Cassie, but anger overwhelmed regret. He could have walked up to that group and disturbed their plan. He could have prevented that girl going through all that pain, and not just the physical pain either, the pain of trying to fit in, of being tricked when you're at your most vulnerable. Aaron thought he knew Cassie, he admired her thoughtfulness, her kindness.

How could she have let this happen?

Aaron laid low for over twenty minutes, dwelling on what he'd witnessed, until all the girls were long gone. His eyes were red and sore from crying. As he stood up to dust down his dirty clothes, he considered what to do next. He had a great desire to run home and hide in his room but he had so many questions for Cassie that he knew, when he started walking, it would be in the direction of her flat.

Random thoughts entered Aaron's head as he walked.

Cassie can see the future. There's a name for that, what is it? But nobody can do that, maybe God, but no one else. Can she see my future? Does she know when I will die? Or when my parent's will die? How does she live like this? Why wouldn't she let me stop them? I could have stopped them, I'm sure. I don't think it's safe to be close to Cassie. She used to make me feel safe and happy. Now I feel very unsafe, very unhappy.

"Wow Aaron. Can't keep you away from here today. People will start to think you two are an item. And look at the state of your jeans, you look like you walked here on your knees."

Cassie overheard the conversation and shouted, "Mum stop teasing and let him in." When Aaron stepped into Cassie's bedroom, in one sense he looked like the boy who'd visited earlier. In another, he looked like a complete stranger. This wasn't because of the smeared green streaks on his jeans and the patches of mud on his top. His face was a potent red, his eyes bloodshot and the earlier concern in his expression was gone.

"Aaron, sit down."

"No."

"Don't worry about getting the cover dirty. Just sit down."

"Cassie, I don't think I can. Right now I'm so mad, it's all I can do to be in the same room as you."

"I know it must've been a shock."

"Shock? You described every detail of what would happen and let me watch, completely helpless. I thought you were nice."

"Aaron, keep your voice down, my mum will hear." He dropped his volume to a whispered shout.

"It's ... it's unnatural what you can do."

Cassie's jaw weakened and her bottom lip twitched. No tears yet, but they were on their way.

"Do you think I don't know that Aaron? Don't you know how difficult it is to be me? Can't you imagine?"

"Why didn't you let me stop them?"

"What would have happened if I had?"

"Well I don't know but-"

"That's it. You don't know, and I don't know either. You could have made the situation worse. They might have gone after you. Rachel's capable of much worse than what she did today.

I can only ever see one eventuality. It's dangerous to act differently, to change the future. The last time I did that, I tried to get away from Rachel and look what happened. Instead of a bust up nose, I got hit by a car and have a broken arm and shoulder and deep scar in my hip, that will *never* heal. I didn't see that coming."

"But you stopped the wasps from stinging me."

"Yes, and for weeks I worried. Perhaps you were meant to be stung. Perhaps in visiting you in hospital, your mum might have been out when someone burgled your house."

"That didn't happen."

"Yes but I didn't *know* it wouldn't happen. As scary as it is, if I know what's going to happen I can face it. Not knowing is even worse."

"I don't understand." His voice was now quieter, sad and dejected.

"That's just it, Aaron. No one does and no one ever will." Cassie raised her knees up to prop up her elbows; her hands covering her eyes. Aaron stood, listening to her sobs, not knowing whether to stay or go.

Cassie's cries were becoming louder, out of control, and Aaron was concerned her mum might come in and ask what was causing her upset. He sat down by her side, half on, half off the bed. He placed an arm around her shoulders. She shuffled so he could sit properly and buried her head in his plump chest. Years of keeping her secret spilled out in her tears.

Chapter Twenty

Laura Robinson brought her ageing Ford Fiesta around the corner of an unfamiliar road in Thornton Heath, a northern district of Croydon. The road was correct: 'Braffield Road' she remembered that, but couldn't recall the number. She neatly (and smugly) parallel parked into a tight spot between a squat Smart car and an ivory Vauxhall Corsa. The Corsa had blacked out windows and a sticker in the back windscreen: a devil's fork in luminous green. Both had their wing mirrors turned in - a local trend. A line of parked cars, on the other side of the street, boasted battle scars. Scrapes and scratches ran along their doors and wings.

I shouldn't have to use my own car for this type of visit.

Papers fanned out of a tan file on the passenger seat. The file had a white label: 'Cassie Janus,' printed in bold businesslike Arial font. She flicked through the papers, searching for the address. She found it beneath her call log - five voice mails left for Miss Atkinson over four days, with no response.

Thirteen Braffield Road, how did I forget that?

She bundled the papers back into the file. The post-war semi to her left was number five. The owners were so sure of this, there was a brass number on the door *and* a ceramic Mediterranean nameplate (spelling out the numbers) to the left of the living room window.

Might as well stay parked here.

She climbed out of the car, quickly becoming grateful for her thick, if inelegant, fleeced jacket which boasted the embroidered motif of Browns bowling alley on the breast. The sun was retreating rapidly, the temperature plummeting.

Sporadic street lights clicked into a low, ineffectual glow. Laura walked along in the orange half-light, Cassie's file pressed against her chest behind folded arms.

She casually glanced into the houses she passed. With their shallow gardens, it was impossible not to see what was going on in front rooms. She assumed most people were out at work, their windows black and lifeless. In others, television sets flickered; kids shows in front of wide-eyed nursery children. A blonde boy with a thumb in his mouth turned and stared back. His mother looked up from her ironing. Laura turned her head, eyes averted towards the opposite pavement.

She squinted in the twilight.

Did I see someone walk out and then step back into that alleyway in front of the Londis shop?

You're imagining things.

The figure, if it had existed, was largely indistinguishable. A man? She thought so, from the cut of the silhouette and its height - Roger's height.

Stop it. Why the hell are you thinking about Roger again?

She knew why. Memories were like uncharged wires, dormant, patiently waiting to jolt into life, to make connections. And when they do, you have no control over which lights come on and which stay dark. She'd recently thought of Cassie, of childlessness, of relationships, of how kind Malcolm is and how ... (at the end of that unwelcome chain reaction) ... how evil Roger had been.

She muttered to herself, "Stop it."

As she approached number thirteen, she was so shocked by what she saw, thoughts of Roger and lurking strangers evaporated. Her jaw gaped and the file slipped a couple of inches in her weakened grip. Her legs refused to move and she came to a full stop some five yards short of the house.

Most of the sofa was obscured, though she could clearly see a man's denim clad leg and bare arm hanging over the sofa's armrest. In his hand he loosely held a partly crumpled can of Red Stripe lager. He would have been sitting in darkness, had it not been for the strong, flickering blue-white light emitted by the television in the corner of the room.

It was the television's unmistakable images, which stopped her so abruptly. She could only imagine the three young women she saw were naked, though the screen only showed their faces. They watched each other whilst waiting for their turn; making dewy eyes at the graphic sight happening in front of them at close proximity.

Laura's stomach turned.

Anyone walking down this street, children for God's sake, would be subjected to this filth. What's wrong with these people? My God, Rachel could be inside.

Her feeling of sickness morphed into rage and she found herself marching towards their front door. In a rational state, she would have walked away and come back with a colleague. They were so stretched that doubling up on visits was almost an unforgivable luxury, but for some house calls there was no other safe option. This was one of those calls. Laura knocked on the front door with an urgency fit for an evacuation.

She heard faint swearing coming from an indeterminable place within the house. To her right, through the living room window, the sofa was no longer in view, though she could still see the television clearly. She hoped he would have turned it off, but the image was merely paused and she felt her stomach go again.

The man who finally opened the door was much taller and broader than she'd envisaged. She guessed he was probably in his mid thirties. He was unshaven and patches of grey sprouted through his otherwise brown stubble. His greasy, shoulder length hair was slicked back behind his ears. The writing on his black T-Shirt had perished into illegible grey flecks. Her eyes skimmed lower. She could see through his jeans that the video had achieved the desired effect. She raised her gaze.

Before he spoke, he straightened his posture and breathed deeply, expanding his chest. He leant forward, over her. If his intention was to make her feel weak and small, it had worked.

"We don't like cold callers."

Laura tried to find confidence and some calm, feeling overcome by a jarring mixture of loathing and fear, "I'm not selling anything. I'm Laura Robinson from children's services." Her fingers habitually located her ID in her jacket pocket. She held it upwards at a comfortable reading distance. His face screwed up in concentration, as though reading didn't come easily.

"Well, did you tell us you were coming?"

"No, I left messages but-"

"So you're a cold caller then. Anyway, what the hell do you want? I'm busy."

"I'm here to talk with you about Rachel. Is her mother in?"

"Yeah, she's in"

"And Rachel?"

"Out playing."

It was getting dark, and cold. A ten-year-old girl had no reason to be out, but at least Rachel wasn't being subjected to pornography in the house.

Not today anyway.

"May I come in?"

Laura you must be mad. What on earth are you doing, asking to come into this house?

"Look it's not a good time." They were interrupted by a screeching call, coming from upstairs, "Lee, who is it?"

He twisted his shoulder to shout up the stairs, "Children's services or something. I'm getting rid of them." As he turned back to face Laura, she could see a woman, presumably Rachel's mother, clambering down the stairs, tying an off-white dressing gown cord around her waist. Laura was curious to see this woman's reaction to her partner's choice of viewing.

Laura, on tiptoe and with elevated chin, called over his shoulder. "Miss Atkinson, I just want a quick chat about Rachel, can I come in?"

"Lee, let her in. You're not going to be long are you? It's just we've got people coming round." Laura suspected this was a lie. Lee put his back to the wall and, making a sweeping gesture with his arm, offered a sarcastic welcome, "Do come in and take a seat in the lounge."

When the paused image of the television came into view, Laura saw Miss Atkinson's eyes roll. It wasn't quite exasperation, but at the least a waning patience. "Lee I've told you to close the blinds when you're watching that shit."

"Oh yeah, I forgot." He gave them a disingenuous smile but resumed his original position on the sofa, without the slightest sign that he was going to take any notice of his partner. She shot him a look, then moved her gaze towards the window and then back at Lee. It was a look that said, 'Don't mess with me Lee, get it done.' He sighed, forced himself out of the chair and yanked the blind's cord. The slats slapped shut. He slumped back down on the chair.

"Now turn that crap off, whilst Miss? ..."

"Mrs ... Mrs Robinson, Laura."

"Whilst, Mrs Robinson's here."

"Perhaps she wants to watch it with us?" He smiled at them both. Laura resisted the urge to walk over to him and slap him across the face, managing a calm response. "No thank you, Mr ... ?"

"You don't need to know who I am."

"I see."

She tried to keep a game face.

Lee's partner fired silent, disapproving daggers in his direction. He sighed, grabbed the remote and turned off the television. Laura was greatly relieved.

"So Mrs Robinson, I suppose this is about Rachel. She's not got herself into trouble has she?"

"No, but there have been a few comments made at school that are cause for concern and I just wanted to talk these through with you."

"What sort of comments?"

"Are you aware of a girl named Cassie Janus?"

"No, never heard of her. Should I have?"

"I don't suppose so, unless Rachel has mentioned her. She was hit by a car, a little over a week ago."

"Oh, poor kid. Is she okay?"

"I hear she's on the mend."

"What does this have to do with Rachel?"

"From what I can gather, Cassie was cycling recklessly in an attempt to get away from Rachel." Miss Atkinson paused for a moment to digest what she'd heard. Her face hardened.

"From what you can gather? I think you'll need to be more specific than that, given what you seem to be accusing my daughter of."

"It was other kids in the school, who said-"

Only one kid actually, if you didn't count Cassie.

"Said what exactly? Actually it doesn't matter what. Whatever they said, it's probably bullshit. You know kids."

The word of one child didn't feel credible. Laura felt her position weaken.

"Look, I'm not saying that this ... this alleged bullying-"

"Bullying?"

"... is happening, but we have to follow up on what's been said."

"Look Mrs Robinson. If there has been a complaint made to the police, and they have evidence that Rachel has done something wrong, then I'm all ears, but this just sounds like some playground nonsense that, frankly, I'm amazed you're wasting tax payer's money following up. I think we're done."

"Are you going to at least discuss this with your daughter?" Miss Atkinson stood up and shepherded Laura through the living room door. "If I decide to talk to Rachel about this, then that's my decision and has nothing to do with you."

Laura squared up to Miss Atkinson in the hall. The lack of respect from this woman, fifteen years Laura's junior, was rattling her professionalism.

"Miss Atkinson, it's as simple as this. If you want me to open a whole can of worms about the toxic environment I've just witnessed, and have the police knocking on your door, then fine, we can go down that route." Miss Atkinson folded her robed arms. Her features appeared sharp now, almost vulpine.

"But I would prefer for us to co-operate in this. It's probably nothing more than a childhood spat that needs nipping in the bud before it escalates. All I am asking is that you talk to your daughter."

"Look, okay Mrs Robinson, I'll talk to her." The door was opened for Laura, a strong hint for her to leave. It's closing cut off her last statement, "I'll be in t-"

Laura stood on the doorstep, relieved to be outside but exasperated by their conversation. She heard Lee shout after her from inside the house, "Be careful out there love. Check the news, you don't want to be walking out alone in the dark. You never know what will happen."

She heard, or perhaps imagined, a self-satisfied snigger. Through the small gap to the side of the blind, she saw Miss Atkinson land a blow with a cushion across the side of Lee's head. Like a lion, bothered by nothing more potent that a buzzing fly, he turned to look at her. Miss Atkinson swore. The television came to life again, its flickering light licking the narrow slits of the blind.

What a family! That poor girl.

As she drove home, Laura struggled to shake a burning image of pornography. She turned on the radio as a distraction. It was shortly before four. The pre-tuned station was a local, commercial one and she'd turned on just in time for an advert from a payday lender, followed by one handling PPI claims.

Desperate people borrowing money at extortionate rates and seeking compensation from irresponsible banks. That's the world we're now living in.

She huffed a sigh, but endured the adverts in the knowledge that local news was imminent.

The top story was the inexplicable death of a well-loved West End producer. His distraught friends and colleagues were being interviewed. After the interviews there was some unhelpful speculation from the reporter about the victim, Peter Eccleston, being openly bisexual and that perhaps it might have been a chance encounter turned sour. The police were issuing little information at this stage but confirmed they were treating the incident as suspicious.

She clicked off the radio and sighed. Two murders in less than a week. This one in Primrose Hill of all places. I thought this city was supposed to be getting safer.

Chapter Twenty-One

An hour earlier, as Laura had been readying to visit Miss Atkinson, Aaron had been at home in his room, reading.

His knees and head propped up his Dr Who duvet, forming a tent. He read in secrecy with the help of his phone's LED light. He'd bought the book from a second-hand bookstall on the market. He swore the lady who sold it to him must have been visually impaired. Her refusal to make the sale, which he'd predicted, never came and he handed her two pounds, making off before the lady had chance to change her mind. The price was steep given its condition. Its pages were overused, flaccid. A few were coming loose.

It was entitled: 'Zodiac - The Shocking True Story of America's Most Elusive Serial Killer.' Aaron had read about Zodiac before but never in so much chilling detail. It was a book he would normally race through, always looking forward to the next page. He read to escape from reality, to different worlds.

Since discovering Cassie's abilities, scary events were less distant. His reading didn't feel like an escape anymore, it exposed the dark truths of his own world, a shrinking, tightening planet. He absorbed every page, expecting a sense of intrigue that never came.

At one point he wondered whether he should be reading this at all. A stranger approached a young couple, vanished and then reemerged, wearing a black hood. As Aaron read the killer's words: "I'm going to have to stab you people," he had to put the book down and take a deep breath.

It's not real, its not real, its not real.

But of course he knew it *was* real and that the killer had never been found.

But America is so far away, that wouldn't happen here, not in England.

But if his books had taught him anything, it was that it *could* and *did* happen in England. His perspective shifted. He now understood Cassie's view and his mother's concern.

What am I reading this stuff for?

"Aaron, Aaron," his mum shouting from downstairs was a welcome distraction.

"Yes Mum?"

"It's Cassie."

"I'm coming."

Aaron's mother met him halfway down the stairs and handed him the phone. He raced back to his room, breathing heavily between words, "Cassie?"

"Yes, Aaron, it's me."

"Have you got a television in your room?"

"Yes."

"Turn onto channel three, the local news."

"Okay, wait a minute." He put the phone down to find the remote. Aaron's room was always a mess; his mother was way past the point of nagging him to keep it tidy. He pushed aside piles of clothes on the floor, uncovering the remote.

The television hummed a low tone as it turned on. On channel three the news was halfway through reporting the murder Laura had heard of on her drive back home. There was a picture of the victim, Peter Eccleston, in the top right corner of the screen, which looked like it had been taken in a studio. A young woman labelled as 'friend' by a caption, was giving an impromptu and tearful eulogy. Aaron, half watching the screen and half watching his step, moved back to the bed and picked up the phone.

"Okay, I have the news on, what's so interesting?"

"I'm sorry about the other day, really I am."

"I know. I'm sorry as well for what I said, but what's up? You sound upset."

"It was just the shock, that's all. You see the man on the screen, the man who was killed?"

"Yes."

"I've seen him. No, that's not right, I've *been* him."

"Huh?"

"You know when I was in the hospital and you called for help? I could see and feel what was happening to that man. He'd been happy, you know, that day. He was celebrating with two young women, I could see his memory of it, but then he was alone. Alone, but not alone ..." Aaron heard her chest heave, rasping. "Cassie, take a deep breath and focus on something else for a moment."

"Trying ..."

Aaron stayed quiet on the line. He knew the signs; she needed some mental distance. He sat on the bed for a minute listening to her breaths gradually slowing.

"I know exactly what happened to him, things that the police will never tell. I can't describe who's doing it - I only see glimpses and shadows, but I know this much." She paused again to breathe.

"He's a monster Aaron, and I don't mean like a Godzilla or Frankenstein." 'Frankenstein's monster' would have ordinarily been Aaron's correction but he wisely chose not to interrupt.

"But like, you know when a child has gone missing and someone says, what sort of 'monster' could do this? Well *that* type. Aaron he did things, things that I could never tell anyone." Aaron felt an uncharacteristic relief. He couldn't bear to hear any more gruesome stories today.

"Cassie, it was almost a week ago when you saw this? Honestly?"

"I swear on my life Aaron. And this isn't the first time." Her voice faltered.

"Cassie, I'm going to speak to my mum and if she'll let me, I'm coming round to see you."

"Thanks Aaron."

Once Aaron had hung up, Cassie sat upright on her bed, distantly aware of the dull pain in her shoulder, hoping desperately that Aaron would be allowed to come.

She *had* to unload the burden of knowing that the killing wouldn't stop.

Chapter Twenty-Two

Laura, surprised the door was locked, let herself in.

"Malcolm, are you in? Malcolm?"

No response.

Oh of course, I forgot he's working late.

Laura admired Malcolm's capacity for work. After eight hours, Laura was fit for nothing but slobbing in front of trash TV. On the rare occasion Malcolm was off work he didn't sit for long, always wanting to finish some job or other.

Thanks to Malcolm's overtime, they'd managed one foreign holiday a year but his recent promotion to sergeant meant no fixed shifts, therefore no 'time' to be over. How was it that, when you progressed, you got less money, regardless of the hours you had to put in? They'd probably have to forgo a holiday next year. Everything had become so damn expensive.

Thinking about Malcolm, she put her shoes and coat in the cupboard. She walked through to the living room, grabbed the television remote and lay back on their sofa. The news was just finishing; she was relieved.

I've heard quite enough, on the radio, thank you very much.

She flicked to a satellite channel running endless reality TV repeats. A show started, promising to transform a house within an hour (albeit with a crew of forty people). As the host explained the owner's tragic backstory, Laura's thoughts drifted.

Two murders in a week. Are they connected? Police didn't think so. Perhaps I'll ask Malcolm why. Wonder when he'll be in. If he's not eaten, there's always the chicken casserole left over in the fridge he could warm up. Could always do some potatoes ...

Tiredness overcame her and these random thoughts turned into random dreams.

"Hey lazy, get up!" Somewhere in the depths of her dream Laura thought Malcolm was above her, lying in an open barn loft, his head and shoulders visible. He smiled down at her. He extended an arm, stretching, inviting, offering to pull her up. His hand should have been within reach, the barn ceiling was low, and yet when she reached out, her arms were short, and shrinking. She was glad to wake before her body shrivelled away to nothing.

When she opened her eyes, his face was close to hers. He was wearing a broad grin. "No time for sleeping, I've got something for you." He was in plain clothes (unusual but not unheard of). He sat lightly on her outstretched legs, straddling her knees, taking the strain of his weight with his thigh muscles. She felt the cold of him seep through the material of her skirt. It was a penetrating chill, the type of cold that comes with hours spent in the winter wind. He took hold of her hand.

"Malcolm. Sorry, must have nodded off."

"You *will* be sorry," his tone was light, playful. "Come with me."

Laura dutifully followed as Malcolm led her towards their bedroom. As she climbed the stairs behind him, the fog of sleep retreated. She'd recognised the look on his face. It was a mischievous look she'd not seen in months. He wanted sex. For Laura this was unusual before bedtime but welcome. He'd been working like a dog recently, why shouldn't they take some time for themselves? Time to indulge a little.

He opened the bedroom door and stepped aside to let her in, his broad white-toothed smile accompanied a theatrical wink as she passed. What she saw made her eyes widen. It reminded her of a wild night they'd spent over a year ago - a night she felt was unlikely to be repeated. The room must have taken him an age to prepare.

"Fancy, falling asleep like that, whilst I'm out working. Lie face down on the bed, you must be punished." His tone was affected. She thought he made a good actor.

Malcolm slept soundly. Laura did not.

What had got into him? He probably just got carried away. I should have shouted up though, letting him know he was hurting me. A little pain was fun though, at first. When did he buy all that stuff? Oh stop whinging. It was just a bit of fun that went too far.

Her pillow was perpetually hot. She turned it and turned it during the night, until there was no cool side left. She prayed for nonsensical, floating, sleep inducing thoughts but when they finally came, the fresh memory of him weighing down on her and pulling at the makeshift gag, stamped them out. When she finally *did* sleep, shortly after four a.m., the sore patch where her lips met constantly brushed against the pillow, waking her frequently.

At six a.m. the 'bong, bong, bong' of Laura's alarm doing an impression of a train station announcement, barely registered with her. Malcolm, however, woke rapidly, swivelling out of bed and reaching up into a stretched bend. He made a sound like a big cat yawning.

"You're not sleeping on the job again are you Mrs Robinson?"

His words brought her round quicker than any alarm could. She pulled back the duvet, freeing a pocket of warm cosy air. She stood up too quickly, swayed and reached down to the mattress for balance, "No, I'm getting up."

Malcolm was showered, dressed and ready for work within twenty minutes. Laura was in the shower when he was due to leave. Her eyes were closed, hair full of shampoo, when, in a moment long enough to dampen his white sleeve, he opened the shower screen, reached round her front and tweaked her nipple. "You were amazing last night, see you later." He slapped her bum and shut the shower door.

Laura felt a burning urge to turn the water off, wrap a towel round her and tell him, in an unsparing voice, what she really thought of what happened last night. Instead she found herself weakly shouting after him, "Have a good day."

She was surprised by the sense of relief that accompanied the distant thud of Malcolm closing the back door behind him.

Chapter Twenty-Three

As Malcolm Robinson was tightening a red silk tie behind Laura's head, too tightly as it transpired, Alfred Tucker was waking from yet another nightmare. He soon wished he hadn't.

He was here again.

What the hell does he want this time?

Every time Alfred woke, it took him a few minutes to comprehend. Maybe, with every awakening, that adjustment time reduced a little. Maybe ... when the sun doesn't rise or set in your world, tracking time is virtually impossible.

The first sensation is the burning in his wrists. He can't see what's causing the pain, because his arms are pulled downwards, strapped to something close to the floor. Maybe to a strut of this makeshift bed - just a guess. The tie has a hard plastic edge which rubs against the tendon above his thumb. He circles his wrists to give short-lived relief.

The second returning sensation is the tightness across his chest. His chin always lifts, reminding himself what the straps look like. It's the type of strapping they use to secure pallets of goods. An old memory (long before prison) returns: a spate of them were being discarded carelessly and the council were getting all het up about it. Kids were tripping, badgers were garrotting themselves, that type of thing. From the numb-needling in his legs, he imagines his thighs and shins are constrained by a similar material.

When he'd first realised how tightly he was strapped, and in how many places, he'd let out a weird half giggle, half whimper. He felt like Gulliver, tied up by an army of Lilliputians. His mirth, if it ever truly existed, had lasted a fraction of one second. There had been no humour since.

What could be worse than the feeling of not being able to move? The not moving itself. He would never have imagined the sores would come so quickly and with such intense pain. The first one came just above his left buttock, then (maybe a day or two later - who knew?) his right shoulder blade. Now it was his leg. The pattern was always the same: a raw chaffing, then more of a dull ache, then a surface tingle, with an occasional stab. Now came the sweats and the shivers as he tried to fight off infection.

And the smell.

He was past the point of begging to be freed. Alfred suspected that if this guy found an abandoned baby in a bin liner, he'd relish tying the bag's cord and throwing it in the back of a bin lorry.

I met some nasty arseholes inside, but this guy's something else.

The hunger was unbearable, but the thirst was worse. One meal and one drink a day (if that's what it was, so hard to know if a day has passed). It was hardly the dining experience he'd dreamt about in prison. Dinner time started with his bed being upended and leant against the wall. He was then spoon-fed cold soups and yoghurts by the overall wearing, masked mute.

So what did he want this time?

Alfred was aware of the mute, to his right. He blinked sleep away, turned to look, not wanting to see, but *having* to. The man held a large syringe in gloved hands. He pointed the needle towards the ceiling and pushed up the plunger with his thumb. He leant over, obscuring the ceiling's strip-light from view. Alfred saw through the serrated eyeholes of his black mask. Green irises circling two deep pits of nothing.

If only I could break free. God help me despite all the 'never agains' I think I'd enjoy beating you into a coma - shakes or no shakes. Just give me a chance, if I could free one arm.

He'd given up making such threats verbally. He wasn't going to waste his breath, or his strength.

Alfred felt a prick and pain like a deep wasp sting, at the top of his lower arm. Then a drawing sensation.

Oh great. Today's fresh offering from the farm of Tucker: Blood.

Chapter Twenty-Four

"Alright, alright. Stop nagging. What is it with you and this girl? You can go round for one hour, and Aaron, I mean it. One hour and I want you back here."

"Thanks Mum, you're a Leg End." 'Leg End' rather than 'Legend' started as a joke. It was now the norm. Aaron didn't notice when he said it. He stood up on tiptoe, landed a firm kiss on his mum's cheek (he knew how to keep his mother soft) before grabbing his green Parka jacket from the coat stand's curling black fingers.

Aaron walked briskly. As he passed terrace house after terrace house, his mind span with everything Cassie had told him. Mingled with Cassie's words were thoughts of the Zodiac killer.

Something was wrong. Something was missing. He couldn't exactly pinpoint it. Something like optimism had vanished. But that wasn't quite right. His focus had permanently shifted. Until recently, his thoughts had been of the now and the immediate future - hours to fill with games, with laughter. Now he explored avenues of horrific consequence, as if the 'now' no longer existed and there were only bleak futures to think of.

Being happy made him who he was. 'Aaron's always got a smile on his face,' 'You can always rely on Aaron to cheer you up.' He couldn't imagine getting back to that state of mind, his memory of being that way was fading. Short hitching breaths slowed his pace.

Being happy is who I am.

Is this what they call growing up? He remembered some (wise?) person saying that, 'When I grew up I put away childish things.'

Sod growing up. I want to be a kid again. I wasn't scared then.

A dog barked from behind a garden gate to his right, its drooling muzzle snarling beneath the slats. Aaron jumped, skipping briefly as if the fright was a natural part of his stroll.

A few doors down, in their front room, a man and a woman were shouting at each other. The woman, in a white untucked blouse (thick creases at the bottom) and navy work skirt, stepped past the man, sweeping ornaments from their fireplace with her forearm. He took hold of her shoulders, turning her. They were nose to nose. Aaron looked away.

He was glad to arrive at Cassie's. She answered the door to him in pink fleecy pyjamas, which were too short. The leg's elastic strangled her shins. She still had the sling, but her arm looked relaxed, she wasn't protecting it.

He dispensed with 'Hi,' slipping past her as if he was being followed.

"Are you okay?"

"Sure."

"Thanks for coming round."

Leanne shouted from the living room over the noise of the television, "Hi Aaron."

Aaron shouted back a polite, 'Hello.'

"C'mon Aaron, let's talk in my room." He followed her along the hall.

"Wow, it's cold in here."

"I know. Mum says we can't have the heating on much. She's not working at the minute."

"Oh I see."

Aaron sat on Cassie's bed in a familiar spot, his hands deep in the pockets of his Parka. Cassie slipped her legs under her duvet, shivering.

The sun outside Cassie's window was fading fast, kissing the edges of the barren autumn trees overhanging their garden. What light there was, came from outside, from behind Cassie's bed. Her features faded into the darkness of her face; an oracle in silhouette. If this were Aaron's house, he would have turned on the light. Cassie's comment about the heating had landed with him. He kept quiet.

Aaron noticed that three of Cassie's Harry Potter books were face down next to a face-up pile on her bedside table. His DS sat next to them in exactly the spot where Cassie had first placed it.

Cassie's words raced from her mouth, "I know I've already said this but really, I mean it, thanks for coming. I know I shouldn't have scared you like I did. I just desperately wanted you to believe me and I couldn't think of another way, without getting you involved ... getting you to see the other stuff I've seen, the worse stuff. And Aaron, I don't want anyone to ever see that, not even Rachel."

"Slow down, slow down. I know I'm going to regret asking this but tell me, from the beginning, what *have* you seen? What has happened and ... and what do you think is going to happen?"

Aaron's use of the word 'think' rather than 'know' hovered in a tension between them. He was thinking about taking it back, of correcting himself when he sensed the tension fall away, and the word vanished into a history of countless, benign words. Cassie carried on, deliberately, taking her time.

"The same person has attacked three people within the last few weeks. He's close as well. He *must* be. I wouldn't be able to see what he's seeing and what they're seeing, if he wasn't close."

"Three times?"

"Yes. Three times. But the first time was weird. No, wait, they were all *weird*, but the first one was ... was different."

"Different, how?"

"It's so hard to explain. A different feeling, a different reason I think. He wasn't excited like he was with the others."

"Excited?"

Aaron's eyes, having adapted to the bedroom's semidarkness, saw Cassie's face draw out.

Her right arm slipped from the sling as she reached up with both hands. The sling hung against her side. She pressed the heels of her hands into the deep sockets of her eyes. Her wrists twisted, rubbing out what Aaron guessed was a powerful, unwelcome recollection.

"Yes, but don't ask me to think about that."

"Okay, then tell me where these things happened. What did you see that you *can* tell me?" Cassie's hands fell from her face. They rested in her lap, palms up, fingers interlocked.

"The first time was in a dark street. He'd chosen an old man who, for some reason, felt briefly free. Before ..." Aaron sat patiently as Cassie struggled to describe something she couldn't comprehend. He noticed her chest pulsing, her sharp sniffing intakes of breath. Each word demanded greater oxygen than it deserved. "The light ... the bright blue light. Then he was in pain and ... and dragging ... awful dragging, his jacket on concrete. His shoulders were cold ... and they hurt but he couldn't feel ... couldn't feel the rest of his body. Then nothing ... I didn't see anything after that."

"Cassie, slow down and breathe."

"I know, I know, I will."

"Now focus on colours. Here."

He picked up Harry Potter and the Prisoner of Azkaban from Cassie's bedside table.

"Take a deep breath and when you're ready, start telling me which colours you see on this cover." He held it aloft and slapped the book's face.

"Red, blue, grey - two shades." Aaron nodded and Cassie continued, her breath slowing, deepening. Gaining control.

Aaron was patient with her, slow, calming. It took over ten minutes, but Cassie said, "I'm ready, I can tell you the rest."

Before recommencing her confession (for that's what it felt like to both of them), she took the book out of Aaron's hand, returning it to its 'recently read' spot on her bedside. She made a hand sandwich, his hand between hers. "You're the only one who truly knows me. You know that, don't you?"

Aaron, unlike any other boy he knew, was happy to be regarded as sensitive, emotionally in tune, thoughtful. Perhaps he was a mother's boy and that was okay. Yet the intensity of Cassie's feelings disarmed him. Her emotional age was so out of step with her true age that sometimes, when she spoke, Aaron didn't know what to say. This was one of those occasions.

"I know ... big softie." He knew his words were inadequate. They were the best he could manage.

Cassie took a sip of water from a glass resting on her bedside cabinet, before continuing. She placed her hand back on his, but lightly this time. "The second time it was different."

"How Cassie?"

"This one was by chance."

"Chance? What do you mean?"

"I mean, he didn't pick them, they chose themselves."

"Cassie, in everything I've read there's always a reason why people kill. It may be some nutty logic, like the-" he paused, not wanting to bring the thought back.

Too late, it's already there.

"Like the Zodiac killer. He was collecting souls to act as his servants in the afterlife. Mad, I know, but there must be a reason."

"Aaron, you're probably right but I just don't know. All I know is that she picked up the card, and that's how she chose herself."

"A card?"

"Uh-huh, a card … you know, for games."

Cassie parted the sea of junk in her bedside cabinet drawer. She pulled out a set of playing cards. She rapidly laid each card on her bed in a ragged overlapping line until she found the Jack of Diamonds. She landed her finger on it so firmly that it bent against the duvet cover.

"That card."

They both looked down at it, the only noise a distant sound from Leanne's television.

"It's a calling card."

"A calling card? What's that?"

Aaron wished he'd never been to the London Dungeons, never started reading about serial killers and, in a small way, wished he'd never befriended Cassie Janus. He breathed a good lungful of air.

"The police say there aren't many killers who use them. But others think they're there and the police don't spot them. Sometimes the killer will leave something at the scene, a message or an object, which is the same for all their murders. They're used to … to brag, I guess, to the police that they did it, sending a message that they won't be caught. The Zodiac killer's were coded messages to the police. Sometimes the 'calling card' …"

Aaron acted out speech marks with curled fingers to accompany the words, 'calling card.'

"… is just the way they kill them."

"I get that … but … then again it doesn't make sense."

"How come?"

"Well the second and third time he did it, he used cards, but the first time, cards had nothing to do with it."

"Perhaps you're seeing different people that just look similar."

"That's just it. I don't really get a good look at him, only the briefest of glimpses, as the … the victims see him. It was so dark the first time I didn't really see him at all. One time I saw his eyes clearly, reflected in a bathroom mirror. They were at the centre of a kaleidoscope."

"A what?"

"You know, one of those things, like a short telescope you look through and twist to make patterns."

"Oh yeah, my cousin Lilly had one of those, she got it for her ... never mind, carry on."

"His eyes were clear ... and horrible. But the rest of his face was ... was swirling - a blur. The third time I only got a brief glance - I was face down most of the time. But I know it's the same person because. I've *been* the killer. Twice ... and I know. That's the only way I can describe it."

Cassie's words were like water pent up behind a cracking dam - the gush inevitable. Aaron felt like he was drowning in the flow.

"Aaron, thank you for letting me tell you all this." Aaron forced a smile. His shoulders hunched and he shrank into the bed.

"Look, Cassie I've been thinking about what you said."

"About what?"

"About how I shouldn't be reading about stuff like this. You were right. We shouldn't be reading *or* worrying about this."

"I don't have a choice about it though, do I?"

Aaron couldn't think of a worthy response, "I know ... I just think you should be going to the police with what you know. *They* should be worrying about this, not you. Perhaps what you know can help them catch him."

Cassie brought her knees up so that her feet were on the bed and wrapped her arms around her shins.

"They want to take me away from Mummy. They think she can't raise me safely. I can't let that happen, she loves me. If I start talking like this to a grown-up, they'll think I've got problems. Aaron, have you ever seen a film where they put mad people in rooms on their own. Not normal rooms, though, the type of room where you can't hurt yourself, no matter how hard you try. Those rooms exist in real life you know.

"Just imagine it ... I go into the police station and say to them, 'A man intends to abduct a teenage boy just because he picked up and rolled dice.'"

"What, what's that about?"

"I've seen it. He'll follow him and it'll happen sometime soon. They won't believe me and then children's services will be round here again and I know they'll start saying more things about me being safe and about whether I'm crazy or not and whether I need a special doctor or not."

"But if it happens like you predict then they won't think you're crazy."

"If they don't find the body they will. But even if they do, what do people think of ... of clairvoyants? Because that's what they'll say I am. They make fun of them and if they're lucky, they'll end up in a circus. And if they're not ..."

Cassie's eyes drifted and Aaron imagined she was picturing eventualities, she had no intention of articulating. He let the silence hang, until she regained focus.

"Even if they do believe me, they'll start thinking the killer must be someone I know, a friend of Mummy's, maybe. Then Mummy will be angry about the trouble I'm causing."

Cassie buried her face in her knees, "Aaron I can't tell anyone and you can't either. The police will catch him eventually, then it will be over."

"And what if they don't Cassie? What if this goes on and on and on and on?"

Chapter Twenty-Five

Laura looked up at their aluminium kitchen clock: seven thirty p.m.. Above the hob the extractor whirred away, doing nothing to remove the aroma of frying onions, mushrooms and pate. The beef Wellington would work out alright, she was sure, but there was something in the smell of hot pate that made her nose wrinkle.

For the first time in their relationship, Laura was dreading Malcolm getting in. He'd sent her a text message an hour earlier saying he'd be in by eight. For a reason that she couldn't entirely fathom, Laura felt compelled to have a nice dinner waiting for him.

At a rare dinner party with friends they'd been asked what they'd choose for their last meal. "Beef Wellington," had been Malcolm's immediate response. Since that night, Laura had cooked it twice: once for an anniversary, and once on his birthday. On both occasions they'd washed the steak down with Merlot, followed up with after dinner mints, and rounded off with after dinner sex.

With that memory, a daunting thought came: her meal choice might trigger his desire for a 'third course.' And perhaps that would be okay. She rubbed her sore lip. If they could get over the hurdle of last night, everything would be okay.

It will go one of two ways. Either it will hang between us in obvious silence and I shall let him know outright how I feel, or we'll totally avoid the subject, eventually forgetting it ever happened until, God forbid, he tries it again.

As Laura daubed pate mixture over fillet with a spatula, her mind wandered. That morning, between house calls, she'd stopped off at the headquarters of children's services in Sawley road, to drop off and pick up case files. On the way to the small open plan office she'd peered through a window cut into the staff kitchen door. Margaret Reid and Vanessa Petford were standing next to each other, making tea. She'd poked her head in to say 'Hi,' and interrupted a conversation about Peter Eccleston's murder.

"Sorry to interrupt, I only wanted to say 'Hello'."

They both offered welcoming smiles. They were, especially Vanessa, the type of people who appear perpetually happy. Laura often wondered what it would be like to be Vanessa for a day - it must be bliss. Laura had convinced herself those smiles and bright eyes were a mask for something else, something less perfect. Somehow that made her feel better.

"Laura, we were just saying, have you heard about Peter Eccleston?"

"Yes, on the news."

"Such a shame," said Vanessa. Margaret hummed in agreement.

"I was just saying to Margaret, that I saw one of his plays, an Alan Bennet adaptation. Mmm ... still can't recall the name. Anyway, I remember him from the programme. I always buy the programme, I know they're expensive, but you just can't resist, can you? And what's an extra fiver when you've paid forty quid for a ticket. Anyway, I remember his name because I once had a maths teacher called Eccleston, Paul they called him. Terrible business isn't it. He was bisexual, you know, Peter I mean, not Paul. Not that that makes any difference, but we were wondering, weren't we Margaret ..." Margaret nodded as she disposed of wet teabags.

"… whether it had anything to do with that lesbian lady who got killed, poor girl. Do you think it's a homophobic thing? Everyone seems to think so."

"Vanessa, I really don't know. I just hope, if it is the same person, they find him and soon."

"Well, amen to that. We were just saying, we wondered if your Malcolm was involved in the case?"

"Sorry Vanessa, Margaret, I really have to go."

"Sure you don't want a tea?"

"No, thank you. See you later."

After that conversation, Laura had tried to put the matter out of her mind and failed. Peter Eccleston's murder was front-page news. She couldn't avoid it. Despite the explosion of iPads and other tablets, London commuters still had a habit of picking up the free Metro newspaper, distributed outside every tube station. She was desperate to ask Malcolm about the case. She had to be careful though - more pressing matters closer to home.

Malcolm's car pulled up a couple of minutes before eight p.m. He walked in with a soft leather briefcase in one hand and a carrier bag in the other.

"Here, let me help you." Laura took the wine. Malcolm took his case upstairs. When he got back down, Laura broke the news; she'd been looking forward to it.

"Beef Wellington's in the oven."

"Great." His smile was polite but cold and his distance both concerned and pleased Laura; at least he hadn't walked in like a dog on heat tonight. As they sat eating and sipping Cabernet Sauvignon Laura made casual enquiries about his day. Three quarters of a glass of wine later, after a few whinges about 'idiots he has to work with,' his bunched shoulders dropped. Laura knew his tolerance for talking about work was nearing its end and surprised herself by asking about the investigation.

"Are they getting you involved in that case with the producer?"

"No, why should they?"

"It's just that people are saying they're connected."

"People, what people?"

"Oh, you know, the press, people at work." He cornered his last piece of fillet and peered at her over his raised fork. It was a look she recognised, Laura you've asked a stupid question.

"Laura. I thought you knew better."

"I'm sorry, I guess they're jumping to-"

"Leaping, Laura, leaping. Let's look at it shall we? There are over a hundred murders every year in London - a city with over eight million inhabitants. I make that about two per week. Dacia Cartwright was killed in Croydon, the producer in Primrose Hill, over an hour away. Dacia was sexually assaulted, the producer, as I understand, was not. Now what precisely is the connection?"

Laura pushed the rest of her dinner (just mash and a finger of mange tout) to one side. She partnered her knife and fork on the side of her plate.

"I don't know, it's not what I'm saying it's just I heard they were both gay and I thought most murders were domestic incidents and-"

"And you know that these are not?"

"Look, I'm not saying-"

"Just forget about it and leave the work to the professionals. I don't suppose to comment intelligently on your cases." Malcolm chewed his last piece of beef and stood up. With his back to her, he walked to the sink and turned on the mixer tap, placing his finger under the stream to gauge its temperature. Laura didn't know whether to apologise or change the subject. They worked in silence, Malcolm washing, Laura drying. When they were finished they made their way to the living room. Laura changed the subject.

"So what did you think of the beef Wellington?"

"Nice honey. But in the future, let's talk before you spend thirty pounds on a fillet of beef, okay?" She agreed - on the surface at least.

For the rest of the evening Malcolm was unusually interested in the television, laughing at 'Fool Britannia.' Laura's occasional smiles were faked. Bedtime loomed.

Chapter Twenty-Six

Wayne was initially pissed off at Mikey for giving him the nickname 'Frankie' after Frankie Dettorri. He hated being short, but he'd never liked his real name and their piss-taking no longer got to him. In fact, he was starting to like the name, which had stuck like windscreen flies in summer. His mother's hatred of people calling him Frankie, was a bonus.

Frankie and his friends were sitting on aluminium chairs, around an impossibly small circular table. A dark green canvas barrier penned them in with six other customers, hunching over their own aluminium islands. It was weird how a stretch of canvas could make you feel like you weren't sitting in the middle of a pavement.

Frankie had moved to London from Newcastle two years earlier and there were two things that stood out about England's capital. Firstly, how bloody expensive everything was and, second, how cramped the takeouts and deli's were. Only in London would you pay six pounds for a carton of salad and have to wait for ledge-space against which you could lean to eat it. He guessed people like him moving to London was part of the problem.

According to what his friends called, 'Frankie's law' there were two types of people in London: those who ate in Pret or Eat, usually in sharp suits, and those who ate in McDonalds or Subway. Frankie and his mates fell into the latter category.

Frankie was about to take a first bite of his twelve inch sub.

"Go on Frankie, get it down yer face." They laughed at him as he took a big bite. Rich and Mikey were in on the joke; Frankie on the other hand, was not.

"Jesus, that's hot, pass'us me coke." Mikey stood up and held Frankie's Coke out of reach. Frankie was desperate to quench the fire burning his throat but wasn't going to give them the satisfaction of watching him jump to reach his drink. He walked inside to buy another Coke. Mikey sat back down next to Rich and they laughed hard, drawing glances from a girl and her mother at the nearest table.

"Come on honey, eat up, I'm freezing," said the woman as she tidied her daughter's colouring sheets and crayons. Mikey suspected their lad's banter was pissing her off.

C'est la vie.

When Frankie sat back down, he took a big gulp of drink, belched loudly and smiled at them, "Bastards, pair of you."

"Thought you liked it hot, man?"

"Piss off. At least I'm not like you two, sat like two skint faggots going dutch cause you can't stretch to a subway each. Peasants." Frankie's comment cut their laughter.

"Anyway, Frankie, how's that girlfriend of yours? Managed to do the deed yet?"

"Keep your nose out. If I told you that, it'd be all over school and you're not screwing this up for me." Frankie reached inside his pocket, pulled out his Sony Xperia smartphone and flicked to a picture of his fifteen-year-old girlfriend.

She was undeniably beautiful. The photo was clearly taken on holiday. She held large white-rimmed sunglasses on the tip of her nose, deep hazel eyes smiling over the rim. Her left arm reached behind her, holding onto the edge of a rowing boat. Behind the boat, a stretch of water ran through a cave into a distant, sun-drenched lake. A beautiful scene of course, but Rich and Mikey were more taken by her bare shoulder - the strap, in Annie's leaning, had fallen to the top of her arm. Arousing greater interest (if they were both honest), were the mini shadows cast by her nipples on her white vest top.

"Just think guys, one day when you grow up, you too might get a girl like that." Rich and Mikey looked at each other and shrugged shoulders, a fake nonchalance. Frankie thought they made crap actors. He smiled and wedged the phone back into his Levis.

"So you *are* doing her then?" Frankie saw the woman with her child shake her head, presumably overhearing Rich's question. She got up and walked off, scooping her daughter up with one hand and pushing a stroller with the other.

Frankie laughed and winked, his friends made whooping noises. "You guys can carry on thinking what you like." As Frankie spoke, he peered into the pot in the middle of the table. It contained an assortment of sachets: vinegar, mayonnaise, ketchup and mustard - the stingy type that never open cleanly. He noticed a peculiar dice, wedged between the vinegar and ketchup, at the bottom of the shallow pot. He tipped it out and rolled it back and forth across the aluminium tabletop. Strangely, the dice had nine sides.

"You guys ever seen a nine sided dice before?" Mikey spotted Frankie's deflection and wasn't going to be put off the scent.

"Hey Rich. Frankie's feeling lucky. Getting lucky tonight Frankie?"

"God you guys are obsessed. You need to get some. Maybe then you'll calm down a bit. Look, I'm going. I'll likely be bunking off so I'll see you guys in the park tomorrow night." Without knowing why, Frankie slipped the dice into the side pocket of his Barbour jacket before heading off in the direction of Liverpool street train station.

So, a teenaged boy. That's interesting. He's short too. I bet he's going to fight, all young bravado and no strength, that's my prediction. But I could be wrong. He might have a knife in his jacket pocket, jingling next to the dice as we speak. He might stab me, or at least try. Now that would be fun.

Frankie, listening intently to Eminem on his Dr Dre Beats headphones, was entirely oblivious to being followed by a man whose Oyster card bleeped a few moments after his. They both moved smoothly through the barrier and onto the central line. As they reached the train, the doors were sliding shut. Frankie darted nimbly between them. The man following him jammed his forearm between the closing doors, drawing looks from other passengers that said, *'there would have been another train in a minute and now we've been delayed, idiot!'* Frankie didn't care, he was immersed in his music and in scanning through pictures of Annie. He paused on an image of her in a red bikini, taken on holiday. Frankie couldn't believe she'd shared that one with him. A lucky boy indeed.

Frankie noticed someone standing behind him, someone who should have been making every attempt to glance in another direction, but was, instead, looking at Frankie's phone over his shoulder. Frankie slipped the headphones around his neck and turned towards the stranger, "What you fucking looking at?" Without waiting for a response, he returned to his music and photos. The man looked away.

Goddamn perverts in this city.

Chapter Twenty-Seven

Next to Leanne, nestled into her bum-weary sofa bed, an old closed Dell laptop (with someone else's Skullcandy sticker on the lid) laid waiting. It silently nagged at her from the corner of her eye; an inanimate conscience. There were two jobs she should apply for. One was in New Look, the other H&M. She wanted neither. It was neither the crappy pay, nor the question of *who's going to be in for Cassie*, that stopped her. It was the fear of rejection coupled with the recognition that her potential at school, like the pain of childbirth, had faded into irrelevance; a minor plot point in a former life.

Fed up of its nagging she looked at it (the Dell Daniel had gifted because its previous owner 'no longer needed it') as though staring alone would get those application forms completed.

Now she understood what Daniel had been on about: 'Sometimes, you just needed to eat your frog.' He'd picked up the expression from someone who'd read a book all about it. The theory was that you should, first thing in the morning, do the job you dread the most, thereby achieving a free, productive mindset for the rest of the day. When Leanne first heard the expression it sounded like bullshit; another piece of *do as I say and not as I do* from Daniel. But today it made sense. Those applications were two fat, wart-infested bullfrogs that just needed gobbling up.

Except the trouble with eating frogs is that TV *looks* better and Bourbon *tastes* better.

Is that really what you need Leanne? More drink before lunchtime. Alcohol you can't afford to replace. Is that going to get you and Cassie out of this mess?

Might help me forget about the mess though.

For how long Leanne?

Long enough.

You've got to get out of this pattern. Turn on your TV, distract yourself with thirty minutes (no more, promise yourself) of Loose Women. Hardly a frog, but better than sweet Tennessee Bourbon.

The local newspaper was balanced on the arm of the sofa. It was unnaturally folded, the job section now the front page. Leanne picked it up as she rocked her thinning, dressing-gown-warmed, behind out of the sofa. She slapped the laptop's Skullcandy sticker with the paper, as though reprimanding her conscience, and turned on the television.

After the forced audience's applause had died down and the first debate was underway, Leanne heard a thud from Cassie's room.

Probably just a book falling on the floor. A heavy book, though.

That girl's spending too much time in her bedroom. When she gets back to school next week it'll be good for her. She needs to get back to normal. That school better look after her this time.

From her bedroom, Cassie heard the muffled Loose Women theme, then applause. The sound distracted her momentarily from Harry Potter - a boy who, due to Cassie's reading speed, was growing up too quickly.

When she tried to refocus on her book, words swam. It wasn't quite the fuzzy, line repeating feeling of reading when tired, more like the way someone with severe dyslexia describes a page of words: jumbled characters of shifting depths and order, letters and numbers in an intimidating dance.

Then the page filled with pictures, but not illustrations of Hogwarts or shifting oil paintings, though the pictures did squirm. It was like a comic strip, in a way, but in another way, it was not. In comic strips there's a jarring between pictures, a shifting in time - the reader fills in the gaps. In this comic the scenes had a mini squirm of action. Each square repeating a blurry smudged movement, handing meaning, like a baton in a relay, to the next. Daniel was the protagonist of the comic strip, Cassie's mother the victim.

A seizure loomed. She couldn't allow it to consume her. She had to warn Mummy. In the moment before it was too late, she thudded the book shut and thrust her forehead into the wall.

The pictures disappeared. All that remained was a stinging lump and a dizziness that would pass. She jumped off her bed and took a haphazard path, out of her room and down the hall. An onlooker might have suspected she'd been drinking. Her hands reached out either side of her, connecting with the walls; re-centring her path.

Five minutes into Loose Women and Leanne had spotted a pattern, a tired formula, she'd not considered before: Raise a controversial question, often relating to a current news story, give opposing views (starting with the serious, then ending with the light-hearted). It was the conversations the viewers wished they were having with their friends, if only their friends were wittier and weren't all stuck in the house on their own, watching Loose women. And with that thought, she determined to turn off the TV, fire up the laptop and put those brain cells to work. That was when she heard Cassie's heavy footsteps approaching along the hall.

How can I make Mummy understand? All I need to do is make sure she doesn't let Daniel in.

"Mummy." She was out of breath, disorientated.

"Yes sweetie?" Leanne turned her head and saw Cassie in her pyjamas standing in the doorway of the living room.

"Let's play games today, just you and me."

"Oh Cassie, maybe later. I have to get these applications written."

Cassie's eyes turned to the blaring television, "Why are you watching TV then?" Leanne got up and turned it off.

"Just give me an hour or so, then we'll play, okay honey. You need to get dressed anyway, you can't stay in your pyjamas all day every day." Leanne became aware of her own hypocrisy, tightening her dressing gown cord as she spoke.

Got to take a risk, got to warn her.

Hurried, impotent words spilled out, "Mummy we *have* to be on our own today. He's going to hurt you."

As Leanne was about to ask Cassie what on earth she was talking about and who 'he' is, there was a knock on the front door and Leanne got up to answer it.

"No Mummy, please don't go. Don't let him in."

Leanne pushed past Cassie, to get into the hall, "Cassie, don't be silly. Have you had a bad dream or something? You look like you've just woken up."

Cassie grabbed a handful of her mother's dressing gown sleeve. "Please Mummy."

"Cassie, let go, go to your room and get dressed." She tugged her sleeve free. Cassie saw the darkness of a figure behind the frosted glass and her mother moving towards the door.

Why wouldn't she just listen to me?

There was something not right. And it was more than the tension between Cassie and her mum, greater than the prospect of letting Daniel in and the inevitable consequences of that decision. It was vulnerability. Cassie felt exposed. When you're in your pyjamas, you don't let people in. That takes trust and familiarity. They didn't know Daniel *that* well. Cassie felt an overwhelming desire not to be near that man, and to be dressed, to be ready to deal with the fallout.

She turned around and ran. Her bedroom door clunked shut as she heard the squeaking cry of the front door's hinges.

Chapter Twenty-Eight

Frankie walked up the left side of the escalators towards the exit of Shepherd's Bush tube station. He stared at his phone, willing his elusive 3G to reappear. He left the escalator's disappearing steps, momentarily taking his eyes from the phone's screen to swipe his Oyster card across the reader. He noted his two pound twenty credit.

Shit better top that up. Later though, on the way back.

Frankie made his way along the pavement opposite Shepherd's Bush Green. He annoyed the sea of oncoming pedestrians, texting as he walked, expecting the sea of people to part for him. Reluctantly, it did. A tall, speed-walking woman in fluorescent Lycra shorts clipped his shoulder with her arm and uttered between heaving breaths, "Watch where you're going," then mumbled, "Dickhead."

Whilst he was effortlessly annoying those around him, he wrote two texts. The first was to his mum, letting her know he was going to be late. The second was to his girlfriend.

Frankie was obsessed with Annie. In the last two months not a single waking hour had passed without him thinking of her. Admittedly, some of those thoughts were typical of a teenage lad: what he would do with her if he only got the chance. But mostly he thought about whether she would be *the* one. He genuinely felt he could happily spend the rest of his life with her. Not that he would ever admit it to Rich, and especially not to Mikey.

Frankie knew Annie was out of his league. He was amazed that she'd gone out with him in the first place, more amazed that she was *still* going out with him. He was no film star and he knew it. She'd not once mentioned his looks or even passed comment about his shitty grades. He loved her for it.

If only Annie's Dad liked me. Or perhaps that makes her want me more? Not sure.

The text to Annie read, 'Hi there. Hope you're not studying too hard. RU free now for an hour? I thought I'd come round and say hi.' Minutes later, Frankie began repeatedly glancing at his phone.

Relax man, she'll get back to you, just chill out.

Chapter Twenty-Nine

Annie knew she should be getting her Spanish homework out of the way, but what does 'should' know? Instead, she did maths. Everyone else in Band Five finding them so difficult made balancing equations all the more satisfying.

She knew she should work at her desk. Her mother had told her that sitting on a bed, hunched over an exercise book, was going to give her round shoulders. Damaging her near perfect appearance was a frightening prospect. Still, round shoulders were a long way off and there was no room on her desk anyway. It was covered in nail varnish and lip-gloss to the right, her television to the left. 'Make up station' was what her dad sarcastically called it.

Stunning looks and a liking for maths were not the only things separating her from her peers. Annie was focussed. For her friends, having the television or some music on "in the background" was the norm. Annie was too ambitious to have the likes of Gossip Girl or The Wanted distract her, damaging her grades. No way. She liked to think of her life dovetailing towards perfection. Achieving eight A plus grades (minimum) was an important piece in the perfect life jigsaw.

And now, another piece was falling into place: the perfect boyfriend, Frankie Archer. Her dad didn't like him, but that was to be expected. What father thinks their potential son-in-law is good enough? Oh yes, even at fifteen she'd already contemplated marriage and its ideal timing.

Her white iPhone, framed by her gold clip-on Gucci cover, was nestled into the duvet. It was on silent. Her elbow, the one that propped her studious chin, felt a buzzing. Her head turned towards the phone. Frankie's text dropped onto her home screen. She smiled, thinking, I'll just finish this equation (can't stop halfway through) then I'll text back. Thoughts of turning on the television were easy to ignore, thoughts of Frankie were not.

Annie bent further, trapping her exercise book between the duvet and her bendy ruler. All titles had to be underlined. All workings out had to be shown too. 'Methodical' was how her father often described her. Annie thought this was a lame description for anyone, but she took the point.

There, all equations balanced. All workings shown, all titles underlined. She messaged Frankie, happy for him to come for an hour. Perhaps today was a good day to lose her virginity. Was an hour long enough? She wasn't sure.

She snapped the book shut, zipped up her Olly Murs pencil case - the one she was becoming embarrassed about but hadn't got around to changing - and took both to her droopy, bohemian school bag. The bag hung from a chair, tucked underneath the makeup station (she had to be honest, her dad was right about that). She slotted, then zipped.

Behind the desk's lip-gloss statuettes, a dressing mirror, tilted on a pine frame, gave a reflection of her pastel blue track suit bottoms. She wouldn't dream of wearing these outside the confines of her bedroom; homework time is important, solitary time, when comfort is important and appearances are not.

On the soft pale material, down the inside of one thigh, was blood.

Can't be. Not for another week at least.

She opened her drawer, looking for sanitary pads, or, failing that, the Tampax she'd tried and not got on with. She was all out.

Annie swore - something else she would only do on her own. Grateful that her mum and dad were out, she walked across the landing and into the bathroom. She expected to find her mother's Lillets in the cabinet underneath the vanity sink. Nothing.

Now what?

She rolled a wedge of toilet paper round her wrist, and held the makeshift pad in place, whilst slipping out of her stained bottoms.

I'll have to go to the shop.

As she crossed the landing, bloodstained joggers in hand, she looked left to the arched window, which overlooked the street. Their house was the second to last down a dead end. It was rare to see anyone and thankfully nobody was outside today, nobody to look up at her embarrassment. She knew they would only see her face and shoulders, but even that would have been too much. For the next twenty minutes, she wanted to be invisible.

She placed the joggers, with her knickers tucked inside, on the floor of her bedroom. She'd folded them to hide the stains, as best she could. She looked down at them, and, with a huffed sigh, used her foot to slide them under her bed.

I'll deal with you later. Guess today isn't going to be the day after all. Probably wasn't the right day anyway, worrying all the time about whether Mum and Dad would disturb us.

Annie pulled on fresh knickers and jeans. She grabbed her brush from the desk, fisted a tail of mahogany hair, and raked through knots with a series of diminishing 'Kkrrrrra' sounds.

She thought about texting Frankie, to say she might be late, but didn't want to lie about why. And she certainly wasn't going to tell the truth.

She snatched her phone from the bed, noting the time.

There's hardly ever a queue in that corner shop, I'll be back in time anyway.

Annie grabbed her bag and headed out.

Chapter Thirty

Leanne recognised Daniel, through the frosted glass. She opened the door.

"Christ, Daniel, what's happened. Are you okay?"

There were crimson smears across his jacket. His hands were cut and bruised. Blood seeped from the split skin of his knuckles.

In her bedroom, Cassie stood with her ear to the door.

Don't let him in Mum, please don't let him in.

Daniel stumbled past Leanne, down the hall, and let himself into the living room. A stench of whiskey hung around him. She followed him.

He slumped down on the sofa, covered his eyes with fingers and swore under his breath. "Daniel, are you going to tell me what's happened?"

"Yeah, but get me a drink first babe, I really need one. A stiff one." She didn't have to ask what he wanted: Jack Daniels over ice.

She stepped into the kitchen, opened the freezer drawer and, as she twisted squares of ice from their tray, thought, *is this the man Cassie warned me about?*

Don't be stupid Leanne, she can't know what's going to happen.

Yeah? Like she couldn't know you weren't at school to pick her up?

Leanne poured two drinks; perhaps whiskey would numb what was surely paranoia. She carried them through, fighting the urge to fill the absence of conversation. The swirling clink of ice cubes on glass decorated the silence, until Daniel finally spoke. Over half his Whiskey was gone.

"It was Brian. He shopped me to the social. We were in the pub together when they called me on my mobile. I've got to go in to see them Leanne. I could go to jail."

"Did Brian tell you he shopped you?"

"No, he didn't have to. I could see it in his eyes. I just flipped. He didn't put up much of a fight; the guilt I reckon."

"Daniel, did anyone see you fighting?"

"Probably. We'd been in the pub since eleven. Pretty quiet. Big Izzy was there with his mates, there were one or two others."

"Oh Christ, I hope he doesn't call the police."

"Right now, I couldn't give a flying fuck about the police - they're hardly going to waste time on a minor punch up are they?"

"I suppose not."

"Anyway ... he got what was coming to him."

Daniel downed the remaining Whiskey and thrust his empty glass at Leanne. Leanne had barely taken a tiny sip of hers.

"Top me up love." She brought in the Jack Daniels bottle from the kitchen and poured him another, a poor measure. He jangled the glass, eyebrows raised. She poured.

"Daniel, what if it wasn't him?"

"What do you mean?"

"Well it's possible, isn't it? He's been a good friend to you and you got over the stealing thing. Wasn't he planning on taking you back?"

"Yeah, but I knew Leanne, sometimes you just know."

No Daniel, you don't know. Cassie, now she sometimes, 'just knows'. But not you, you jump to conclusions. You're too eager to use your fists; you should have stopped to think. As I look at you now I don't know how I got mixed up with you.

134

Somehow I've got to get away from this relationship. It's not good for me. Or Cassie.

Leanne looked down at her whiskey and decided to stop drinking. This thought wasn't with the lightness of a New Year's conviction, made through the fog of a hang over. It was that deep self-loathing determination, the sort that comes with getting so drunk you can hardly remember a vicious argument with your child. Her distance and the way she hung her head, lit a fuse in Daniel.

"Wait. Why are you going on about it not being Brian?" She continued looking down, avoiding his gaze.

"You can't even look at me. It was you wasn't it? Not Brian, it was you!"

Leanne snapped her head towards him.

"Daniel, you must be wasted. What the hell would make you think that?"

Christ, he's so loud, Cassie's hearing every word. She must be so scared. I'm scared.

The pain in her left cheekbone came with a force that twisted her body off the sofa and onto the floor. She landed on all fours. Perhaps his knuckle connecting with her cheek bone sounded, to him, like a dull thud. From inside Leanne's head, it was a deafening crunch. Dancing specs of bright light obscured her sideways view of the mantelpiece.

Leanne's instinct was to get away and she tried to get up, to run. She lifted one knee to stand but felt his tight grip on her ankle, stopping her.

The rough carpet pile scraped her chin and chest bone as he dragged her backwards. He held her neck in a tight grip, pushing her cheek flat to the floor. Leanne felt his hatred through the brush of breath on her ear as he spoke.

"You know what, it's no wonder so many men kill their partners. Two women a week. Did you know that? And that's just in the UK."

Leanne couldn't help but inhale the Whiskey-laced air escaping his lungs.

"And it's all because we can't trust you lying bitches. I thought you were different, but no, you're just the same as all the rest. Couldn't resist stabbing me in the fucking back could you?"

He'd lifted her neck a few inches then pushed it down hard to accentuate the word, 'back'.

Leanne's face was so pressed into the carpet pile that, even if she could think of a reply, she couldn't speak it.

She heard a sound like unbuckling.

"What service do you require?"

"Police and ambulance. He's attacking my mum."

"What's your address?"

"Fifteen Abbot's close."

"Stay calm honey. I'm sending someone now. Stay on the line." A brief pause.

"Where are they sweetheart?"

"In the living room."

"Where are you?"

"In my bedroom."

"Does he know you're there?"

"I don't know, I don't think so."

"Can you get out of the house without being seen?"

"No, I think they left the living room door open."

"Listen carefully sweetheart. You're being a brave girl. Help is on its way. I want you to hide under your bed and not make a sound, do you hear me?"

Cassie whispered softly, 'Yes.'

"Take the phone under the bed with you, stay on the line and be quiet. Help will be there in less than three minutes."

Those minutes were the longest of Cassie's life. She would happily have endured three minutes of anything else: the stings of wasps, a beating from Rachel. Anything but the sounds of her own heaving chest, punctuated by distant thumping and the cries of her mother.

Chapter Thirty-One

Frankie paused to take out his phone and change the music to Daft Punk. As he did so, despite the failing light of the autumn afternoon, he saw a man standing among the thick roots and fallen leaves of an oak, at the edge of Shepherd's Bush Green. Or at least he thought he had. The figure's stature had echoes of the pervert who'd looked over his shoulder on the tube. It was so dark he could have been mistaken. By the time the tree came into clear focus, as he squinted in the Green's direction, all he could see was the immense girth of the oak.

As he walked, the tree became closer, twenty yards away on the opposite side of the road. He kept his eyes on it, his head slowly turning right, in line with his shoulders. He wished his neck had the flexibility of an owl's as he conceded, looking forward again.

What's up with you Frankie?

A rational thought that he was being paranoid didn't stop a strange tingling between his shoulder blades. He rolled his shoulders backwards to shake off the sensation. He continued along the street, the disco rhythm of 'Get Lucky' injecting a bounce in his step. He was glad to be moving quickly.

A few hundred yards down the road, his pocket buzzed. Frankie's pace dropped to a stroll, and he pulled out the phone, hoping to see Annie's response. The message read, 'I'm free until six, I've got the house to myself, you close by?' Appearing too keen was a mistake ... still. He responded instantly. 'Ten minutes away, see you soon.'

He pressed send, wearing a smug grin. He was walking in the direction of Annie's house. A punt that she'd invite him had paid off, saving him from doing an about turn, to head home. He was about to press play on 'Get Lucky', when his screen's reflection showed someone walking, perhaps fifteen yards behind him. This time he *was* sure. It was the man from the tube.

He slid the headphones around his neck and turned on his heels, with half formed thoughts of confrontation. A couple, walking awkwardly, held each other too tightly and laughed in their stagger. No one else was near.

Where the hell is he? Jesus, am I really being followed? Don't be stupid.

Only seconds had passed since that unnerving reflection. To duck out of sight that quickly, he must have either stepped into the corner shop (a Tesco express ten yards ahead on Frankie's right) or into the side street beyond. Frankie was caught by indecision; to carry on walking or to search out and confront a man who was probably minding his own business. He decided to put his mind at rest.

Frankie walked slowly, away from Annie's, looking through the shop window as he moved. He saw customers at self-service tills, and a shop assistant interfering with a machine (presumably giving permission for someone to buy alcohol). None of these people had recently walked in. Even if they had, they didn't look like Frankie's man.

He took a nervous, wide path around the end of the side street, looking intently for someone either making a retreat, or hiding in waiting.

It was a ridiculous notion, but the thick band of his headphones felt tight around his throat, the right bin pressing uncomfortably against his Adam's apple. He ran a finger under the band to release the pressure. That tingling returned with intensity, now running the length of his spine, an itch that needed to be scratched. He wanted to make windmills with his arms to dispel the sensation, and to take huge lung-filling breaths. He wanted to, but didn't, not wanting to look stupid or scared. A teenager's self-consciousness could trump even the deepest fear.

Puddles of water from an earlier downpour, offered shimmering reflections in the cold wind. An elderly woman, wearing a rain-hood, wheeled a tartan shopping trolley behind her. She was the only person in sight.

Nobody's following you, you idiot. Get yourself to Annie's.

He turned and walked quickly now, faster than the beat in his headphones.

I'll keep my distance. If I don't find the right moment, I'll track him down tomorrow. It's not going to be easy to find him again, and he is the one. *Best do it now if I can. Only if I can.*

I wonder if that's his house he's walking up to. No, don't think so, he's ringing the doorbell. If someone's in, I'll have to wait.

Now's the time. Yes, he's distracted, peering through the glass of the door. Get into position, behind the wall.

Okay, there's no answer. That's it, if no one's in, he'll walk back towards me, then I'll make my move. He's tried the door again. Oh, kid. Give up, no one's home.

Chapter Thirty-Two

Laura wasn't looking forward to giving Leanne an update on progress. The only upside being the proximity of their homes; it would take less than five minutes to get there.

She hummed along to 'Don't Stop Me Now' playing on Radio Two, figuring that by the time the song ended she'd be pulling up outside Leanne's.

A wailing siren, accompanied by flashing lights in her rear-view mirror, drowned out the radio. She stopped humming and took her foot off the accelerator. She drifted left, taking a decelerating path, close to the curb. The ambulance passed. A thought came to her, the same thought that always accompanies the sight of an ambulance: *I hope they're alright .... I hope it's not someone I know.*

As she turned left down the narrow street, she saw the ambulance parked at the far end of the road. She wasn't sure it was outside Leanne's flat ('Cassie's flat' was more honestly the way she thought about it) but was beginning to suspect it. Pessimistic 'What if' scenarios crowded her thoughts.

Opposite the ambulance, on the other side of the road, a Volvo police car was parked, facing Laura's approaching car. Blue lights rippled silently along its grill. She avoided blocking the tight escape path of the ambulance, pulling up in front of the police car.

A uniformed officer met her at the door with a raised palm.

"Sorry, nobody's allowed in."

Laura heard a man's voice, low and drifting along the hall from Cassie's open bedroom door. He was encouraging 'Luv' to 'come out'. Laura couldn't imagine where from. She also heard grunting exertion followed by a metallic clunk, coming from the living room. She angled her head to see what was going on, but could only make out vague reflections in the glossy sheen of the open living room door; a sofa, some movement.

"I can help." Laura showed the officer her ID card. "The girl your colleague is talking to, and her family, have been referred to me. I know them well. The girl's name is Cassie Janus. Her mum's is Leanne. Please, let me through."

"Wait here." The officer walked down the hall, past the living room door, towards Cassie's bedroom. His head disappeared around the bedroom's doorframe, he said something Laura couldn't hear, then reappeared, gesturing her to approach as though he were signalling traffic.

Before Laura had time to move, a stretcher was wheeled from the living room into the hall, blocking her path. Two paramedics flanked their patient. They looked at Laura like she was a hindrance, "Excuse us please."

Laura stepped back, away from the doorstep. The paramedics trolleyed past. A word escaped the stretchered woman who (due to a metallic blanket and an ice-pad across one side of her face) only vaguely resembled Leanne, "Cassie." Her uncovered eye fixed on Laura. "Is Cassie okay?"

Laura took hold of her hand, in an arm wrestler's grip. "I'm sure she's fine but I'll check on her. I'll make sure she's looked after."

Laura moved with the stretcher to the ambulance.

"You have to let go now."

Their grip broke and Leanne was rapidly wheeled inside, along the centre of the ambulance. One paramedic jogged to the front of the ambulance, the other jumped in the back with Leanne, shutting the double doors behind him.

The first thing Laura detected in Leanne's flat was the sweet musky aroma of weed. The smell didn't surprise her. In her job, you got used to it.

The anonymously coaxing Policeman and the one whom Laura met at the door, were now talking outside Cassie's room. Laura didn't catch much of their conversation, but did hear the words, "Still won't come out."

"Please gentlemen, let me speak to Cassie."

"Be our guest."

Laura stepped into Cassie's bedroom. A three quarter height pine veneered wardrobe faced her, its right door open at a drooping angle; the top hinge's screws working their way out of chipboard.

To her left, against the wall, was a bed. It was smaller than an adult's, and Laura imagined Cassie's feet hanging from the end at full stretch. Apart from the bed, the wardrobe, a bedside cabinet (matching neither the wood of the bed nor the wardrobe's veneer) the room was empty.

This is more like a hostel than a child's room.

"Cassie, sweetheart?"

There was only one place in the room she could be. Laura gathered her navy skirt above her knees and crouched down, a benign distance from the bed.

Cassie lay on her side, under the bed, facing Laura. Both hands clutched a black portable phone to her chest. If she'd been on her back, it would have been the pose of a sleeping vampire. She wore jeans that were too short, stopping an inch above the elastic of her socks. Her t-shirt was a grubby white and the label tongued out, licking her chin. Cassie gazed out between greasy pointed clumps of hair that gravity made fall across her face.

The sight of this fractured, shaking child made Laura understand what that overused expression, "Broke my heart" actually meant ... what it felt like.

She attempted to make eye contact, but couldn't. It wasn't like Cassie was looking over Laura's shoulder, or even through her. More like she wasn't looking at all.

"Cassie, sweetheart." Laura extended her hand slowly, with the fearful respect of someone rescuing an animal, one that's cornered and afraid.

"You remember me, don't you Sweetheart. It's Laura."

Cassie let go of the phone and took Laura's hand.

Chapter Thirty-Three

Frankie's shoulders slumped.

She said she would be here. She said.

He looked again at the message.

She said!

He turned to walk back along the path, which ran the length of the house.

I know I'm lucky, that Rich and Mikey's parents are struggling and I get more or less what I want, but Annie's parents are in a different league. Look at this place. Who can afford a four bedroom detached house a short tube ride from the centre of London. This place is beautiful. Annie's beautiful.

Forgive her for this Frankie, she probably just had to go out, but why didn't she drop me a text? I'd understand if ...

His thoughts were interrupted by the thick forearm of a man whose muscle bulged, exerting pressure across Frankie's face. Another arm clamped the back of his head. Frankie kicked back with what he thought were shin-crunching blows. His attacker stayed firm, still, strong.

Over the rough, crumpled material of his attacker's jacket sleeve, Frankie saw Annie appearing a few yards away around the end of the fence. She wore a big grin which collapsed into gaping terror. Then the pressure was gone. Frankie's head hit the floor. His last memory played out like a movie, shown in landscape, designed in portrait. He saw ankles turn into booted calves, then into a hooded man, obscuring his view of

Annie. He wanted to scream, 'run' but the darkness overcame him.

Chapter Thirty-Four

Half an hour after Laura had coaxed Cassie from under her bed, Detective Frank Simmons arrived. He felt like he'd missed the action. The paramedics were long gone. He'd spoken briefly to his two uniformed colleagues, who'd told him about Daniel Fisher being taken into custody. The case was watertight. Just the kid's and Miss Janus's witness statements to take. If ever there was a case the Crown Prosecution Service would support, it was this one.

Frank stood with Laura in the living room. He leant against the sofa, his meathook hands making dents in its upholstery.

"How's the kid?"

"I'm not sure it's sunk in yet."

He walked past Laura, pushed the kitchen door open a crack, and looked at Cassie from a discrete distance.

Cassie sat at her kitchen table, hands on her knees. Her glass of orange juice was half empty, greasy finger marks around its rim. She looked blank, as though her brain had shut down in self-preservation.

He pulled the kitchen door to, and moved back to his position near the sofa, beyond the reach of little ears.

"You got a good look at Miss Janus didn't you?"

"Uh-huh." She nodded.

"How long do *you* think she'll be in the hospital?"

"Difficult to tell. She was bruised and battered, but still had some strength in her. If I was a betting person, I'd say a few days. They'll probably just keep her in for observation."

Laura was glad to see a familiar face. She'd met Frank ten months earlier at Malcolm's official Christmas do (the unofficial one was strictly 'no partners'). She remembered the night clearly. Malcolm had drifted away from her as the evening progressed, talking to notably scarce female colleagues. She'd tried to ignore his behaviour and put it down to the drink.

Frank had approached her. He was broad-shouldered with thick forearms, without being brutish - a gentle giant. He made kind comments about how Malcolm's leaving her was clearly a sign of temporary insanity, assuring her that Malcolm would come to his senses and return at any moment. They'd chatted for the best part of an hour before Malcolm returned, later than predicted.

Frank's comment broke her recollection, "You got here quickly."

"It was pure dumb luck. I was ..."

Laura caught sight of drops of blood a few inches from her right shoe, soaking into the pile. She shuffled left.

"... on my way to see Miss Janus when I saw the ambulance."

"Not sure what to do with the kid, are you?"

"Not really. I could find her a temporary foster home with a family I know but ..."

"But?"

"I think she needs some familiarity, some continuity, you know?"

Oh God, I would love to take her in, just for a few days. I know I shouldn't but I would, for this kid, I would. Can't do it now though, things are too weird at home.

"Malcolm always says you get too attached."

"Does he now?"

"Frank, could you stay with Cassie for ten minutes while I make a few phone calls."

"Sure."

Laura stepped into the hall, mobile phone in hand, whilst Frank walked through to the kitchen. Cassie recoiled at the sight of him and stared into her drink.

Frank was confident and comfortable with adults but never quite knew what to say to children, particularly girls and especially in a situation like this. "Hey kid. I can understand you not trusting anyone at the minute but, for what it's worth, Mrs Robinson will make sure you're okay and I'm sure your mum will be back on her feet in no time."

Cassie, still looking down, mumbled the only urgent question: "Where is he?"

"Don't worry about Daniel Fisher. He's locked up right now and I'd bet my pension that he won't get bail. Do you know what that is?" She nodded.

"I can't say that you'll *never* see him again, but I can say for sure that if you do, it won't be for a long, long time."

Outside, in the hall, Laura was talking to Aaron's mother on the phone.

"I know Mrs Hall, but I'm sure it will be for just a few days ... I have a single blowup bed I'd be happy to lend you ... it's really just that I don't want to put Cassie through the trauma of foster care under the circumstances if its just a few days and I hear that Aaron and Cassie get on so well and she doesn't have any family she can stay... yes I understand that but she is a sweet kid. I know her mum has problems, but I'm sure she would be eternally grateful for this small favour. The school speak really highly of you and ... oh you will? That's fantastic Mrs Hall. I'll see that she's okay here and bring her round this evening with some clothes. I'll be there by six, I hope. I can't thank you enough. Yes, goodbye and thank you. Bye now, bye."

Laura walked through the living room and into the kitchen. She smiled at Frank who was leaning against the work surface, holding a glass of water. Cassie sat perfectly still, in complete silence.

"Frank, thanks ever so much, but could you leave us now?"

"I guess so but we'll have to talk to her sometime in the next few days."

"Of course, plenty of time for that. See you soon."

"Say hi to Malcolm for me."

"Will do, but I'm sure *you* see more of him than *I* do at the minute."

Frank's eyebrows gathered and he glanced sideways at Laura as he made his way out of the house, towards his unmarked Subaru Impreza. Laura was oblivious to his look; her thoughts were with this poor girl.

Laura sat opposite Cassie, letting the peace of the house settle for a few moments before she spoke. Laura slid the half finished orange juice to one side and held her hands out palms up, as if begging.

"Cassie, give me your hands." Cassie pulled her arms from under the table and laid her hands in Laura's. They were stiff and warm, like they'd been sat on for a long time.

"Cassie. I know the last thing you want right now is to talk and that's fine, really it is. We only want what's best for you and so does your mum.

I'm afraid you won't be able to stay here for a few days though. Your mum will need a short while to recover before she can come home."

"Mummy's going to be okay isn't she Mrs Robinson?"

"Yes she is. Please Cassie, call me Laura."

"Where am I going to stay?" Cassie's eyes were wide and glassy. Laura saw her reflection in them. It was a look of fear Laura was used to, was virtually *immune* to - in most cases.

"I've arranged for you to stay with Aaron for a few days. Would you like that?"

Cassie's face broke into a smile.

Chapter Thirty-Five

Their unconscious bodies lay in a heap, propped up by the leg of the telephone table, in Annie's parent's hall. Frankie was on top.

On the table lay a note: '*Annie, we'll Be back by six. We'll make tea when we get in.*' It was five forty-five p.m..

Enough time to kill them carefully, to arrange the evidence, and leave? I don't think so. There wasn't supposed to be two. Have to leave.

He grabbed the car keys from the telephone table, slipped his rolled up hood into a deep back pocket, and peered outside. A Volkswagen Beetle, parked on the drive, had gone unnoticed in the rush of adrenaline. Even in the semi-dark, he could see the fake flower poking up from the dashboard. He couldn't quite make out the colour of the car; perhaps pink. No time to worry about anonymity.

I have to move, now.

Frankie was first. He took him by his ankles and dragged him down the path. Frankie's skull knocked repeatedly against the concrete, the loudest thud coming as his head dropped over the front doorstep.

The boot was full of junk; an automatic car pump, a shovel, a blanket. He sighed, slinging them over the parcel shelf into the back seat before picking Frankie up off the drive and throwing him. A grunt escaped Frankie's lips as he hit the boot's floor.

He can't be coming around yet, must have just been air escaping. Now for the girlfriend.

By five to six the Beetle was reversing out of the drive. He resisted the temptation to speed.

"Andrew."

"Yes honey?"

"I'm sure the car we just passed is mine."

"Don't be daft, there are hundreds of Beetles in London. I bet it just looked like yours." Andrew was used to Pamela's irrational fretting. 'I've left the gas on.' 'Did you remember to lock the door?' They could never go out, even to the supermarket, without her having some concern or other.

"I didn't see all of the reg' plate, but the end was the same as ours, I'm sure."

"You'll see, in a moment we'll pull into our drive and it'll be sitting there, just where you left it."

They pulled their BMW X5 into the driveway. A street light sent shadows of neatly clipped bushes across the garden - shadows that should have swept across Pamela's car but stretched over their empty driveway instead.

A dark void was where the front door should have been. They jumped from the car (leaving the BMW's doors wide open) and ran across the grass, Pamela's heels rapidly sinking and unplugging. They reached the door together shouting, "Annie, Annie." Pamela walked inside, her shoes dropping damp grass-cuttings on the hall carpet.

"Pamela, call the police."

Andrew turned on the outside light and inspected the entrance. He saw dark smears on the step and doorframe. He bent down, using the light from his phone to take a closer look. He ran the tip of his index finger across the scarred aluminium of the frame, then pulled his stained fingertip into the light. He dropped the phone. Its light went out.

"Pamela."

Andrew turned his head, holding up his finger to the light of the hall, wanting and not wanting his wife to see what was surely Annie's blood. Her attention was elsewhere.

She held the phone to her ear, muttering, "Come on, come on." The burgundy of her Ted Baker suit exaggerated her pallid complexion, all of the colour having drained from her face.

Chapter Thirty-Six

"C'mon Cassie. Let's get a bag together. We'll pack enough for four days, just to be on the safe side. How about that?"

"Okay."

"Are your clothes in your room?" Cassie nodded and sprung off her kitchen chair, as though the prospect of going to stay with Aaron had erased her ordeal. Cassie led the way to her bedroom.

The top of the wardrobe was level with Laura's chest. She stood behind Cassie who was dragging out a rucksack whilst skilfully negotiating the broken wardrobe door. Cassie's clothes, though most were too short, dragged on the bottom of the wardrobe.

They worked together, parting hangers, Cassie at the left of the rail, Laura at the right, both looking for suitable clothes and finding few.

"Jesus Christ!" Laura's hand was at her chest. She was looking down at scattered clothes, on the wardrobe floor. A toddler's hand poked out from between a pair of crumpled jeans and a vest top.

"It's just Katie, Mrs Robinson."

Cassie took Katie's hand, rescuing her from the sea of out-grown clothes.

"Look."

It was the creepiest doll Laura had ever seen. If it possessed clothes, they'd long since vanished, as though a dressing-up game had been abandoned in mid-flow. Frayed stitching just managed to keep its left arm in place. Someone (presumably Cassie) had scrawled on its eyelids. Scratches of black ink had faded to blue over time. One eye was shut entirely, the other half-closed.

"Mrs Robinson."

"Yes Cassie?" She was struggling to take her eyes off the doll, which Cassie held in her arms as though she was cradling a baby.

"When can I go to the hospital to see Mummy?"

"I'm sure you can go tomorrow morning."

"Who'll take me?"

"Don't worry, I'm sure Aaron's mum will and, if she can't, I'll take you myself."

Laura crouched down next to Cassie, looking into the rucksack at two folded tops. They looked up at the wardrobe again. It was crammed with clothes that were either too small or were bought for Halloween.

There must be some dirty clothes somewhere. This can't be it.

"Do you think your mum would mind if I put some clothes through the wash?"

"I guess not."

"Come on, you can give me a hand."

Cassie sat Katie on the bed, upright and against the wall - a position Katie hadn't taken for years.

They found a small wedge-shaped plastic laundry basket (the type that neatly slots into corners) in a kitchen cupboard. Laura tipped it up, next to the washing machine, creating a large heap to salvage from.

They knelt next to the diminishing pile, routing and shoving darks into the chrome mouth of the washing machine. It was the type of sunny afternoon that made chores feel light. Cassie carried on shoving but Laura's progress was halted by a jolting question.

"Mrs Robinson, why do grown-ups like to hurt people?"

How on earth do you respond to a question like that?

"It's not just grown-ups Cassie, you should know that. And it's not many people either. Most people are nice."

"Some people are nice. Aaron's nice. You seem nice. And I know that Rachel is a bad person and she hurts people, but not like grown-ups do. Grown-ups hurt people really badly."

It wasn't the sort of conversation you could have over laundry. Laura turned off her knees and sat on the floor cross-legged. She couldn't remember the last time she'd sat like that and hoped she could get up okay. She put her hand on Cassie's arm, to make her stop, to listen.

"Cassie, do you mean Mummy's friend, Daniel?"

"Him and others. Somebody in London is hurting people really badly."

"Oh sweetheart, I know it's difficult to understand, but London's a huge place and the good things that people do never make it onto the news ... so it's too easy to think bad things are going on around you, and I would understand how you'd think that, with your mother being in hospital and everything. But trust me Cassie, these things are not very common. Your mum was unlucky."

She looked at Laura. Their direct eye contact lingered. It was like Cassie was examining something potentially poisonous, something she was about to eat.

Cassie ceased her silent cross-examination without comment and force-fed the washing machine again. They worked in silence for a couple of minutes.

Cassie Janus, what's going on inside that mind of yours?

"I understand what happened. He was drunk and Mummy said something he didn't like. He got mad and couldn't control himself. Sometimes Rachel's like that. She gets mad and lashes out."

"Well I suppose we all get angry sometimes, but that doesn't excuse what happened to your-"

"What I don't understand is why someone would tie someone up, someone they don't even know and start putting stuff in them and choke them to death." Her tone was so matter-of-fact, she could have been reading a shopping list. Laura took hold of Cassie's hand.

"Cassie, stop, let's sit down at the table for a minute." Laura turned onto her knees to get up. Cassie noticed Laura's rising stumble, and offered her an arm to lean on.

They sat down opposite each other. Laura squinted against a square of sunshine cast by the kitchen window, and shuffled her chair into a better position. She reached out, keeping a tight hold of Cassie's hands.

"Cassie, listen to me, where did you hear that from? Is someone trying to upset you?"

Cassie looked at the tabletop, "No, why would someone do that? I read about it in the paper."

She looked back up with a forced smile, "Shall we switch the washing machine on?"

Laura felt sick, unnerved by the inhuman ease with which Cassie had snapped out of that plain, childish, matter of fact description of murderous abuse. She wanted to confront what was clearly a lie - the papers never reported graphic details like that. But hadn't Cassie been through enough for one day?

"Okay Cassie, do you know how to do it?"

"Yes Mrs Robinson."

She can't have just made that up, and she definitely didn't read it. Somebody's told her that to frighten her. Perhaps it was a misguided scare story to keep her from talking to strangers. I could believe that of her mum. This girl needs a normal environment, to be with responsible parents. I've got to do something about this.

Chapter Thirty-Seven

"Laura, turn the oven off and get your coat, I'm taking you out for dinner."

His words came before their back door was even closed. Laura looked down at her creased work skirt. It had one of those unidentifiable white smudges that black material attracts.

Such a long day. The afternoon spent with Cassie had been mentally exhausting. Laura's boss, Angie, had called just as she'd arrived home. Laura's referrals were stacking up. Angie was pleasant enough, but obsessed with numbers. Her questions were never about the people they were helping, they all centred on case clearance rates, open case loads, risk management. Ugh. Talking to her could suck the energy out of the best of days. A real mood-hoover. Laura just wanted to shove something in the oven and crash on the sofa.

One minute I'm being complained at for how much I'm spending on food, the next, we're eating out. But he's making an effort. We rarely go out. It'll be good for both of us.

"Okay Malcolm, just give me five minutes to change."

Laura and Malcolm ended up at Zizzi's. It was almost perfect. Their waiter, Marco, was attentive, friendly and had those come-to-bed eyes, a thought Laura kept to herself. He lit two tea candles in porcelain pots at their table, as Malcolm looked over his menu at Laura, smiling.

Perfection would have been a restaurant filled with couples. Next to their table, a man sat on his own, grazing on Antipasti. White headphones, nestled in his ears, led to an iPad on a folded triangular stand. His chuckling at YouTube videos was overly loud for a restaurant.

Malcolm didn't mind Italian food, but much preferred Indian or Thai. Laura loved Italian; his suggestion of Zizzi's was a kind gesture - kind and appreciated.

The waiter poured them both a glass of Chardonnay. Laura offered her glass forward and Malcolm raised his in response. She thought he looked gorgeous tonight in his clean white shirt, in the flickering glow of candlelight. "Malcolm thanks for this, this is great."

"Laura, we've had a breakthrough today. I owe you a big apology." Malcolm was grinning, a sparkle in his eyes.

"How come?"

"We were cross referencing DNA samples from unsolved cases and guess what?" Laura shrugged.

"There's a DNA match across the murders of Dacia Cartwright and Peter Eccleston."

"Sounds like great progress. Do you know who it belongs to?" Malcolm looked towards the man with the iPad, then back towards Laura. He whispered, "An ex-convict, Alfred Tucker."

"Do you know him?"

"No but someone on the team does. Do you remember Jerry?" When Malcolm said Jerry, only two images came to mind: Jerry McGuire then Jerry the Berry from Phoenix nights.

"It's not ringing any bells."

"You *will* remember him, he got hammered at the Christmas party last year and started pinching and slapping women's arses until they finally kicked him out." Laura still couldn't remember, she must have missed the commotion whilst talking to Frank.

"Oh him." Easiest to lie.

"Well, Jerry's coming close to retirement and he remembered the case clearly. This guy, Tucker, served a sentence for second-degree murder. He was released a few weeks ago, two days before the Cartwright murder. *And* he failed to turn up at his halfway house. He's got to be our man."

"Sounds like it. Do you think you'll catch him?"

"Now that we've identified him, I'm pretty confident. We've released a picture of him to the media today. It's only a matter of time now. Strange though."

"How so?"

"There's absolutely nothing connecting those murders other than this evidence, well, other than the sexuality aspect which you mentioned, tenuous at best. We're struggling for motive."

"Well Malcolm, with the hours you've all been putting in, you deserve it, you really do. I hope you find him soon." Laura raised her glass again, Malcolm reciprocated and the chink reverberated loudly from their wide, half-filled glasses. Malcolm smiled, then his expression shifted into an uneasy one, perhaps a look of shame. He put his hand against Laura's cheekbone, caressing it and then gently stroked her cheek to one side of her mouth. "I *am* sorry, you know. I noticed the mark on your mouth. I didn't mean to hurt you. I'll be more gentle in future."

At last he's mentioned it and apologised. Such a sense of relief.

"Malcolm, I love you."

"You too sweetheart. You too. Anyway ... here's me banging on about my day, how was yours?"

"Weird, Malcolm weird." Laura paused, unsure whether to share what Cassie had said.

Oh what the hell, it seems like a good night for getting things off your chest.

"I've been making sure that this girl, Cassie, is okay. She's been through a tough time, poor kid. She was just getting over being injured in a car crash when her mother's boyfriend attacked her."

"The girl?"

"No, her mother. But it was while she was in the house."

"Oh Jesus, poor kid."

"I know. And to make matters worse someone, probably her mother, has been scaring her with stories about these murders. She told me things that *no* kid should hear."

"What did she say?"

"I might tell you later but its probably best discussed at home. You know what … let's try and forget about work for the rest of the night. Let's order, I'm in the mood for Risotto."

Malcolm opened his mouth, closed it and looked at the menu again. His eyes were looking without reading, a distant focus. He placed the menu between his knife and fork.

"Okay, let's order. But you've heard all about my day, and I want to hear all about yours."

Chapter Thirty-Eight

As Frankie's eyes opened, the world was a blur. He had the strangest memory of art class at school. Their teacher had told them to squint their eyes and look at an image as they turned their heads quickly. It was supposed to help them understand what impressionism was all about; blurred objects. For several minutes that's all Frankie had, unformed impressions.

The dull ache from the lump on the back of his skull was drowned out by the monotonous stabbing sensation across his forehead, which beat to the rhythm of his heart.

"Where the hell am I? What in God's name happened?"

Was he dreaming? A distant voice penetrated his fog. The voice was familiar, beautiful in fact.

Urgency dispelled the allure.

"Frankie, thank God, can you hear me?" He wanted to say that he could, but when he parted his lips no sound escaped, only air. "Frankie, sweet Jesus, Frankie, don't drift off again. Wake up. We've got to get out of here." Consciousness crept back and blurred objects merged, coming into focus.

He saw Annie opposite him, perhaps ten feet away, sitting on the stone floor, her back against a brick wall. The bricks were either black veined or crumbling. Sometimes both. Her arms were elevated, pointing upwards at forty-five degree angles from her shoulders. Two sets of handcuffs caused her arms' elevation, looped through thick iron shackles, which were screwed into the wall.

Her cuffs were tight. As she wriggled Frankie saw red marks on her wrists emerging and then hiding again behind the cuff's steel. Her tangled brown hair looked like it hadn't been brushed in days. She was still wearing the jeans he'd caught a glimpse of over that arm (*oh God, the arm, I remember now*) only now they were shredded. Ragged strips made her jeans more closely resemble a grass skirt. Denim grass.

Above her knee, dark streaks - dirt or something - ran down her thigh. Frankie breathed deeply, finding the strength to speak, but as he opened his mouth all that came out was a wheezing cough, expelling dust and the smell of stale paper from his lungs. He tried again.

"I can hear you. Has he hurt you?"

"Yes ... no ... I don't know. I woke up like this maybe half an hour ago. My legs are stinging, but I'm okay ... I think. I heard shuffling and mumbling outside the door but it's been quiet for the last twenty minutes. Can you get free? These cuffs are too tight, can you move?"

Frankie looked at his arms and the realisation came that his situation entirely mirrored Annie's; his arms were raised and he too was chained to a wall. He tugged against the steel. The chains were firm - no give - digging painfully into his wrists. He looked back at Annie, trying not to show what was running through his mind.

We're going to die in this room.

"Annie, what *is* this place?"

"I'm not sure. I've been trying to figure that out. Look at the door." She motioned her head to her right, drawing Frankie's attention to the thick door to his left. It had a large metal circular mechanism. He imagined, on the other side, there would be spokes like those on the wheel of a ship, which would assist in turning the enormous lock. Towards the edge of the door he saw symmetrical twin keyholes, equidistant from the concrete floor. One keyhole was eight inches or so from an enormous hinge, its twin was where a handle would have been, if this were an ordinary door.

The door, the smell of old paper, brick walls and the empty shelving all combined to stir a thought.

"Annie ... I think it's a disused vault ... or something."

"Maybe, but what place has a vault like this?"

Frankie scanned the room again. He was looking for vents but couldn't see any. He looked back at the door again. A rubber seal ran its perimeter.

How does air get in? Correction ... does any air get in?

A sinking feeling in his stomach must have played out on his face. Annie, as ever, was in tune with his thoughts.

"Frankie, how much time do you think we have?"

They were distracted from the question by a series of clanks, both loud and distant, like the first rumbles of thunder twenty miles off shore.

Chapter Thirty-Nine

The unfamiliar patterns in Aaron's curtains, swollen by the light of the moon, were spooking Cassie, keeping her awake. They were curtains that surely Aaron's mum would soon replace; they had no right to be in a boy's bedroom. In the daylight, the patterns were beige representations of flowers with thorny stems intertwined. At night, they were faces that formed and vanished as the curtains wafted in a draft. The windows were the tight-sealed PVC type, but the storm wouldn't be silenced. It was close to gale force and grew stronger as the night wore on.

Despite the noise of the wind she also heard the ticking of Aaron's Mickey Mouse shaped alarm clock. Against her better judgement, she swore the ticking was getting louder.

The longer Cassie lay there, staring at nothing, the harder it was for her to drift off to sleep. She tried to look away from the fleeting faces in the curtains but found herself strangely drawn to them and the more she looked, the louder her heart became and the more rapidly she breathed.

She was drifting towards a seizure and yet she felt a calm acceptance, a tender confidence. She *would* survive and *would* wake. The terrible visions *would* plague her but maybe Aaron was right, she *could* help the police. Perhaps she could risk changing events. Perhaps this was who she was; a good 'different' if she could use her gift to stop these murders.

Is this really where I'm going to spend the rest of my days, locked up in a cell after just being released from one? Have I really pissed God off that much? How long has it been now, two weeks, three, four? It's so hard to get a sense of time passing, when you have no windows.

Chapter Forty

Without the buzzing strip-light Alfred would have been lying in total darkness. And sometimes the man, who 'tended' to him, did turn it off and those days were the worst.

I don't think I've seen him now for a day or two. Surely he can't risk leaving me in here much longer, he's going to kill me soon - sick son of a bitch. That's if the infection doesn't take me first. Who the hell is he? Must have some sort of medical background I reckon, the way he drew my blood, the narrow tubes he had for my spit. God only knows what he's doing with it.

I just wish I could sleep now. I hate sleeping on my back, and that's without the sores. The newest one, on my back under my ribs, is killing me. Maybe, if I pull the straps hard enough, I can break the leg of this bed. Can't be that strong, it's only a camping bed. But even if the leg gives way before the bones in my wrist, what then? There's still the bars to get through. What the hell is this place? The smell gets right to the back of your throat. It smells like wet, rotten cloth. Yeah that's it like someone has pulled linen cloth, used for mummification, from around a corpse and left it out for years.

Wait, what's that? Quiet, distant, but definitely a sound, a human sound. The first sound I've heard in weeks that doesn't sound like him, doesn't sound like the persistent rush of the blood in my ears either, or the ticking of rats' claws on concrete. Is that someone crying out? It's so faint, am I just imagining it?

"Hello, is someone there?" Alfred wished he still had young man's lungs. Every time he shouted out the effort brought a deep coughing and his chest felt so weak. Between each outcry he paused, hoping to hear something in response. He thought he heard someone, but it was so faint and mostly his heartbeat drowned out the sound. After an hour of shouting and listening, his body relented to tiredness.

When Alfred awoke it was for less than a minute. He was aware of a stinging sensation in his arm, then a sinking grogginess. His mouth was being held open and there was a scraping inside his cheek. Then nothing.

Chapter Forty-One

The faces in the curtains had vanished and outdated impressions of flowers had returned in their place. The sun was rising but it wasn't the light that woke Cassie, it was Aaron's Mum, knocking on the bedroom door and shouting, which brought her round.

"Come on Aaron, Cassie, you're going to be late."

Aaron sat up, momentarily opening his eyes then laid back, turned over, bunched his Dr Who duvet over his head, mumbled and promptly fell back to sleep. Cassie sat up, her bum-cheeks meeting the carpet through the half-deflated blow-up bed. She rubbed sleep from the corners of her eyes.

She became aware of a stinging on both sides of her tongue, right at the back where molars clamp down. It was a feeling she recognised, an injury she'd suffered before, though this time it didn't hurt nearly as much. She wiped the side of her mouth with her arm, smearing half-dried blood across her pyjamas sleeve. She looked around, disturbing the duvet as she turned. Her movement uncovered a few spots of blood on the cover. They'd dried into a brick colour, darkest at the edges.

I must apologise to Aaron's mum and tell her I had a nosebleed. I don't want her to know I had a fit in the house, that would frighten her. I'm going to live here as long as possible.

Cassie decided to stand up and get dressed. It was her first day back at school and she didn't want to be the one to make them late.

Aaron's room was strange, in a good way. There were so many things designed for a younger kid's room, the Mickey Mouse alarm being one. There was a Mr Potato head and oversized building blocks on top of his wardrobe. A space hopper sat in the corner, and a stuffed lion looked comfortable, nesting in a Star Wars beanbag.

Forming a strange counterpoint to the toys was a poster of Rihanna in a white dress. The front of her dress gaped so much, revealing a zebra print bikini, that Cassie could only imagine she'd put the dress on back to front by mistake.

Cassie's clothes were temporarily stored in Aaron's wardrobe. Mrs Hall had given them ample hanger space. Cassie pulled out a white school shirt from the rail. Laura had ironed it; no creases.

In the last few months, Cassie had become conscious of her body. Her mother saw this as progress; Cassie did not. Looking back, it was good not to care who saw you naked. She couldn't pinpoint when self-consciousness kicked in, growing up sort of creeps up on you. But there it was, she now cared, it was undeniable. You had to keep your body out of the sight of boys, and not look at theirs. She knew that this was because of sex but she'd only skimmed the surface of that word's meaning. She knew the mechanics that was all. She got changed with her back to Aaron's bed.

As she fastened buttons, she looked again around Aaron's room. The enormity of his computer drew her attention. It sat proudly, centre stage on his desk, looking like a widescreen television except for the wireless keyboard and mouse, which marred the illusion.

Above the desk his forty-two-inch Sony TV was mounted on the wall. Cassie could now see why Aaron spent so much time in his room. It also occurred to her that Aaron's parents must be well off or, to be crude and probably more accurate, filthy rich.

Aaron stirred. He rubbed the top of his head, which made his hair an even greater mess. His head turned right towards Cassie's bloodstained pyjamas, which were folded on her bed. "Cassie, where are you, are you okay?"

"I'm right here sleepy head." She was warmed by his concern.

He really is a great friend.

"Your mum's been calling you, better hurry. I'm off to the bathroom to clean my teeth. Come on ... get up and get dressed. I'll knock before I come back in."

Aaron swivelled so that his feet landed on the floor, straight into his StarWars slippers.

When Cassie returned Aaron was looking into the mirrored front of his wardrobe, fiddling with a green clip-on tie. Cassie distracted and surprised him with a question. "What sort of building do you think might have rooms with bars, other than a prison?"

"Cassie Janus, you do ask me some random stuff, but that one's just an all time great. It's seven forty-five in the morning, I've just about got my eyes open and you're asking me what buildings have bars, other than a prison!"

"I'm serious Aaron. I saw something last night."

"Did you have another fit?"

"Yes, but please don't tell your mum. I'm getting control of them, I can feel it. Every time I fit, I can see more clearly and sometimes I can stop the fitting altogether. Not last night ... I know ... but it wasn't a bad one. Please Aaron, please don't tell your mum. Promise?"

"Okay Cassie. But what's all this about rooms with bars?" They were interrupted by Aaron's mum letting them know that toast was ready and if they didn't get down to eat it soon, they'd have to go without. There was no way Aaron was going to skip breakfast.

"Never mind Aaron. We'll talk about it later." They cantered down the stairs, "Nice computer by the way."

"Thanks, Mum and Dad bought it for me for Christmas."

Wow, all I got was a Furby, bought off Ebay.

Chapter Forty-Two

That afternoon at exactly five o'clock, Laura Robinson stood outside Mr and Mrs Hall's house, bringing their brass knocker down with the right force - a polite assertiveness.

Aaron's mum answered, in a housedress and 'Yummy Mummy' apron.

"Hello Mrs Hall. Sorry to disturb you. Is Cassie around? I'd like to have a quick chat with her, if that's okay?"

"Sure, she's upstairs with Aaron. I'll call them. Do come in."

As Laura thoroughly wiped dirt off her soles onto the doormat, Mrs Hall shouted for Aaron and Cassie to come down. They bounded down, side by side.

Laura looked up at them. *As thick as thieves.*

Mrs Hall had a minor confession to make, "Oh, I took Cassie to the hairdressers, just for a trim."

Laura could tell. Cassie's fringe now stopped halfway down her forehead; a little severe. Mrs Hall must have had a similar thought, "You don't think Leanne would mind do you?"

"No, I'm sure that's fine."

"Aaron, why don't you get your homework out for half an hour, Mrs Robinson would like to speak with Cassie."

"Oh, Mum, do I *have* to?"

"Yes you 'have to'. It'll be good to get it out of the way. Your folder is where you left it on the mantelpiece. You can play with Cassie later."

"O-kay Mum." Aaron's shoulders slumped. He climbed down the rest of the stairs. At the bottom he turned, looking up the staircase towards Cassie, and lifted a weak see-you-later hand. She waved back. Laura smiled.

I've made the right call asking Mrs Hall to take Cassie in.

"How are you? Have you been good for Mrs Hall?" Cassie nodded.

"She's been as good as gold. Had a slight nosebleed in the night, but nothing serious. And if one good thing has come out of this, it's that Aaron's tidied his room for the first time in ... well forever."

Aaron's voice carried from the living room. "Muuuum, I heard that."

Laura's snorting laugh took her by surprise.

"Cassie, why don't you come down and take Mrs Robinson through to the kitchen, I'll make sure that Aaron keeps out your way for a while. Help yourself to a drink. Cassie knows where we keep the mugs and glasses. She's really getting used to the place, aren't you Cassie?"

"U-huh."

Mrs Hall followed Aaron and pulled the living room door shut behind them.

Cassie poured herself lemonade and sat on a stool at the breakfast bar. Laura fixed herself a tea and, with her hands warming around the mug, sat down opposite Cassie. The narrowness of the breakfast bar brought their faces naturally close.

Laura noticed a cork board organiser, with a dry-wipe panel on the side. A 'to do' list, five items long, was printed neatly on the white panel. The writing was perfectly aligned with embossed square tick boxes. At the top of the list: 'Clothes shopping with Cassie.'

"So Cassie, I hear your mother's recovering well. The doctors have said it's best she doesn't have visitors today because they've given her strong painkillers. They'll be reducing the dose overnight. You should be able to see her in the morning.

Okay?" Cassie didn't say anything but nodded and gulped her lemonade.

"How's it been living at Aaron's house? Do you like it here?"

"I love it. Aaron's mum's been great."

"Getting much sleep on that blow-up bed?"

"Some."

Laura wanted to ask about Cassie's mother scaring her with gory stories. They sat in silence, drinking for a minute whilst she considered her approach.

"Cassie, I've been thinking. Look, you seemed worried yesterday when we spoke about … the murders. There's been a lot of talk, a lot of speculation. Do you know what that means? Speculation?"

"It means when people talk as if they're sure about something that they don't really know about." Laura was floored by the articulation.

"Well yes, Cassie, that's exactly what it means. A lot of people have been talking about what happened, without really knowing. Sometimes people say these things because, when they don't have all the facts, they like to … to fill in the gaps of the story. Sometimes people do this to frighten others, in a strange joking way, or to warn people to be careful. Is that what happened with you Cassie, did someone say those things to frighten you?"

Cassie's forehead pinched, forming deep lines. She was clearly bemused by Laura's question, "No, nobody said anything."

"Because you know, sometimes grown-ups tell us these things to make sure we don't go off with strangers, that we're aware of the dangers."

"I told you, I read it in the paper. I'm not stupid you know. I wouldn't go off with a stranger."

Laura smiled. "I'm sure you're not. 'Stupid' is definitely not a word that people use to describe you Cassie, quite the opposite. Look … I know you're saying you read about it to protect someone. I know you wouldn't lie unless you had too.

The things you described don't get reported in the papers and no child has any business knowing or thinking about those things. I need to get to the bottom of where it came from."

"Oh." Cassie suddenly understood. She stared into her glass, swilling it, reviving its fizz. She was weighing up how much she could trust this woman. On the surface she was kind, but - it was such a big truth. Mrs Robinson had an amazing ability to sit comfortably with silence. Cassie felt decidedly *un*comfortable.

"Mrs Robinson, if I tell you, you have to swear not to tell anyone else, anyone at all."

"Oh Cassie, I can never make that promise, but I *do* promise I'll only tell if I feel I really have to, and only if you say it's okay."

"If I give you permission?"

"Exactly."

"I have a gift." When the words came out, Cassie felt an unexpected pride. She sat tall, straight backed, on her stool.

Laura slowly lowered her mug, placing it carefully on the breakfast bar.

"Go on Cassie."

"And I've had it as long as I can remember."

"What's your gift?"

Cassie looked intently at Laura's eyes, examining them, trying to look beyond them. She was searching for any small sign of dishonesty and saw none. That was when she let the words escape, words that could never be unsaid, or denied.

"I see through the eyes of other people. I see what's happening to them and often I see what's *going* to happen. I know so much about what's happening because I can see it, through their eyes and through his." Cassie waited for Laura to be filled with a look of doubt, scepticism or horror.

Laura had considered that Cassie's knowledge of the murders might be another symptom of what Miss April had described; her inexplicable powers of perception. She'd almost dismissed this possibility, almost, but not entirely.

Laura gently loosened Cassie's grip on the glass and took her hand, "It's okay, I know you're telling the truth."

"You do?"

"It's what made you tell Miss April about her boyfriend, wasn't it?"

"Yes."

"How often does this happen?"

"Lately, all the time."

"Look Cassie, I can't imagine what it's like for you, having all of that swimming round your mind. I'm not going to ask you to talk about it if you don't want to. But if there is something you've seen that's disturbing you, that you need to talk about, then you can talk to me Cassie. You can trust me."

"I think I might be able to help the police."

"In what way?"

"They're going to think it's Alfred, but he's not done anything wrong. He's being hurt too."

Laura withdrew her hands, trying to absorb what Cassie was telling her. Mrs Hall poked her head around the kitchen door. "Sorry Mrs Robinson, are you just about done? It's just ... I need to prepare dinner and my husband will be back shortly."

"Yes that's fine. Cassie, I'll take you to the hospital tomorrow, to see your mother, if you'd like that. We can talk some more then."

Laura could have pushed the issue, taken Cassie to another part of the house, to discuss it further. She chose not to, anxious to be alone with her thoughts.

Why is it that just when you think you've got things under control, your work, your health, your relationships, there's always something to knock you off centre.

Today that 'something' was the tiniest crack in a concrete case against Alfred Tucker.

Chapter Forty-Three

An hour after telling Laura about her abilities, Cassie felt light, agile in both body and mind. She sat next to Aaron at dinner, with Aaron's mum and dad. Aaron's dad was quiet, but friendly and polite. He looked like a man who enjoyed his food.

Aaron's mum did most of the talking, enquiring about what school had been like, when the next tests were and whether they'd done all of their homework.

"Mum, every night it's the same, quit with the interrogations."

"Aaron!" It was Cassie who interjected. "Your mum's just taking an interest in you, isn't that right Mrs Hall?"

"Yes that *is* right." Mrs Hall nodded twice, once to 'is' and once to 'right.' She smiled at Cassie.

Cassie understood Aaron. Having an attentive mother had never been novel for him. He took her for granted. It was a fact, not a criticism. He'd never known any different. Cassie had. And all she could think about was how perfect it would be to live there forever.

Cassie's thoughts then turned to her mum, who was alone in the hospital; not knowing what state she'd be in when she visited in the morning. The guilt, flooding in, washed away that feeling of lightness, for a while.

We'll have to make the best of it together, that's all. I'll just have to be more independent than most kids.

Cassie was daydreaming, wondering why Mr and Mrs Hall hadn't had more children, when Aaron asked his mum if Cassie and him could be excused to play in his room.

"Of course sweetheart. You two go and have fun, but first, you need to help stack the dishwasher." Aaron was about to complain when Cassie jumped up, "Of course we can Mrs Hall."

"Thank you Cassie. Hey, you two. Once we've got cleaned up. Why don't we all go bowling ... oh Cassie ... I forgot. If your arm's up to it."

Aaron's dad spoke for the first time in over half an hour, "You'll have to go without me, I'm afraid. There's work I need to do."

"What about you two. Are you up for that?"

Cassie got that feeling, the one that only came with picking up the next Harry Potter. A feeling she thought she'd never have again, now that she'd read all seven. And her arm was a lot better. It would hurt but she could cope. She *would* cope. She turned to Aaron in desperate nodding persuasion. Neither Aaron nor his dad looked like the bowling type. Aaron's words sounded more resigned than excited, "Yes, thanks Mum, that would be great."

They couldn't get a lane until seven - an hour to play. But playing wasn't on Aaron's mind. He was thinking about a 'room with bars' and had been, on and off, all day. School had been a trivial distraction from something that felt more important.

Aaron sat down at his desk. Cassie carefully moved the lion (Aslan) from Aaron's beanbag, placing him on the bed. He laughed at her.

"It's not real you know, you don't have to be that careful. He won't bite."

She smiled, stuck her tongue out at him, and pulled the beanbag next to his seat. She felt low, but comfy.

She wasn't comfortable for long. Aaron's questioning soon took her back to her latest vision, back into Alfred Tucker's world.

Rachel burning that poor girl, exactly as predicted, had dispelled Aaron's disbelief in Cassie's abilities. Precognition was clearly illogical, implausible, yet still, there was no doubt.

Aaron viewed Cassie's visions like road accidents: you know it's a bad idea, but you can't help taking a look.

"Let's go through this again. What exactly did you see?"

"I saw a man trapped in a room with bars. At first I thought it was a prison but the room had a filing cabinet and a table. Whatever the room was used for, it looks like it hasn't been used in a long time. What sort of a building would have things in it like that?"

"Are you *sure* it's not a prison?"

"Pretty sure. Aren't prison cells usually narrow, just big enough to live in. This was much bigger, like it could have caged a tiger or something."

"An inside Zoo enclosure?"

"No, there was no light. They wouldn't have kept animals down there."

"Down?"

"Yes, I don't know why *(descending footsteps?)* but I just got the sense it was in a basement of some kind."

"Someone's built themselves a cell in their basement?"

"Maybe, but it felt more office-like than that."

"A bank?"

"What makes you say that? I didn't see any money, there weren't any safes."

"My mum once worked in a bank, in the centre of Croydon. They closed it for a week or two while they were decorating. They had to get a special firm to clear out some rooms in the basement because of the ... what was the word Mum used? 'Spores', I think ..., something like mould.

Anyway, my dad took me there when the staff were busy getting ready for the opening - we had to drop off a package for

Mum. Dad got talking to this man, Mike something or other. Mike was the manager. He asked if I'd like to take a look around. Dad was keen but it sounded deathly dull to me.

I was right about the office part, that *was* dull, but when we went downstairs into the basement, it was amazing. There were two big rooms, one with bars and one which looked like a vault. The one with bars had filing cabinets and shelves of papers as well as huge bags of coins in tall cabinets. To show me, they had to call a lady, because two people had to open the vault door at the same time."

"Aaron ... you might just be right. I don't think it's too late to help him. How do we find out where it is?"

Aaron smiled, "I have an idea." He reached under the metal strip at the bottom of his computer screen. Cassie couldn't see what he'd pressed but the computer fired into life, accompanied by an affirming chime.

Cassie watched in amazement; within a minute, the computer was ready to go. Aaron typed 'Bank branch closure, London.' into Google. Nine million results in .58 seconds. "Cassie, this is going to take forever."

"Let's start looking through them." Cassie rolled out of the beanbag and stood next to Aaron's chair.

After half an hour of searching, they both sighed. *Needle in a haystack,* was the thought playing in Cassie's mind, no doubt in Aaron's too.

"Cassie, can't you just tell the police what you know and leave it to them?"

"What ... that I had a dream about a man in a bank's vault?"

"Guess so." It did sound stupid when she said it out loud. He changed tack, "Cassie, it's a long shot, but do you think he has a phone on him?"

"Not sure, but I wouldn't think so, why?"

"Most phones have GPS trackers."

"Okay, now you've totally lost me. Aaron fetched his shiny new iPhone from his jeans pocket and held it up. "You see this?"

"Showing off again Aaron?"

"Get lost Janus. Most phones are the same nowadays. They've got something in them called 'Global Positioning ... something' anyway, I can log on now and tell you exactly where my phone is." Aaron busied himself opening another screen and typing passwords. "Look Cassie." He pointed to a throbbing blue blob on a map. There I am.

"Aaron, you know where your phone is, it's here. What's so great about that?"

"Think about it Cassie. If I was ever missing, my mum or dad, or the police could find me. As long as I had my phone on me..."

"If your mum could work out how to log on."

"Oooh, harsh Cassie. Harsh but fair." He smiled at her. "So if this man ..."

"Alfred."

"... Right, Alfred ... had a phone on him ... okay, it was a long shot but I thought I'd ask." Their amateurish investigation was cut short by the sound of Aaron's mum.

"Come on you two. We don't want to miss our lane."

Wow when your house is as big as Aaron's, your mum gets good at shouting.

Chapter Forty-Four

As the drug wore off, Alfred dreamt that he was standing on a table, a hood covering his head and a rope around his neck.

That's when the dream retreated and reality picked up the baton. His shallow breaths forced a dry, acrid warmth to rise behind the cloth, stinging and bringing water to his eyes. His hands were tied behind his back with something tight, hard, pinching. He heard someone nearby: regular, relaxed breathing and the dull brush of shoe leather on dusty concrete.

"Whatever you're going to do, get on with it, do it quickly. Don't think you scare me for a minute. Life's been shitty to me and I don't expect it to stop now. God and I are going to have a long conversation and I'm looking forward to it. So go on, do it, just make it-" His words were interrupted by the sound of table legs scraping on the floor. His feet were dragged backwards until they lost contact with the table. His neck took the burden of his weight. The ties around his wrists clicked and fell away but his arms had no strength or impetus to reach up. Alfred's struggle was weak and brief.

Chapter Forty-Five

Bowling wasn't exactly the idyllic family evening out that Mrs Hall had envisaged. Cassie, on the other hand, was having one of the best nights she could remember. Despite arriving five minutes late, they found a group of giggling teenaged girls in their lane. That didn't matter - there was no rush.

"Not to worry kids. Let's change our shoes and get a drink."

Cassie stood on tiptoe, her elbows on the desk. There were numerous shelves holding a mixture of boots, shoes, trainers and, of course, an inadequate supply of blue/red bowling shoes. Aaron was lucky; they had his size. His head was next to Cassie's thigh, as he knelt, fastening laces. "Wow Aaron, you're making hard work of that."

"Isn't he Cassie. For years he wouldn't wear anything without a Velcro strap, and this is the result."

Aaron paused and looked up, "Would you two just leave me alone."

"And what size are you young lady?' The question came from a man behind the counter, clearly just out of college despite his thick beard. He had ear stretchers you could see right through. Cassie tried not to stare.

"Six."

His forehead wrinkled, and he leaned over the counter, coming uncomfortably close to Cassie. She lifted her elbows, stepping back.

"You might just be right, little miss big-feet. You're lucky, you've got our last six." He spoke from underneath the counter, reappearing with Cassie's shoes.

"There you go." Cassie passed him her worn out Reeboks in return. Perhaps she just imagined him holding them at arms length.

The lane came clear at seven sixteen. Cassie was sensing Mrs Hall's agitation.

She's got a low tolerance for things not being perfect.

Aaron clearly knew his way around the electronic scoreboard. Cassie was grateful, this whole experience was new to her.

"And just where are the bumpers?" Mrs Hall slapped her hands against the outside of her hips as though this was the latest incident in a history of corporate negligence.

"Mum, tell me you didn't ask for bumpers."

"Of course I did, don't you remember last time?"

Cassie had never seen Aaron go so red, "Mum!" He shook his head. Cassie, not really understanding what was going on, was amused despite her ignorance. She'd never been happier.

When you can do what Cassie can, sometimes the best of days turn sour. They'd each taken three turns to bowl. Mrs Hall was winning, Aaron a close second. Cassie had scored a three (beginners luck), then two, then nothing. The weight of the bowling ball wasn't helping. It had rekindled the ache in Cassie's right shoulder, which worsened with each round.

It happened at the start of round four. She walked onto the lane, her slight fingers desperately gripping a purple bowling ball which she expected to drop at any moment. Her optimistic hope was that it would reach halfway down the alley before slumping into the gutter.

The walk felt different this time. Before, she'd been acutely aware of the sounds from the other lanes: the clatter of strike upon strike in the semi pro's lane to her left, the jeers of teenagers mocking each other to her right. Sounds deadened, as though she was swimming underwater and the noises came from the poolside. She shook her head to regain clarity. She wasn't speeding up as Aaron had suggested, and she heard him say something behind her, too muffled to decipher.

She reached her arm back, then realised that the mechanical arm hadn't placed the bowling pins down. She paused, her toes on the edge of the line she wasn't allowed to cross. She knew she should take a few steps back and try again, but her legs were paralysed by what she saw at the end of the lane.

The mechanical bar, which usually held bowling pins by their necks, brought down a looped rope instead. The noose held greying black hair; the back of someone's head. The rope turned with the speed of a rotisserie until Alfred Tucker's dead, rolled-up eyes faced Cassie.

She screamed, dropping the ball on the side of her foot. Peripheral clarity returned as the ball rolled into the gutter. She could hear again, and became conscious of teenagers laughing.

Laughing at me?

Cassie felt hands on her shoulders.

"Cassie, Cassie, are you okay?" The voice was Mrs Hall's.

When Cassie had screamed, Mrs Hall's attention had been elsewhere, pointing out that Aaron's lace was coming loose. Cassie insisted that she'd called out in pain, at the bowling ball hitting her foot and had done a good job of putting on a limp as Mrs Hall helped her back to her seat.

Aaron knew better. Cassie Janus was not the sort of girl who squeals when a bird unexpectedly flaps its wings, jumps when a door slams or cries out in pain. That scream was what his gruesome books described as 'gut wrenching.' There had been something else. He was certain.

"When we get home, we'll take a good look at your foot Cassie." Mrs Hall glanced in her rear-view mirror as she spoke. Her eyes were then back on the road, driving with the care of a parent taking their newborn home from the hospital. Cassie and Aaron sat in the back, an empty seat and folded down armrest between them.

"I think its getting better Mrs Hall, just a bruise I think."

"All the same, let's be sure."

Cassie looked to her left, out of the window at an enormous billboard. It advertised an eagerly awaited film to be aired next Valentine's. There was a man and a woman on it. The man appeared to have a hand around her throat and Cassie couldn't tell if the woman objected. Cassie became aware of her right hand kneading her thigh muscle, as Aaron tapped her knuckles with his phone.

She turned, seeing a note he'd written:

'What's up? What did you see?'

He tapped again and offered her the phone, encouraging a reply. She took it from him and typed:

'Alfred's dead.'

After Mrs Hall had examined Cassie's foot from a dozen angles under the intense kitchen spotlights, she declared all was well and gave them a thirty-minute bedtime warning.

They sat on his bed, Aaron on David Tennant and Cassie on a Dalek.

"Cassie"

"U-huh."

"This man, the one who's doing these things. Is he like you? Can he know what you know?"

"No ... I don't think so ... I'd not really thought about it."

"Tell me something honestly. No bullshit."

Cassie hadn't heard him swear before, "Aaron, your mum might hear."

"I don't care. Tell me, are you scared?"

"Honestly? I'm terrified." Aaron took a lingering moment to absorb her authentic frailty.

"Cassie I want you to have something."

"What?"

Aaron got up and opened the bottom drawer of his desk. He picked out a phone, a lot like his but more square and not so shiny.

"Here." He passed it to her. "My mum was going to have it when I got my 5C but she couldn't work out how to use it. It's my old phone. It has the GPS thing just like my new one and I think it's got a little credit left on it. Pay as you go, so use it wisely. And, it's bound to need charging."

"Aaron, I couldn't, really. It must be worth hundreds."

"A hundred and ten-ish on eBay. But it's not making us any money sat in my drawer. If I ever get round to selling it, which I doubt, I'll ask for it back, okay?"

"Thanks Aaron." She gazed at it for a while, enjoying the screen's smoothness with her thumb, then slipped it into the pocket of her jeans. They hugged each other. Neither wanted to let go.

Chapter Forty-Six

An armed unit backed Malcolm: eight men carrying nine millimetre submachine guns. They were responding to an anonymous tip-off alleging that Alfred Tucker was squatting inside.

The building had closed three months earlier after an armed robbery. The bank's executive saw the robbery as an opportunity to consider the branch's future; the location didn't have the footfall it needed and the branch was losing money. They decided to close it. It was about to be sold to one of their competitors, according to local rumour.

Four officers dressed in black, protected by body armour, stood each side of the building's front entrance. Malcolm stood nearest to the double doors, peering through a crack between two plywood boards.

He saw no movement inside and authorised one of the officers to enter forcibly. The double door had thick panes of wood with bevelled trim. It took five attempts before the metal enforcer overcame the lock. Strong hinges rebounded the doors back at the men. They easily brushed off the blows. Malcolm moved in behind them. The unit spread swiftly, breaking into pairs. They secured the bank of tellers' desks, two interview rooms and the manager's office.

A security cabinet, mounted on the wall above the manager's desk, was wide open. Deep silvery scratches scarred its green metallic lid. Inside the box, keys hung from hooks. One of the men ran the tip of his weapon across the keys. Three of the hooks were labelled, but empty.

"All clear," their hushed communications came through the hiss of radio static.

The team of eight reformed near the stairwell and Malcolm ordered half of them to ascend to check out the first floor and the others to join him in securing the lower ground. The descending team held torches parallel to their weapons and the light bounced from the stairs to the stark walls and back again. At the bottom of the stairs a long corridor stretched to their left and right. They split.

Malcolm took two men to the right, silently signalling the others to head left. The men who followed Malcolm were almost indistinguishable, both in their mid thirties, anonymised by their helmets and uniform. Malcolm knew neither of them well.

They searched a storeroom, found nothing, and headed further along the corridor. He stopped with his back to the wall. The next door to check was to his left. He made eye contact with the colleague who mirrored his position, on the other side of the door. Malcolm raised his hand, ordering a pause and turned to the remaining team member. The man's thick monobrow and keen eyes were prominent through the grill of his visor. He stood, facing the door. Malcolm noted the man's eager twitching as though he were about to be let out of a trap.

Malcolm tipped his head towards the door, received a nod in response from his monobrowed colleague, and the door was kicked open. Malcolm smiled.

This guy loves his job. You can see it in the eyes.

A stench hit them the second the door clattered open. Something was rotting in there.

Malcolm hung back, leading from behind, his teammates ventured forward in the dark. Under torchlight the team were only getting glimpses of the scene. The metal bars, painted green, appeared as indiscernible vertical lines. It wasn't until the torches had swept a few times over the bars' uniform shape that their purpose became apparent: to protect the bank's most valuable assets.

Malcolm remained near the door as the two men moved further into the room. They stepped over the bottom of what seemed to be an iron cage. Their torches fixed upon the yellowing bedclothes of a single camp bed, before moving up, revealing Alfred's dangling legs. "Oh Lord," one of them muttered as Malcolm hit the switch. The long fluorescent tube flickered for a moment before clinically exposing every detail of the room. "Don't touch anything. We need to seal this room off."

"By the look of him, I don't think it's him we can smell. This happened recently." Monobrow made the observation; his colleague was (scared) quiet.

"I think I've found the cause of the smell." Monobrow poked the barrel of his rifle behind a filing cabinet, using the tip to drag something out. He held up a half decomposed rat which strangely clung to the barrel, its stiff body curled, back arched.

He tapped the barrel on the concrete, depositing the rat. He looked up and spotted a rickety aluminium-legged table in the corner of the room. On it was an A4 sheet of typed paper, "Looks like he left a note." By the side of the paper sat a bunch of keys.

"Back up, both of you. Let's not risk contaminating the scene." Malcolm led by example, stepping back into the hall.

They were disturbed by one of the officers who'd broken off left at the bottom of the stairs. He'd backtracked to find Malcolm.

"They're here." The officer turned, and Malcolm followed.

Malcolm heard the distant screams of a girl. His striding turned into a run as he headed towards the sound. At the end of the corridor he met the vault's entrance. The door was eight inches of thick steel, with a circular locking mechanism. It was half open and Malcolm saw, through the doorway, a teenaged girl handcuffed to steel brackets, which were screwed into the brick wall. She wore little and what she did wear was torn and dirty. Her lips were blue, dried and cracked.

Her shivering was so fierce that she appeared to convulse, desperately trying to breathe but losing all the breath she'd gained, with each chilling scream. The sound came with staggering regularity. As Malcolm stepped into the room he realised why her screams weren't diminishing. On the opposite wall to the girl was a teenaged boy whose skin had no life; tanned yet greying. His head hung down and his chin was dipped in the blood that had clearly spilled from his throat and covered his Barbour jacket.

Two officers stood either side of the girl. They attempted to dislodge the brackets, tugging violently, rushing under the pressure of her screams. The officer, who'd discovered the rat, arrived at the back of the room and made the connection instantly. "Sergeant Robinson, the keys in the other room."

"Sure, get them."

The officer returned with the keys and swiftly tried them, one by one, on the cuff securing her left wrist. The others stood, blocking her view of the boy.

As the men finally freed her second arm, Malcolm placed a jacket over Annie's front to help restore some sense of dignity. He tried to reassure her, "You're safe now, we've got you, you're safe."

The coat drowned her. She shivered beneath it, eyes wide, whimpering.

Chapter Forty-Seven

It was nine o'clock in the evening. Hilary April was blowing out the scented candles around the edge of her bath when she was disturbed by a loud knock at the front door. She hurriedly wrapped a dressing gown around her, tying the cord as she raced downstairs. She hated being disturbed in the evening, particularly since living on her own.

Arriving at the bottom of the stairs, Hilary scooped up her glasses from the telephone table. She saw a police car parked in her drive and slipped on the front door's security chain.

What could they possibly want? I wish I didn't live in such a built up area. All my neighbours are sure to be gossiping about this tomorrow.

Hilary opened the door to the clanking chain's limit. A woman and a man stood on her doorstep. Both wore police uniforms. They held their identification up, above the gold links of the chain. Hilary freed the door and opened it. "I'm detective Sergeant Rebecca Jackson, this is Constable Jacobs. Are you Miss Hilary April?"

"Yes, what is it?"

The last time she'd dealt with the police was during Mark's conviction for sex offences. The depravity of her partner's sick habit, filed safely away for the most part, came flooding back. Her head and shoulders involuntarily shimmied. "There's a matter we would prefer to talk about inside, if that's okay."

"Sure, come in."

They followed Hilary into her living room.

"We're really sorry to disturb you so late into the evening Miss April. We won't take up any more of your time than is necessary." Hilary became suspicious of Sergeant Jackson's overly apologetic opening.

"Please, take a seat. How can I help you?" As they sat down Hilary leant forward, pulling her dressing gown together over her knees, conscious that she'd not had time to put on underwear.

It looked like Sergeant Jackson was going to lead the conversation. "It's about Mark Adams."

He's been in prison for months now. What could they possibly want to tell me about Mark?

"What about him?" Her tone was terse, fearful.

"I'm sorry to say he was being transferred from Wormwood scrubs prison to Oakwood prison in Wolverhampton when he escaped from custody."

She was disturbed by a powerful concoction of recollections; of holding that memory stick in her hand and of Mark in bed with her, running a cold finger along her spine.

"How?" Hilary's arms, clutching her stomach, began to shake.

"Miss April, are you okay?"

"I asked *how*. How could he have escaped?"

Sergeant Jackson gulped and looked at her colleague. Hilary detected embarrassment between them. Jackson turned towards Hilary again and attempted to explain.

"We believe that he received assistance from within the prison service. It appears that the manifests were altered both at Wormwood and Oakwood, so that he was never expected and therefore not reported as missing for some time. A full investigation has been launched."

"Oh my God. What do you mean, 'some time.' How long has he been missing?"

"We found out today. The transfer was attempted three and a half weeks ago."

"What the hell! You lost a convicted sex offender for over three weeks without knowing about it?"

"Actually it was a security contractor-"

"I don't care who it was."

What if he comes looking for me? He knows where I live. He'd be crazy to come back here. But he is crazy. He's proved that. And you knew it all along, deep down, if you'd only bothered to stop and examine his behaviour for one minute-

Wait, why the hell are you beating yourself up? This is their *fuck up,* they've *got to sort this mess out. Hell, the prison service has* one *job to do: keeping prisoners locked up - and they can't even do that. Is this what we pay our taxes for?*

"How in God's name could you have let this happen?"

"Miss April, you're understandably upset but if you could try to keep calm, we'll explain what we're going to do about the situation." Sergeant Jackson moved over towards Hilary, resting on the sofa's arm. She misread the situation, reaching to put a reassuring arm around Hilary who shrugged off the gesture.

"Look, I'm as calm as I guess I'm going to be until he's caught. Exactly how are you going to ensure my safety?"

Jackson sat back down again. "If you agree to it, your house will be guarded twenty-four hours a day for the time being. Constable Jacobs will be the first and will stay here once we're finished." Jacobs smiled at Hilary though his look didn't impart great reassurance.

"I can't imagine what my neighbours are going to make of that but I guess I don't have much choice, do I? What are you doing to find him?"

"We've notified police services nationwide. A photo will be issued to the media shortly. We're confident, with enough publicity, we'll find him quickly. This is the last place he'll return to, so please think of our presence here as a precaution, nothing more."

Two hours later, Hilary lay in her bed. Sleep was an impossibility. She stared at the long shadows racing across her ceiling cast by leafless branches flexing in the intense wind.

Her thoughts flitted between the police officer who stood outside her front door, braving the elements, to a memory of Mark's face the last time she'd seen him; unrecognisably filled with anger and bitterness. Was there also a vengeful intent, or had her mind coloured that in after the fact?

How could I have been so stupid as to get involved with someone like that and not realise it? Why did it take the words of Cassie Janus to make me see what he was really like?

She bent a pillow around the back of her head, covering her ears. She buried her face in the mattress and let out a groan, fear and frustration momentarily drowning out the relentless storm.

Chapter Forty-Eight

"What do you think Doctor? Is she strong enough to make a statement?" Malcolm towered over the consultant who was just over five feet tall. They were standing in a corridor outside the ward in which Annie Mendoza was recovering from her ordeal.

The consultant spoke in a Malaysian accent, "She has minor internal bleeding and some bruising, but these are not really of concern. She's suffered a severe trauma though, mentally she's not in a good state. If it's absolutely necessary then I'll allow it, but I'd sooner you wait a few days if at all possible."

"I understand, but we really need to know if what she's seen backs up our evidence. If it doesn't, there's a possibility we still have a predatory killer at large and I'm sure you can understand we need to rule out that possibility."

"Okay Sergeant but fifteen minutes, no more. Make it clear she can call a break whenever she needs to."

"Of course."

The doctor left him to continue her rounds and Malcolm stepped into the ward. There were four beds each side of the ward, only two were occupied. To his left, in the corner nearest to the door, an elderly lady snored lightly. In the opposite corner, Annie lay on her side, facing the far wall. Her bedside table was filled with cards. Among them stood a large vase crammed with gerberas; deep oranges and reds.

Malcolm approached her with care, speaking softly. "Annie, it's Sergeant Robinson. Do you remember me? I was one of the officers who found you." He sat down, tucked his hat under his arm and drew up a seat a few feet away from Annie's bed. He waited, wondering if she would turn round to face him. She craned her neck and glanced at him. Her eyes were red and puffy, her face still pale but not as deathly as when he'd last seen her.

"I don't mean to bother you Annie, and I know this must be really tough for you, but there are a couple of questions I need to ask." She turned further away, silently dismissing him with her back.

"Please Annie. We need to make sure the person who did this to you can't hurt anyone else."

She turned onto her back and sat half-upright.

"I don't think I can do this right now."

"Don't worry I'm not going to make you go through it all now. I just want to reassure you and clarify one or two points. I'll only stay for fifteen minutes. You can have a break at any time." Malcolm pulled out his notebook from his jacket pocket and flipped it open.

"What do you want to know?"

"Well firstly, I just wanted *you* to know that the person who did this is no longer alive."

He was expecting to see some relief on Annie's face but instead her lower lip bowed and tears welled in her eyes.

"Good. Did one of you kill him?"

"No, he took his own life and left a note, confessing."

Annie's shoulders slumped, and her neck bent forward. Her chest heaved with every breath. Her fringe masked her face as she rubbed at the marks on her wrists.

"We just need to confirm the authenticity of his confession. The note said that he went after Frankie and that you disturbed him. Is that correct?"

Annie turned away again, pulling her covers up to her chin. Two shallow nods.

"Don't worry, I'm not going to show you anything now, but if you saw a picture of him, would you recognise him?"

"No, he always wore ... wore something covering his head."

"And his hands? Any distinguishing marks?"

"I really don't want to have to think about this again."

"I understand but this is my last question, then I'll leave you to rest. *Did* he have any marks that could identify him?"

"A tattoo of a star on his wrist. Nothing else, okay? Please sergeant, I just want to be left alone."

"Of course. You've been really helpful, thank you. From what you've described, we've got the right person."

Malcolm rose from his chair, "The doctor said visiting time will start soon, will your mum and dad be coming in to see you?"

She nodded.

"Good. Thanks again Annie, I hope you're feeling better soon. We'll be in touch when you're back on your feet."

Chapter Forty-Nine

Laura repeatedly glanced over at Cassie who sat in the passenger seat of Laura's Fiesta. Cassie clutched the blue envelope of the get-well card Mrs Hall had bought for her. It said 'Mummy' on the envelope in the clear handwriting of a child who's learned to write, and not yet learned to rush. She gently bent the corner absentmindedly as she stared out of the window. They hadn't exchanged a single word in the last five minutes.

They would be at the hospital soon and Laura didn't want to miss this perfect opportunity to put Cassie's mind at rest about the murders. She was struggling to think of a way to put it that didn't sound like, 'you were wrong.'

No easy way to start this, just talk to her.

"Cassie."

"Uh-huh"

"Did I tell you that my husband Malcolm has been looking into these murders you were talking about?"

"No, you didn't."

"Well, and please don't tell anyone else about this, promise?"

"Promise."

"He says they've found the person responsible?"

"Really? And it wasn't Alfred?"

"It *was* Cassie, really it was him." Cassie looked out of the window again, seemingly reluctant to discuss it further.

"I know you don't think he's the one doing it but he wrote a letter, confessing. His DNA ... do you know what that is?"

"Of course."

Why did I even ask?

"Well his DNA was at each crime scene and he was found in a disused bank, where … " Laura was babbling. She'd criticised Leanne for scaring Cassie and was now in danger of doing the same. Cassie finished Laura's sentence in a bland, matter of fact tone, "Where those kids were imprisoned and attacked."

"Well, yes."

"I know."

"What?"

"More than you."

The conversation had distracted Laura. She caught sight of a red sign with a white H, disappearing over her shoulder. She glanced in the mirror and whispered a half-sigh, 'Haa."

"We're going to have to turn around."

Two turns later they were back on track. Cassie was becoming frustrated at Laura's lack of belief.

Well if it takes me scaring her to make her believe like I had to with Aaron, then so be it.

"Alfred was quite calm when that table was pulled from under him. Quite relieved really, to be dying. He was starting to become quite upset by the crying of those kids. He wanted to save them, but he couldn't get out of his cell."

"Cassie, look, now I *know* you are making this u-"

"He was also sick of the man coming and taking things from him, like he was part of an experiment he didn't understand. He always left with a tube full of something."

"Cassie stop."

"And he never wrote a note, he couldn't have. He was tied down. There, that's all I know."

"Cassie, sweetheart," Laura took her hand off the gear stick and stroked Cassie's arm, which tensed up at her touch.

Cassie couldn't bring herself to look at Mrs Robinson as she talked and so she spoke as if conversing with her own reflection in the window.

"Mrs Robinson, other people trying to give me comfort about the future is pointless. I know the future and it's not safe, for me, for you, not for anyone in London. I'm sorry to have to scare you like this but I'm not going to pretend everything is alright, when it isn't."

Laura pulled into the car park in front of the hospital. She wound the window down, reached out and pulled a ticket from the machine next to the barrier. Cold air flooded into the car and she shuddered.

"Cassie, let's go and see your mum. We can talk about this later." Cassie knew 'talking about it later' would be entirely pointless. Mrs Robinson no more believed her now, than Miss April had when she first heard about her boyfriend. Something was going to have to happen to make her believe.

Laura waited in the corridor, though she couldn't resist occasionally shifting her position to look along the ward. She saw Cassie hug her mother gently and hand her the card. There were no other cards, no flowers or gifts of any description by Leanne's bedside.

She really is entirely alone.

Laura stepped out of sight again (*they need their space*) imagining Cassie's attempt to hide shock and horror at her mother's appearance.

Her mum's injuries were hard to look at; her jawbone, cheeks and temple covered in swollen lumps of assorted shades of blue and purple. Her bottom lip was badly inflamed. With every few words her eyes shut tight, bracing against the pain.

They spoke for a quarter of an hour before Leanne laid back and closed her eyes. Cassie kissed a scarce flesh coloured patch on her temple, whispering, "I'm okay, take as long as you need. Get better Mummy," before heading back to where Laura stood waiting. As they walked back down the hospital corridor

Laura said, "Cassie, I don't think your mother will be out as quickly as the doctors first thought."

"I know. That's okay, she's safe in here."

Chapter Fifty

On Wednesday nights, Malcolm insisted they go out and do something active together. Laura hated this but knew that the exercise did her good. She loathed it so much because, despite her best efforts, he always won. It didn't matter whether they played squash, badminton or even table tennis; she couldn't match his pace or his power. They hadn't been for a couple of weeks, his workload hadn't allowed it. This week though, she'd felt the pressure on her husband diminishing.

On the drive to the leisure centre they discussed the mounting evidence against Alfred Tucker.

"It's not only the DNA. The girl who survived has managed to identify him from a distinctive tattoo and her story entirely matches the description of events he laid out in the note."

"I can't understand what possesses some people, I really can't. Did he say why he did it?"

"He didn't say too much about his motive, except that he'd been controlled by others for years and it was about time *he* was in control."

"And that was the only way he could get a sense of control? Just doesn't make sense, does it?"

"We've got our man." Irritation crept into his tone.

"I'm not disputing that. I'm just saying that anyone who does ... something like that ... it's just impossible to relate to their motivations."

"I see what you mean." Having arrived at the car park, they made their way to the reception area. The night was especially cold and Laura hugged herself as they walked. He put an arm around her. "I'm just glad this case is over. I don't know how long it would have gone on if he hadn't, you know, ended it."

"You were getting close, weren't you? He probably sensed he'd be caught and ended it before *you* could."

"You're probably right." He squeezed her shoulders and kissed her temple.

"Love you Mrs Robinson."

"Love you too."

Laura was grateful to be inside in the warmth. This feeling was short-lived. Two games of squash later she was wishing they'd turn the heating off. Despite her mind being elsewhere, she was fairing better than usual, taking at least five points off Malcolm in every game. She never came close to beating him, though. Every time he was in trouble, he flexed those thick forearms and the ball would whizz by in a blur.

Between games they sat side by side against the scarred Perspex wall, recovering and sipping water. After the third game she posed a question, plagued by what Cassie had said about Alfred. She uttered the words against her better judgement, regretting them immediately.

"So how does a case like this work then? Because the suspect is no longer alive, he obviously can't be tried." She paused to gain breath, "Is the case just closed then?"

"If we have enough evidence to be sure of the suspect's guilt, then yes."

"Because, if he had lived, it would have been up to a jury to decide whether his guilt was beyond reasonable doubt, wouldn't it."

"Of course."

"It's only just struck me, that's all. The comparatively low level of scrutiny given in cases such as these, compared to cases where the suspect has survived. That's all."

"Low level of scrutiny? Do you know how many police hours have been put into pouring over every detail of this case?"

"I didn't mean-"

"C'mon Laura. I don't want to argue about this, let's play again. Best out of five."

She wanted to ask him if there was the slightest possibility Alfred was innocent. She had to be certain there was no way someone could have fabricated the letter and planted DNA, to pin the murders on Tucker. Then she stopped to contemplate the weight of evidence.

Cassie's wrong. She must be misinterpreting it, whatever she's seen. She's just a young girl after all.

They played through the remaining games to a predictable outcome, the subject of Tucker's guilt having been laid to rest.

Chapter Fifty-One

"Look Leanne, I know that she's your daughter, but you really shouldn't have just turned up like this. You should have called. Mrs Robinson said it would be a couple more days at least, before you'd be home."

Leanne wore jeans, a vest top and a thin pale blue hoodie. Her arms were wrapped across her front (sleeves pulled over knuckles), and she was attempting to rub the cold from the back of her arms. Her balance shifted from one foot to the other and back again. Her swollen lower lip trembled. A Puma holdall with red cracked leather was in a state of collapse at her feet.

"Well Mrs Robinson was wrong. I'm here to collect Cassie, I have a taxi waiting." 'Robinson' sounded closer to 'Rovinson,' her bulging lip hampering speech. Mrs Hall looked over Leanne's shoulder. A black cab was parked up at the end of her drive, engine running. The driver sat, thumbing through the Sun newspaper.

God knows how much that's costing her. Can she really afford it?

"Look, let's send the taxi on its way. You can come in, then Cassie won't have to pack in a rush. When she's ready I'll drive you both home. Please come in. Have you got enough money for the taxi?" Leanne's shivering stopped, and her chin dropped to her chest. She took out a canvas British Heart Foundation purse and fanned out the note compartment. Nothing.

"I could have sworn ... actually, I'm a little light." When she looked up, she began rubbing the back of her neck.

"Come in, I'll see the taxi off." Leanne waited inside the hall, the back of her legs pressed against the radiator. Mrs Hall passed the driver a twenty and half jogged back up the drive.

"Come through to the kitchen. Would you like a drink?"

"I really want to get Cassie settled back at home as quickly as possible."

"I can understand that but twenty minutes won't hurt. I'll make us a drink and tell Cassie you're here. Tea?"

"Milk two sugars, ta."

Once upstairs, Aaron's mum walked up to his bedroom door and was struck by a sobering thought.

It won't be long before I have to knock first. They grow up too fast.

She poked her head round the door. Cassie and Aaron were huddled around his computer. Aaron's fingers darted instinctively across the keyboard and the screen went black. Christine resisted the urge to ask them what they were up to.

"Cassie, I have some good news. Your mum must be feeling a lot better ... she's come to see you. She's downstairs in the kitchen. I think she wants you to go back home. Why don't you come down and talk to her."

Cassie felt a mixture of emotions, each one bubbled up and then vanished only for a new one to surface: disappointment, happiness, fear, emptiness. There was an awkward silence between the three of them, each one knowing that a normal reaction would be for Cassie to leap up and rush downstairs in glee. It was all Cassie could do to respond, "Oh, okay."

She followed Mrs Hall downstairs and into the kitchen. One look at her mother told her she wasn't well enough to be home, not yet. The bruising had reduced but her right eye still looked like someone had slipped a golf ball under her skin. Cassie doubted her mother could see properly. She couldn't manage a smile but walked over to her mother and dutifully slipped her arms round her waist, trying not to hug her too hard.

Christine gave them some space, busying herself making tea, while they talked.

Leanne took hold of Cassie's shoulders and held her at arms length. "Cassie, honey, is everything okay?" Cassie couldn't understand her concern.

"Yes Mummy. Everything's fine."

"Have you had your hair cut?" Her tone was hard to discern; curious verging on accusatory. All went quiet. Christine was taking an age to get milk from the fridge, stalling with her back to them. Cassie looked towards Mrs Hall. Then realised she was going to have to explain, "Yes Mummy. My fringe was getting in my eyes. We went to Supercuts. Do you like it?"

Leanne lifted Cassie's fringe then dropped it as if to prove it wouldn't fall far enough.

"Bit short isn't it?"

"Are you sure you should be out of the hospital Mummy?"

"It wasn't doing me any good being stuck in there. Too much time on my hands, I needed to get out and focus on something. There's nothing wrong with me that time won't mend. No sense in taking up a hospital bed. I have a bed at home." 'Sofa bed' was Cassie's correction but she decided to keep quiet.

"Look Leanne, I know you'll have a lot to sort out. I really don't mind if you want Cassie to stay here for an extra night to give you a bit of time to get things in order." Cassie stood directly between the two women. She sensed she might soon start feeling like the rope in a tug of war.

"Look, I'm really grateful you took Cassie in at such short notice. I can't bear to think what children's services would have done with her if you hadn't. But Cassie's rightful place is at home and the sooner we can get her there the better. Now, earlier you kindly offered to drive us round there, if the offer still stands, I'll help Cassie get her things together and we'll both be out of your hair."

Christine was slotting a milk carton inside the fridge door. "Of course it stands. It's just you look like you could do with a little more recuperation time, that's all. Cassie's been as good as gold." The fridge door slammed shut.

"She always is." Cassie felt a knot grow and tighten in her stomach and the back of her head began to ache. Neither woman noticed Cassie's pupils' flickering eclipse.

"And I'm just saying I don't mind, if she would like to stay longer she can, that's all." Christine walked towards Leanne, offering her a steaming mug, with a smile. Leanne took it, her lack of thanks was deliberate; she was there under sufferance. If only she'd had money for that taxi. She looked down at the hot liquid wondering how she was going to get it past her lip.

"I'm sure Cassie's as anxious to get home as I am, aren't you honey? Honey ... Cassie ... Christine, she's going to have a seizure."

Cassie fell back, away from Leanne. Christine moved in an instinctive blur, slipping her hand under Cassie's neck to stop her head hitting the tiled floor. Leanne froze for a second before proceeding to move all objects out of Cassie's way: barstools, dining chairs and the kitchen bin all got quickly dragged into the hall.

"Christine, we need cushions. Where?!?"

"The lounge, through the hall." Christine gestured to a position over Leanne's shoulder.

Leanne hurriedly grabbed an armful of tasseled red cushions off the living room sofa, and returned to the kitchen. She placed them under and around Cassie's head and shaking body.

"We need to move this table away from her." Christine nodded and they each took an end of the dining table. Christine noticed Leanne's wince as they laid it down flush to the wall.

"This is the worst she's had in a while. It's my fault. I didn't realise I was stressing her. It's *all* my fault."

Christine wanted to tell Leanne not to be so hard on herself and that she understood how difficult it must be, bringing up Cassie on her own. She couldn't find the right words so both women stood in silence, watching Cassie twitch, occasionally shoving cushions back into place.

Christine heard Aaron's footsteps on the stairs. "Aaron, go back to your room." It wasn't the tone she'd intended. She was going for 'serious' and instead achieved, 'panicked'. He shouted back, "Mum is everything alright?"

"Everything will be fine. Go back to your room. I'll be up there in five minutes and I'll explain, I promise."

Aaron stood on the stairs, momentarily tempted to defy her, to creep down and take a peak at what was happening. An overriding trust in his mother's judgement propelled him back to his room.

Chapter Fifty-Two

Cassie's seizure was subsiding. Leanne had moved her into a recovery position as the convulsions had eased. She lay in the centre of Christine Hall's black tiled floor, protected by excessive space around her.

"Leanne, I know she's suffered from epilepsy in the past but Mrs Robinson said a seizure was very rare nowadays."

"It used to be. Now I think it happens and she doesn't even tell me. Sometimes I know because now and again she'll bite her tongue and I'll find blood on her clothes, but I'm sure other times it happens and I'm none the wiser." Their earlier squabble seemed trivial now, childish, almost forgotten. Christine put her arm around Leanne, gently squeezing her shoulder. "Bringing up a kid is hard enough without this eh?"

Cassie let out a weak, 'Uuuuurgh.' The skin on her right temple slackened and her visible eye blinked into a half-knowing state. Christine moved to help her up. "No, leave her. It's better if she comes round slowly, in her own time."

It took a further five minutes before Cassie was sitting upright. Leanne sat with crossed legs on the floor, by her side. As Cassie gained full consciousness an expression of deep recognition, of knowing, spread across her face and she reached out to grab her mother's arm, twisting her skin in an Indian burn. "Ow, Cassie you're hurting me, what's wrong. Are you okay?"

"Mummy. Call Mrs Robinson." Cassie's face connected a memory for Leanne. It was a rare look of genuine terror, she'd only seen once before - the memory of it flooded back.

She'd been putting on makeup after a day's drinking, readying herself for a night in the King George, when the mirror's drifting and her nauseous stomach forced her eyes closed. She'd laid her head on the carpet and slept, her face a few inches from the mirror.

And she'd dreamt. Perhaps there were many dreams, but the only one that anchored in memory, was of Cassie stepping in a puddle, which was strangely also a deep well of tar. Cassie sank into it, chest high, then chin high. Leanne reached into the tar, trying to grasp slippery arms. Cassie was screaming. When she did manage to get hold, Leanne wasn't strong enough to help. Either something had hold of Cassie's ankles, or they were weighed down somehow. The image from which Leanne woke was a bubble of tar ballooning from Cassie's nostril - her last breath.

Terror had instantly broken Leanne's sleep and flushed alcohol from her brain. She'd opened her eyes, confronted by her own face in the mirror. And the look of pure horror she'd had then - *that* was the look Cassie had now, as she sat on kitchen tiles, gripping Leanne's arm.

Christine wanted to ask why. Why on earth should they suddenly need to call Mrs Robinson? There was greater understanding from Leanne who, having learned a painful lesson, would do exactly as her daughter instructed. "What do you want me to say Cassie?"

Christine was missing something; the whole conversation was irrational.

"Tell her not to go home, that she needs to come round here now."

"What if she can't or won't?"

"Then she'll die."

Christine ended the long and uncomfortable silence. "Cassie, your Mummy and I are going into the living room for a few minutes. We'll be right back and we'll bring the phone with us, okay?"

"Hurry." Cassie's tone was flat. She looked distant, detached.

Christine hooked her arm under Leanne's, encouraging her to her feet and out of the kitchen. They moved through the hall and into the living room, shutting the double doors behind them.

"Are you really going to make that call Leanne?"

"Yes."

"Look, she's just come round from what I imagine is a pretty severe seizure?"

"Yes, it was."

"And when people come round from something like that they can feel confused, disorientated?"

"Of course."

"Then don't you want to take ten minutes, to calmly discuss with her what she thinks is going to happen?"

"No."

"Leanne for God's sake you're making no sense at all. Think about the consequences. If you make that call to Mrs Robinson, what do you think her reaction will be?" Leanne's expression was blank. No words were going to permeate her determination; Mrs Hall was wasting her time.

"I'll tell you what she'll think, Leanne, she'll think that a mother hasn't been able to cope with some dreamlike fantasy her daughter has had. Do you want her thinking that you can't cope?"

Until then their conversation had been furtive, but Leanne was certain the next part would be heard throughout the house. She couldn't contain her volume.

"Christine, you've known my daughter for a few days. *I* have known her all my life. Cassie has an uncanny knack of knowing what's going to happen. I always thought she was just intuitive, you know, the way some people are and lucky in her guesses, in her predictions." Christine folded her arms.

"And I expect that Mrs Robinson will react just how you're reacting now and she might think I'm mad and completely ignore me. If she does then my sanity will be the least of her worries."

"Leanne this is crazy, do you honestly think there's even the slightest bit of truth in what she's saying?"

"Christine, look at my face."

Leanne took tight hold of her own chin and jutted her neck, presenting it to Christine, ignoring the painful spasm it sent through her cheek.

"Take a good look. Cassie warned me not to let him in, just before *this* happened. I sent her away and the look on her face was one that said, 'it's inevitable, I've warned you.' Now maybe nothing will happen to Mrs Robinson and maybe something *will*, but I'm not prepared to take the risk. If I do nothing and Mrs Robinson ... if something happens to her. What do you think Cassie's going to think of me then?"

Christine appeared to have no answer, so Leanne decided to spell out the situation. "She will hate me even more than she does now. I'll be lucky if I even *have* a daughter. Now, can I borrow your phone?"

Christine walked into the hall, shaking her head. She brought back their portable landline. The comment she made as Leanne took it was supposed to remain a thought, but she couldn't help herself. "You'll be lucky to *have* a daughter, if you *make* that call." Leanne dismissed Christine's protest and walked back to the kitchen.

Cassie, having moved off the floor and onto a bar stool, jumped down and met Leanne with a hug that hurt her ribs.

"I *don't* hate you Mummy. Thank you for believing me." Without realising it, Leanne had gone a long way to repairing years of neglect and hurt. Sensing the importance of the moment, Leanne resisted the urge to suppress tears. They rolled down her cheeks, landing on the line of Cassie's neatly parted hair. Leanne bent over, holding Cassie tight. She rested her swollen cheek against the top of Cassie's head. Her hair smelled clean, fresh, the way a young girl's hair should, the way they were going to keep it.

"Cassie, do you want to speak to Mrs Robinson or should I?"

"Would you Mummy?"

Chapter Fifty-Three

"For God's sake." Laura Robinson was mumbling under her breath. She rarely swore, but today she was on the brink. *Why am I so pissed off?*

It was a combination of things, one of those days where every minor setback amplifies the last. It started with the kitchen bin liner splitting over the pavement, just outside the back door. Scraping carrot peelings and dry teabags off concrete, particularly in work clothes, at seven in the morning, didn't bode well for the rest of the day.

Angie had phoned her whilst Laura was driving to her first house call. Three times she'd rung. Laura had lost patience and pulled into a side street, which was almost impossible to park on, even with Laura's Fiesta.

She rang Angie back, and what did she get? A ten-minute rant about how Laura now had fifty-seven files that were either not diarised for review or closed. Laura had tried to hold back the words, but couldn't. "Angie, that'll be fifty-eight very soon - while I am having this conversation, I'm not working ... get it!" Then there had been the silence, followed by Laura's apology. There really wasn't any reason to be so rude, as Angie kindly pointed out.

Then there was the work itself, two house calls to parents who, of course, couldn't see any cause for concern and were infuriated by even the slightest hint that they weren't model parents. In a way, Laura couldn't blame them, but constantly empathising with their views was exhausting.

She'd looked forward to the last call of the day, to a woman called Mrs Matthews, who'd been relocated from Middlesbrough to Croydon as part of a witness protection scheme. Mrs Matthews appreciated that Laura was only trying to help her and her daughter Violet. Laura dreaded signing the Matthews family off her caseload, even if it would help keep Angie off her back. You needed one or two like Mrs Matthews to cope with the rest. So, to cap the day off, who wasn't even in for the prearranged visit? ... Mrs Matthews.

To make matters worse, Mrs Matthews's house was on the outskirts of Laura's patch. It would take over an hour and a quarter to get home in rush hour traffic. Surely there were easier ways to earn a living?

Then there was the bloody wiper blade. On the way home, the rubber had split. It was constantly dangling and dragging across the windscreen. Its scraping was starting to give her a headache and the rain was too heavy to turn the wipers off.

Yep, sod it. "What a shitty day," she declared to the nodding Churchill dog on her dashboard. She was stuck at a red light, a few turns before home. She rubbed her left thigh as she waited for the light. It was burning from an hour of clutch pumping.

It was then she noticed the buzz of her phone on the passenger seat. She glanced away from the traffic lights to see who was trying to reach her. It was a text message. The lights were finally getting ready to change, but Laura's eyes were still on the phone. The message read: "Pick up your voicemail urgently, you're in danger." The message was so distracting that the car behind had to sound its horn to cajole her through the green light.

She considered waiting until she was at home to pick up the message, but instead, deciding 'urgent' might be just that, she pulled up at the side of the road under a huge decaying billboard. For the first time in her life, she'd parked on a double yellow line, two wheels mounting the pavement.

She grabbed her phone and stared at it like she'd picked up a five legged rat. Both the missed call and the text came from unknown numbers. She dialled her voicemail.

"Mrs Robinson, this is Leanne Janus. It's difficult to explain over the phone but we have reason to believe your life is in danger. Please *do not* go home (then Cassie's voice in the background, 'Mummy tell her to come here.') Come to Mrs Hall's house I'm here with Mrs Hall and Cassie, we'll explain when you get here, but please *don't* go home."

What the hell sort of a message is that? Tell me not to go home and then don't even tell me why. I'm less than two blocks from home and a good twenty minutes from Mrs Hall's. I'm going home to offload to Malcolm. I'll open a bottle of wine and tell him all about what a shitty day it's been. Why do I put myself through this? Day in day out, dealing with all these peoples' problems. Miss Janus has finally lost it. No, I'm tired of doing what everyone else wants me to do, I'm not listening to that woman.

Laura drove home but, as she slowed down to approach their drive, doubts crept in.

You have a duty to Cassie, Laura. Leanne shouldn't even be out of hospital and if she is with Cassie, in that state, you have to make sure Cassie's okay.

She picked up speed again and drove past their house.

When I get there I'll send Malcolm a text, telling him I'm going to be late.

By the time Laura arrived, she'd missed two texts from Malcolm. The first read: "Got back early, lamb chops for dinner. Hope you won't be long." The second: "Why are you ignoring me? Where the fuck are you?"

Laura parked on Mrs Hall's extensive drive, closer to the house than she'd intended; closer than was polite. She was in no mood to back up. She pulled the hand-break on without depressing its button. She liked the raking clicks it made. They matched her mood.

Laura fired a text back to Malcolm, trying to conceal the full extent of her anger: 'Sorry, I'll be late. An urgent case has come up. Eat without me, I'll warm mine up.' She broke her usual habit of ending the text with 'Lx.'

She slammed the car door shut behind her, marched to the front door and rapped the brass knocker hard five times. It opened instantly. All three stood in the doorway. Leanne and Christine had similar half smiles. Cassie, hugging the top of Leanne's arm, wasn't smiling at all. She looked like she'd done something wrong and was about to be told off.

"Leanne, have you discharged yourself from the hospital?"

"Yes, but-"

"Forgive me for being more than annoyed at the message you left me. I hope you're as worried for your sanity as I am."

"Look Mrs Robinson … Laura … I called you because Cassie begged me to." Laura looked at Cassie's face and paused, gradually calming; deep breaths restoring her ability to listen.

"Please, come inside so we can talk properly." Christine led the way into the living room. "Do take a seat." Laura sat down as invited. The two-seater fabric sofa made a 'humph' beneath her. There was an identical empty sofa opposite. Laura twisted in her seat. Leanne and Christine had held back, near the door. Leanne was whispering something to Christine.

"I'm going to leave you to it." Christine walked out, gently shutting the living room's double doors behind her like a retreating butler.

Cassie and Leanne walked hand in hand to the empty sofa opposite Laura. A deep coffee table partially filled the chasm between the sofas. In the centre of the table, a metallic figurine of an African tribesman looked out of place next to a ceramic bowl filled with deep red Potpourri.

Laura leant forward in her chair. She wasn't staying long, no need or desire to make herself comfortable. "Okay, Miss Janus. I'm all ears and Cassie, feel free to speak up, I understand you wanted your mummy to call me?"

Cassie turned her head to look up at her mum. Leanne reached over Cassie's knee and took hold of her hand. She gave it an affirming squeeze and nodded, "Go on. It's okay."

"Mrs Robinson. I'm sorry I scared you. I needed to protect you from what was going to happen. You see-"

I don't think I can listen to another word this girl's got to say. I like her ... Christ I might even love her, but I'm not in the mood for this.

"Cassie ... sweetheart. You've got to stop believing these thoughts you keep having. I know at times they seem real to you, but they're only *thoughts*."

"Laura, I think you need to hear her out. If I'd done the same, if I'd taken the time to listen to her, I wouldn't have ended up in hospital."

Oh brilliant. Now her mother's delusional as well. Why are you letting , no ... encouraging Cassie to indulge in this?

Laura took a deep breath and inwardly counted to ten far too quickly for it to be effective.

"Okay, Cassie, I'm listening."

"Sometimes I only see pieces, only partly understanding what he's doing. But today, I saw him ... " Cassie bowed her head and covered her eyes with her palms in an effort either to block out the image or concentrate on its memory; Laura couldn't tell which. Then she looked up and the words rolled out.

"... Saw him tie a bag around your head. You couldn't breathe."

And then Laura *did* sit back, but not to get comfortable. She was trying to calm the rant that wanted so desperately to come out. Laura knew, on a better day, the rant might not be so strong, that listening would have been easier. She was determined not to explode into a rage.

She's just a kid after all and its not her fault you had a crappy day.

Just a kid.

"Cassie. I know you've seen that. And I'm sure some of the dreams you have seem to come true but I'm equally sure that others do not. I'm safe at home, Cassie. There's not a place on earth where I'd be safer. *Please*, stop worrying about me."

Cassie stood up straight. So straight that Laura thought she'd grown a few inches overnight. Her eyes were wide, feverish. Laura held her hands up, in praying position, against her chin, pretending to cogitate over Cassie's words. She wanted her hands near her face. Just in case.

Come on Laura. Scared of a nine-year-old girl?

Leanne looked up at Cassie, "Sit down honey, please." No response.

Without looking down, Cassie reached to the table and picked up the figurine by its legs. Her eyes were still trained on Laura's.

"Put it down Cassie." If Cassie felt any discomfort from lifting the object with her still-mending arm, she wasn't showing it.

Cassie momentarily shifted her gaze, staring deep into her mother's swollen face. Leanne recoiled, sat back and softened her tone. "Don't Cassie, please, whatever it is you're thinking of doing, don't."

Cassie faced Laura again. Laura turned her head to one side, and lifted her hands, ready to deflect a blow that surely wouldn't come. Surely.

"It *will* happen. And you know him, you know him *well*."

"No, Cassie, I'm sorry. I've listened to enough."

"You haven't *listened* to a word. You know I'm right. You *know* I'm right. He's going to take a bag and ..." Cassie raised the figurine over her shoulder. At perhaps fourteen inches tall, the figure dwarfed Cassie's hand. Her grip on the statue's legs turned her knuckles white. Taut tendons webbed her neck. "And tie it with a band around your throat. You'll be naked and ..."

Leanne turned out of the chair, stood up and held her hand out to Cassie. "Enough now, give it to me."

"He'll not take pictures this time, though he really wants to. But you will see them. *All* of them."

Cassie stood, shins pressing against the coffee table, leaning towards Laura.

"Enough Cassie, listen to your mother, put it down."

"YOU LISTEN!" Cassie punctuated her final word by slinging the metal figure over Laura's shoulder. Laura flinched and, realising it had passed her without contact, turned around on the chair in time to see the figure hit the double-glazing with a boom. A chip flew out of the glass, skittering along the hearth, coming to rest in the deep carpet pile.

A school picture of Aaron, propped up on the window ledge, was squashed flat by the tribal elder who miraculously came to rest in a standing position, upon the image of Aaron's head.

"Miss Janus. I'm going now. I suggest you give Cassie some time alone to calm down. I'll be in touch."

Laura heard Christine rapidly thudding down the stairs and they met for a moment at the door to the living room. "Mrs Hall, if I were you I would bill Miss Janus for the damage. Thank you for your help but I have to leave now. I suggest Cassie goes home with her mother, once she's had time to calm down." Laura slammed Mrs Hall's front door as she left.

Chapter Fifty-Four

The rain had returned. It was lashing down sideways in winds that Laura was beginning to think might never subside. The cold of the night air clashed with the warmth of her breath. As she drove, the windscreen continually misted up. She had to lean forward and wipe furiously with her sleeve to preserve some visibility. That damn wiper blade was still nagging at her.

Why did you even go round there? Laura, they don't pay you enough for this. Just go home, try to make it up to Malcolm (that stupid text message though, who does he think he is?) for being late and missing dinner.

That kid has issues. How could you be so naive as to think that all she needed was some maternal attention? When the dust has settled and I write up my report on this I'll have to give serious consideration to recommending a psychological evaluation. Having disturbing dreams is one thing but being so convinced that it's real, is another. I don't think I know the half of what Cassie must have been through to make her so delusional (wasn't delusional about Miss April's boyfriend though, was she?)

'It will happen. And you know him. You know him well'. For a second there I believed her, believed I was in danger. My God, she was adamant and again, so graphic. Shake the thoughts from your head, Laura, don't you lose it as well.

After parking on the driveway, Laura rushed to their back door, holding the coat's collar to her neck and bowing her head to save her face from the rain.

I'm going to apologise the second I step through the door.

"Sorry I'm so late. Couldn't be helped." No reply. The house was silent, other than the flurry of rain ticking against the kitchen window. Laura dumped her coat and bag on the work surface. She was walking out of the kitchen, towards the living room, when she heard a sound coming from upstairs. It was the distant creak of a chair, or perhaps their bed.

He's probably in the bedroom. Oh tell me he's not setting the room up like he did before, please God not tonight. I'll just say 'no', that's all there is to it.

She was about to go up but stopped herself, pausing, with one foot on the bottom step and her hand on the banister, listening intently. Her conscience told her to shout up again, letting him know that she was home. But she didn't. She closed her eyes to concentrate on sounds. She heard a squeaking creak, similar to the last, but this one was definitely not from the bedroom. He was in the study. Then another noise which reminded her of someone using a tabletop to straighten the edge of a pack of cards; a ragged tap.

This is not the way married couples act, sneaking up on each other. What if he mistakes you for an intruder?

A part of her, a nagging part that would not be silenced, *had* to be sure that Malcolm was harmless, that Cassie was wrong about him (presuming he was the man from Cassie's dream - how many other men did she 'know well?')

I'll watch him closely over the next twenty-four hours. I'll find him acting normally. He won't lay a finger on me and that will be the end of the matter. How could you even imagine him hurting you? It's the memory of Roger, messing with your head.

But he made your mouth sore, and Cassie's been right before.

Start now. Just walk into the study and say 'I was shouting you, you mustn't have heard.' You'll find him catching up on paperwork, that's all.

Laura pushed the study door open. "Christ Laura, you gave me a fright. I didn't hear you come in."

What she saw made her forget her rehearsed speech. She stared at the array of photographs laid out on their desk. "I was sorting these for the file, but it can wait, let's get your tea heated up. I bet you've had a hell of a day, you can tell me all about it." His arm formed a protective semi-circle around the photos and he slipped them off the desk, into his case. He closed the gold clasps and flicked the combination wheels.

'Hell of a day?' I wouldn't know where to start. How could he act so casually, especially after that text!?

Laura followed him downstairs in a daze. "Sorry you had to see those honey. Crime scene photos can be pretty grim. I guess I'm just desensitised to it."

"I understand. Didn't mean to startle you."

Do I understand? I know two teenagers were attacked and one survived, so what pictures would I expect to see? Okay, there was one of the boy, he had blood all down his front and he was chained to a wall. That was shocking enough, but understandable - they have to collect that evidence. But I'm sure I saw ... yes I saw a picture of the girl, shackled, half naked and bleeding. Surely when the police found her, they wouldn't have taken pictures like that. They would have freed her in a second, not stood around taking photographic evidence. Laura, it's just the stress, you must have imagined it. You only saw the photos for a brief second and there were so many of them.

Perhaps you were mistaken.

I wasn't.

Must have been mistaken.

I wasn't.

When they got downstairs, Malcolm did something he'd not done in months. He put music on. He liked vinyl and frequently talked about how it was becoming popular again, that digital music lacked soul. But today he took hold of a CD.

He hid the cover from Laura. She tried to look over his shoulder, but could only see the living room lights, reflecting off the bottom of the shiny disc in a mini rainbow. He dropped it into the drawer and pressed play. He turned to smile at her as the drawer whirred shut. The first few bars of 'Somebody to love,' came on. It was on too loud, given the adjoining wall, but the volume stayed as it was.

Malcolm walked over to Laura, placed his hands on her waist, then pulled her to him, wrapping his arms around her. His warm cheek pressed against her ear. "Sorry about that text earlier, I just wanted your dinner to be perfect. Silly really, I was just frustrated. Forgive me?"

"I forgive you."

He kissed her. "Come on, let's get you some food. We'll leave the doors open, so we can hear the music."

I can't cope with this. Act normally. Keep the conversation mundane; nothing out of the ordinary. Don't let jumbled thoughts spill out of your mouth. Just get through the night with him, like you've done thousands of times before. Then tomorrow you can dig deeper, satisfying yourself that he's just the normal, hard working husband that you know he is. My God, Laura, how many other men would put up with your tempers when you come home from work? How many would sacrifice the prospect of having their own children to be with you? Don't let him go over a stupid mistake (not mistaken).

The microwave pinged a few minutes later. Laura found it weird, her eating, Malcolm sitting next to her sipping water. She was grateful for the music spilling through from the living room, drowning out the sound of her chewing and negating the need for conversation.

"Tell you what, while you finish your lamb, I'll make us each a fruit salad." Without waiting for an answer, Malcolm opened the fridge door, retrieving a punnet of strawberries and a bag of white grapes. He closed the door and picked a pineapple out of their wire fruit basket. As Laura chewed through her overdone lamb, she watched him run their largest steel kitchen knife against a sharpening rod. He sliced through the pineapple in a motion that looked easy.

Laura watched, hypnotised by the rocking of the blade working through yellow pineapple flesh. With each motion, the steel lightly scarred the wood of the chopping board. Within a minute they both had a bowl of chopped fruit resting on the work surface.

Malcolm had used the last of the grapes. He moved to put the plastic bag in the bin, then stopped, placing it on the worktop. She wasn't sure whether it was the sight of him with the knife or the plastic bag, which brought back Cassie's voice.

'Take a bag and tie it with a band around your throat.'

The memory made her inhale deeply, lodging a piece of dry, half chewed lamb in her windpipe. She struggled for breath, clawing at her neck.

Is this what Cassie saw, did she get confused? Am I going to die here tonight, not from some homicidal attack but from my own dumb luck?

Malcolm realised what was happening.

"Laura, nod at me if I'm right. Do you have lamb stuck in your windpipe?" She nodded furiously. He walked round the back of her.

Where's he going? He's walking so slowly. Is he going to leave me to die? Is this a happy coincidence for him?

Laura's vision became narrow and speckled with black and white - like the static of an old television. She bent over, her palms on the table. The skin on the backs of her hands matched the hue of her veins. A strange memory came in as consciousness drifted out. It was of a word she'd heard only once, during a first aid class: cyanosis.

Then she felt his thick forearms clamp around her and the knuckle of his thumb dig into her diaphragm. He heaved three times before the piece of lamb finally projected from her throat. The half chewed lamb first clung to, then dropped from the curtain fabric. It came to rest on their stainless steel draining board. Laura fell forward onto the table, gasping for breath like a free diver coming back to the surface after ten minutes under water.

"Laura, are you okay?" Malcolm rubbed her back with the heel of his hand. She was finally able to speak, "Yes Malcolm, oh my God, you saved my life." She turned and hugged him tighter than she'd ever done before.

How could you ever have doubted him?

Chapter Fifty-Five

Later that evening Malcolm Robinson slept soundly in his bed, breathing a regular, rumbling snore. On another night Laura might have blamed his snoring for her insomnia. Tonight she was kept awake by the photo she'd seen him scoop into his briefcase. The image haunted her every time she closed her eyes.

Her thoughts swung back and forth with the monotony of a pendulum, from ... *he saved your life for God's sake and you repay him with suspicion* ... to ... *that girl had been tortured and he had a picture of it. Surely for security reasons, he wouldn't even be allowed to bring evidence like that home* ... and then the pendulum swung back again. Early that evening she'd had clarity of mind but as she lay, battling sleeplessness, her thoughts were out of control or, more accurately, in control of her. She muttered in frustration, "Jesus Christ Laura, get a grip and get to sleep." Another thirty minutes passed as she stared at the digital clock on their bedside table.

I need to get up and do something. I'm going to warm some milk - might help me sleep.

She moved carefully, each motion slow, measured and furtive. She sat on the bed, her eyes adjusting to the light. She distinguished two lumps on the carpet, which her feet reached out to confirm were her slippers. If she hadn't needed to be so quiet, she would have let out an "Ahhhh," as the furry lining banished a chill from her toes.

She wore a thin satin nightie and looked around in the shadows for her plush dressing gown. She distinguished the wardrobes from the wallpaper; subtly different shades of dark grey in a pitch black room. She thought she'd left the gown hanging from the knob of the wardrobe door, but the grey was uniform, no other texture.

Could have sworn I left it there. Might be in the wardrobe. Opening it and fumbling around will be too noisy. I'll have to go without.

She was familiar with the location of every creaking floorboard and took a silent path towards the bedroom door. The handle worried her as the mechanism squeaked loudly in the daytime never mind in the early hours of the morning when every sound is amplified. With relief, she realised the door had been left ajar and it opened with the whisper of MDF clipping carpet pile.

So far so good. Laura, why the hell are you so afraid to wake him?

She knew exactly why.

Can't get that damn image out of my head.

She reached to turn on the landing light, her fingers hovering over the switch. The bedroom door was still open, a slither of gap between the door and the frame.

The noise and the light might disturb him.

She stood still for a moment, her toes curled over the edge of the top step, with so many thoughts swirling uncontrollably.

Perhaps those aren't the only pictures he has. What if there are images on the PC? You've never really used that computer, have you? It was supposed to be our computer, but it's always been his, really. Can you even remember your own log on? Why did he insist on us having separate user accounts? Something about the unusual settings he prefers. Sounded like bullshit then, didn't it? Sounds the same now. I bet Miss April thought she knew her partner before she saw those pictures. I bet with a couple of attempts, I could guess his password. He's still snoring soundly. He hardly ever wakes in the night, I could check without making a sound. The study's far enough away from the bedroom, he wouldn't hear a thing.

She looked across the landing towards the study. She moved nearer its door, gently rolling her feet from heel to toe with each step; rich with time, unable to afford noise.

It felt like winter was upon them. The heating had long since turned itself off and she glimpsed her breath's slight mist. Her skin tightened and goosebumps formed on her arms. As she reached out for the door handle the stupidity of what she was attempting struck her.

Come on, Laura, if he really did have images of girls who've been abused, would he really keep them where you could find them, behind a password that you could guess? If there is something on there that he wants to keep hidden, the password will be the last one you'd expect. And why would you want to check this when he's in the house? If you want to pry, do it tomorrow while he's out. Just go downstairs, make a drink and bide your time.

She was stepping back towards the stairs when she heard the click of their bedroom light turn on, followed by shuffling footsteps. Her heart hitched, stealing a breath; she wasn't sure if she could reach the stairs before he opened the door.

She just made it. His ordinarily neat black hair was pushed into a wedge and his eyes were half shut. He stood in checked boxer shorts, scratching his stomach and looking at her as if she were an apparition in an ongoing dream.

"What's going on?" It was a question full of confusion not accusation. She instantly felt guilty, vulnerable and exposed. These feelings weren't helped by her short, thin nightie, which clung to her chest. She became conscious of her nipples having hardened in the cold air and she instinctively pinched material away from her skin. She hoped his slitted eyes were still sleep-blind.

"Just getting a hot drink. Not sleeping that well, that's all. Want one?"

"Uh, no. No … going back to bed." His response was so slow and unsure that she wondered if he was truly awake.

Laura stood in front of their range cooker, stirring frothy milk that was coming to the boil. She was grateful for the warmth of the steam and the flame. It was a slow process, but she didn't mind. It gave her time to formulate a plan.

In the morning, I'll find a reason to get him on that computer, whilst I'm there. I'll study his fingers carefully. He doesn't type that *quickly, it should be easy. Then once he's gone to work, I'm going to call in sick and log onto the computer to see if there's anything to be concerned about. If I don't find anything, then great. If I do find something … well … I'll have to report him. Either way I'm going to meet with Frank to talk this through. I just need someone else I can trust, someone who understands, someone who can be rational about all this, because I sure as hell can't.*

Chapter Fifty-Six

Laura had finally drifted into an uneasy sleep a little after four a.m.. As a result, when Malcolm's alarm rang out at six, she hovered in that not-awake-not-asleep state. Thoughts of last night's conjured plan seeped in. Like a mother disturbed by the screams of her baby in the night, Laura was instantly awake.

I'm not going to have much time and I need to go through with it.

By the time Malcolm was out of the shower, Laura was sitting on his black leather chair in their study with the door open. The desk had two shelves you could bump your knees on whilst typing. On the top shelf was a cheap black A4 printer, on the bottom, on the shallow shelf, was a scanner whose cream top was yellowing. It was old, unused.

The computer's base stood on its side, to her left on the desk - a big rectangular black tower. The screen's frame was silver. It mismatched the black of the hard drive, as Malcolm had bought it separately; specially. It was far wider than the ones Laura used at work. She wasn't good at guessing the size of these things (TVs, monitors). Forty-two inches? She wasn't sure.

The screen was incredibly thin. She could never quite bring herself to ask how much it had cost. She waggled the mouse, which clicked the screen into life.

Laura's fingers pecked aimlessly at keys, accompanied by a barrage of exaggerated tuts. She shouted, "Malcolm!"

He looked around the doorframe, struggling to thread a stubborn cuff link.

"Yes, what is it?"

"Could you give me a hand with the computer?"

Malcolm joined her in the study. He breathed a loud sigh through his nose. "Laura, you know I'm in a rush ... and what are you shouting across the landing for at this time?"

"Oh, yeah sorry. Guess I was a bit loud. Anyway, this won't take a minute. I've just realised that if we're going to get Matthew's present bought and sent out to America, then I need to order it today. I can't find anything in town so I thought I'd look for something online. For the life of me, though, I can't remember my login."

"Tuh ... I can't believe you've left it that late. Budge over and I'll set up another log in for you." With some difficulty, Laura slid the chair a few inches to her left; the casters protested against the carpet pile. She watched his fingers intently as he logged on as the administrator. A minute later he was done.

"There, your password is password1, best change it to something less obvious, when you have a minute." He walked out of the study and hurriedly made his way back to the bedroom. Laura opened up the web browser and typed in the names of potential gifts for a six-year-old boy, doing a good job of faking interest in the search results. At six-thirty he returned to the study to give Laura a peck on the cheek and say goodbye. "Don't be late for work honey."

"I won't. I'm nearly done."

Laura had no intention of going to work.

At seven thirty I'm going to ring Angie and tell her I'm not coming in today. Oh lord, I hate telling lies. I'll hate her whinging more, though. What will a day off do to the team's case numbers?

You've not got the headspace to worry about that now ... Laura, put it from your mind.

Now, what did I see him type?

She logged out of her user account and attempted to log into his.

Think, Laura, what pattern did you see?

He'd typed a little quicker than she'd expected.

It was short, too, and wasn't really a word. Hard to guess, easy to enter.

She typed out: 'Cutrel.' The screen shimmied and froze. Laura was sure of the start, uncertain of the end. She tried again.

'Cutrek,'

Yes, that was it - I'm in. Now, what do I need to look for and where?

It occurred to her that her computer skills were fair at best and she sat for five minutes, trying to work out where to look for images. She navigated the folder structure and clicked on file names at random, each appearing to be a genuine description of the content: holiday snaps from their trips to France, pictures from Malcolm's Christmas party and one or two selfies taken in their living room (some clearly snapped after excessive quantities of red wine).

Laura was reprimanding herself again for her suspicion when a thought broke her guilt.

Miss April found files on a memory stick. Could he have one hidden, or an external hard drive stored somewhere? Even if he did, am I really going to turn the entire house upside down, looking for something possibly smaller than a matchbox that I don't even know exists?

She remembered a time when she'd tried to open a letter on a work PC. The letter was stored on a memory stick and the stick was no longer protruding from the base unit. She recalled the mouse path clearly: File>Open Recent> then she'd clicked on the file name and a message had popped up telling her that the file location had changed.

How did I manage to even attempt to open it, if it wasn't accessible? What did I do? Recently used files in the application - that was it. But what application?

Laura used a spotlight search to look for photographs. Two entries under the sub heading 'application' for the term photo: iPhoto and Photoshop. iPhoto contained nothing but the innocent images she'd already reviewed. However, Photoshop had the strangest filenames listed under File > Open Recent. The first one was '2i4o5w4h3i6nz35t2n1d5q' the second one, 'p26n2q4w5y3d1k2u2m4g5y' and so on. There were at least twenty indecipherable file names. She clicked on a few. Each time she received a message: "The document could not be opened. Its location may have changed." She deduced that these files must have been stored away from the main hard drive. She was far from convinced, however, that this was any cause for concern.

Perhaps it's some kind of police encryption protocol. These might genuinely relate to his job. Frank will know.

She wrote down '2i4o5w4h3i6nz35t2n1d5q' on a scrap of paper and shoved it into her dressing gown pocket. As she did so a text came through to her mobile from Leanne Janus. It read: 'Mrs Robinson, Cassie is really sorry that she lost her temper. She just wanted me to text to apologise and ask if everything is okay.' Laura wasn't in the frame of mind to write a lengthy response so she replied: 'That's very sweet, but everything's fine.'

She logged out of Malcolm's account, being careful to shut everything down without saving any changes. After calling in sick, she got dressed and found Cassie's case file. Inside was Frank's mobile number.

Chapter Fifty-Seven

"Jack, come here boy, Jack!" Paul whistled loudly but his black Labrador was nowhere to be seen. He squinted into the early morning sun along the diagonal path Jack had taken across the farmer's field.

Must've seen a rabbit, the pace he went off. I better not have to trudge through that field to find him.

Janet had told him to take the dog later but he'd insisted on getting the walk out of the way. Now he was sure to be late and an 'I told you so' conversation with Janet was the last thing he needed.

"Jack, come here now. Jack! Jack!" Paul took a deep breath and headed out over the field, wishing he'd worn wellingtons. He swore under his breath.

A faint mist rose from the furrowed soil, last night's rain slowly evaporating in the morning sun. Paul took uncertain steps, the mud slipping away beneath his ankle-high boots. He lost his footing, regaining balance with windmill arms.

For God sake, Jack, where are you?

Now a good thirty yards into the field, Paul shuffled round in a circle. He resembled a ship's lookout, a flat hand resting on his forehead shielding his eyes from the sun.

Finally he caught sight of a black tail. It was poking out of a ditch some fifty yards in front of him. Jack's tail wagged and jerked back and forth as if the rest of the dog's body, entirely out of sight, was trying to recover something. Paul headed in Jack's direction, his shouts of "Come boy," entirely ignored.

As he got closer to the ditch, Paul saw sticks and other debris rushing along, perhaps two feet below the bank.

Must've really come down last night.

"Jack, what is it? What've you got?" As he neared, Paul closed his eyes, convinced that when he opened them again he would realise he'd been mistaken. He wasn't that lucky.

Jack's powerful jaws had a tight grip on the dark blue canvas inside leg of what appeared to be an overall. The intermittent motion of the dog's tugging revealed a rolled down sock and an ankle; the skin pale and speckled with silt. "My God."

Once at the dog's side, Paul could make out the upper body, despite rushing driftwood distorting his view. The body bent with the flowing water and Jack was in a battle with nature, preventing it from floating off. Part of Paul wanted to force Jack to let go but then a sense of duty overcame him.

He reached down, grabbing the material of the other leg, to help Jack. They pulled the body far enough out of the water to rest it on the bank. Whilst the man's face was still obscured by water, his neck was exposed and Paul saw why the skin was so pale. Blood must have escaped from the gaping wound in his neck.

Jack was still tugging at the body. Paul prised the Labrador's jaws open, forcing him to release the material. The dead man's leg thumped onto the soil. Paul slipped Jack's lead back on. He patted his pockets and cursed at not finding his mobile.

Left it on charge in the kitchen.

Paul swore frequently at the bounding dog. Its taut lead frequently pulled him off balance, as they made their way off the field and onto the main road.

Fifteen minutes later when Paul stumbled through the front door, he heard Janet shouting from the kitchen, "You're late." He didn't reply, heading straight for the phone in the hall. Over the dial tone he heard his wife again, "Jack, where the hell have you been? Paul, he's filthy, why did you let him come through in this state?"

Janet walked into the hall, finding Paul's lack of response inexplicable. One look at him, the mud all over his boots and jeans and his pale expression, made her certain that something was wrong. "Paul what the-" He held up an arm, halting her interruption.

"Police please."

Chapter Fifty-Eight

Hilary thought she was probably going stir-crazy. The phrase Cabin fever also came to mind. The school had been incredibly understanding about her taking some time off but there was only so much work she could do from home and she loathed daytime television. Reading killed some time but her concentration was frequently broken by thoughts of Mark's whereabouts.

Both Mark's parents had died tragically whilst on holiday in Indonesia, victims of the Boxing Day Tsunami (*or so he said, Hilary, don't make the mistake of taking anything for granted.*) He had no friends she was aware of. So where else could he go?

He's probably sleeping in an outbuilding somewhere.

Yours?

No the police checked when they first started protecting me.

Have they checked since though? He could have sneaked past them. It's possible, isn't it?

She slammed a hardback copy of 'Mr Mercedes' face down on the coffee table, frustrated at her inability to keep track of the storyline. She opened the front door, looking for Jacobs. There were three men in the tag team of protection working in shifts. Jacobs was the only one whose name she remembered. She liked him. The others were hunkier, stronger, but Jacobs had a kind face and the spindly assurance of a ballroom dancer.

He greeted her with a smile. "Good morning, Miss April." It sounded strangely like the greeting of her pupils at registration.

"Can I get you a tea or coffee?"

"Thank you, tea please."

"And … can I ask a small favour?"

"Certainly, what can I do for you?"

"Could you check the shed and the garage, one last time? I know it's silly but it's best to be sure."

"Of course."

Constable Jacobs had been overly friendly since the day they'd broke the news of Mark's disappearance. She put this down to the embarrassment they'd felt on behalf of the authorities for allowing a sexual deviant to escape.

Jacobs disappeared down a path along the side of the house, emerging near the garage door. As Hilary put the kettle on to boil, she watched him out of the kitchen window. He twisted the handle, and pushed the top of the door. It swung wide open, retracting against the ceiling. He moved piles of junk, exposing places where it might be possible to lurk. The garage was half filled with boxes, most belonged to Mark. She struggled to remember what was in the others.

Why do I carry all this crap from one place to the next? Perhaps I should have a clear out.

Jacobs moved more boxes aside. His movements appeared circumspect.

Is he nervous? Some protection!

Hilary cursed her paranoia, as she reached up to her left, pulling two mugs out of the narrow cupboard. Over the whirring and bubbling of the kettle and clunking of mugs, Hilary failed to hear steps behind her. It wasn't until she reached for the kettle and felt a hand upon her shoulder that she realised she wasn't alone.

Chapter Fifty-Nine

Cassie stood in the doorway of her bedroom. She gripped her rucksack loosely, its tightening straps dangling over her Reeboks. She'd thought a lot about this moment over the past two days, anticipating what it would be like to be home again.

It's too easy to judge your surroundings as inadequate when you've tasted better. Cassie knew that she'd been seduced by Aaron's computer, by his fitted wardrobes, his beanbag, his new phone, his plush bathroom even by Aslan. All of these things stacked up and Cassie knew that when she came home she would feel like she'd lost something, something good.

She walked to her wardrobe, bent in front of it and pulled the few clothes out of her rucksack that hadn't gone straight to the wash. Unlike Mrs Hall, Cassie's mum only washed clothes that were *actually* dirty. She held one hand under the wardrobe door before pulling it open, conscious of the broken hinge. But, as it swung towards her, the door didn't feel like it was dropping. It had been mended ... of sorts. A white shiny substance, with the texture of bubbling lava, had been pumped behind the hinge's screws. It was holding, for now.

She's tried to fix it. When did she do that? That must have been difficult, with only one good eye. Oh Mummy you should have been resting.

After Cassie's seizure in the Halls' kitchen, Leanne had relented to Christine's request, letting Cassie stay for an extra night. Leanne had said, on reflection, 'perhaps it would be good to get a few things sorted.' Fixing the wardrobe must have been one of those things.

After hanging up her tops and folding her jeans onto the lowest shelf of her wardrobe, Cassie looked for her pyjamas. They were usually scrunched up under her pillow, but today were folded neatly in the middle of her duvet. She picked them up and leant over, placing them across her face. She breathed deeply, her nose buried in the material, feeling strangely like a kid from a Lenor advert.

Clean and soft.

The pyjama bottoms were too short but she didn't mind. It wasn't as cold as when she'd last been home. She reached behind the cream padded headboard and touched the radiator. Warmth.

Mummy put the heating on. She wants it to be nice for me.

Cassie was happy. Happy, but exhausted. It was only seven thirty but, despite the time, she climbed into bed. The covers smelled as fresh as her pyjamas. Katie sat, resting against the wall. Cassie grabbed her. She would cuddle Katie to sleep, not caring how babyish it seemed.

Random pleasant notions came. Sleep approached. "Night Mummy," she whispered, expecting it to be just a thought. Her last wish, before drifting off, was to sleep without nightmares.

For once, she got her wish.

Chapter Sixty

Frank had agreed to meet Laura in Eat on Broadgate, near Liverpool street, at two forty-five p.m.. Laura was ten minutes early and bought the strongest, sweetest latte they served. She waited upstairs.

The seating area was mid refurbishment. Half the room was painted in a grey primer, which merged into the old colour, mustard yellow, with a jagged join, as though the decorators had stopped brushing the instant their shift had finished. Vinyl tiles were missing from the perimeter of the room, leaving adhesive rectangles she imagined her soles would stick to. The tables were unusually empty.

I'm not sure this place should even be open.

As she waited, she dwelled on how evasive she'd been with Frank.

' ... something I really need to talk through with you.'

'What's this about?'

'It's not something we can discuss over the phone.'

When he'd agreed to meet her, she'd sensed his reticence. She'd heard, or maybe imagined, a touch of impatience as well.

Frank was five minutes late which gave Laura ample time to both doubt and trust her suspicion of Malcolm in equal measure. When Frank arrived, she put an arm around his cream chunky wool jumper, and surprised herself by kissing his cheek. She was pleased he wasn't wearing a uniform or a suit. He wore jeans and Adidas trainers; entirely nondescript.

More informal, less conspicuous this way.

Laura kept her voice low. "Thanks for coming Frank." He nodded and smiled, as he laid leather gloves in an 'X' on the table.

"Before we start, can I get you a coffee?"

"I'm good thanks."

She imagined her heavy smile gave away her disappointment. Her prepared opening line, a segue into the real conversation, escaped her. Five minutes of waiting in the queue downstairs might have given her enough time to recall it.

Oh for God sake, just tell him.

"I'm suspicious of Malcolm."

Frank's brows gathered and he lightly scratched at his earlobe.

"Okay ... suspicious about what?"

"When I tell you all about this, you'll probably think I'm mad, or paranoid or both and that's fine. Sometimes you just need to say something out loud to think things through, you know?"

"Come on Laura, what is it?"

"It's a number of things really, all of which probably sound silly."

"Go on."

"Well firstly there are these files on our computer: image files. When I say, on the computer, someone has opened them, possibly edited them on our computer, but stored them somewhere else. I'm guessing they're on a memory stick or hard drive. When I try to open them, it says they're not there anymore."

"Deleted?"

"I guess. Anyway, the file names are really weird as well, like they're encrypted. Does this look like any sort of encryption you're aware of?" Laura pulled out the scrap of paper with '2i4o5w4h3i6nz35t2n1d5q' written on it and passed it to Frank who studied it for a second, shaking his head, lips upturned.

"Doesn't look like any type of encryption we'd use. I can get a cryptologist to take a look though, if you'd like."

"Would you? Can you do it discreetly, without Malcolm knowing?"

"I would think so. But I wouldn't feel comfortable doing it based on what you've told me so far. My hunch is that something else is worrying you." Laura gulped down a large mouthful of coffee, nodded and then closed her eyes, thinking very carefully about what to say.

"I walked in on Malcolm in our study the other day. He was sorting out some photographs. He said they were taken as evidence from the crime scene where that man held those teenagers."

Frank leaned towards her, forearms resting on the table, flattening his gloves.

"If that *is* what he had, depending on how explicit and identifiable the subjects were, those photographs would have to be signed out."

"That's just it. In my job, you get to see a lot of things; things you wish you didn't have to. Things you can't un-see. But I've never seen anything as ... as cruel, as ugly."

"From what I've heard, the scene was pretty gruesome." Laura felt patronised.

"I know that Frank," she lowered her volume still further. "But I swear to God, in one of the pictures the girl was tied up, with her jeans cut up so that ... " She paused, not really believing what she was about to say, needing him to be as concerned as she was. "So that her breasts and genitals were showing. She looked terrified and had cuts all over her."

Frank's light and sympathetic face darkened as he leant in further. His upper body cast a shadow across the table. With shoulders hunched, he looked half the size of the man who'd walked in five minutes earlier. "Laura, how sure are you about this? A number of officers attended the scene. Are you suggesting a conspiracy?"

"Frank, honestly, I'm not suggesting anything other than he had that photo. Perhaps the killer posted it to the police, or shared it online. I really don't know, I only know that Malcolm has it and I want someone to say that it was discovered as part of the investigation and that I have nothing to worry about."

"So why *don't* you think that Laura? Why are you so worried? I don't think you're telling me everything."

Laura paused, thinking about whether to tell him what Cassie had said.

Surely my credibility with him will instantly evaporate if I confess to letting the bizarre fantasies of a nine-year-old child get to me. That means I have to give him something else. I'm going to end up telling him about what happened in bed the other night, I can feel it. Oh God.

"Frank ... there's some really personal stuff you know. I need to know that none of this this will go any further. It has to stay between us, do you promise?"

"Of course Laura."

"Malcolm's been acting completely out of character lately."

"In what way?"

"In many ways. Some, I'm sure you'll say are perfectly normal, others are not. Until they found Tucker, this case took over his life. He was practically living at work and he's really touchy whenever I bring it up. You know when something's nagging at you and you can't put it from your mind?"

Frank nodded.

"Well these murders have been like that. In a way that's stupid, isn't it. It's such a big city, these things are going to happen. I guess we all hope they're rare events but they're not, not really. But knowing a thought's a stupid one doesn't make it go away. I just keep going over the same ground. Why are the papers so interested in this if it's so commonplace? And that gets me thinking that these *are* strange, rare events - people murdered with no family suspect. There's *always* a family suspect. You examine their faces at police-lead press conferences, don't you ... are they overly distraught, are they not distraught enough? I guess that's why everyone's talking about them; brutal murders in rapid succession, no close relative jumping into the frame. When I put that to him he spoke to me like I was stupid."

"You're not suggesting he ... he has something to do with these murders are you? You know that case is sewn up, don't you?"

"God no. I'm not suggesting *that*, just that he seemed overly sensitive about it."

"Well, I don't know why. We've been investigating-"

"We've? I didn't know you were involved?"

"Why would you?"

Laura shrugged.

"I was initially assigned the Eccleston investigation. What I was going to say was that we've been investigating a connection since shortly after the second murder. Malcolm's been working hard. We've *all* been working hard. But 'living at work.' Forgive me Laura, but that sounds like an exaggeration."

"Well ... that's what it felt like to me."

Laura, who'd half lifted her coffee (the cup's dregs were far too sweet, even for her) stopped for a moment and then put it down. She was about to initiate a barrage of questions, which Frank sensed and pre-empted.

"Look Laura, this confidentiality works both ways, right?"

"Absolutely. Now, what do you mean 'connected', in what way?"

"I spotted it ... and the DNA eventually backed me up."

"Spotted what?"

"A calling card. And quite literally. Guess the bastard thought it was funny. I suggested we share resources across investigations. Soon after, we were working on the same team." She scratched her neck and looked towards the stairs without seeing, contemplating what she'd heard.

"The first victim, Dacia Cartwright, had a playing card, the Jack of Diamonds, in her bag. Dacia's girlfriend said they'd found it discarded near a department store. Tucker's prints were on it, virtually a hundred per cent match. The second victim, Peter Eccleston, had a full deck of cards in his coat pocket. Archer, the third victim, had a nine-sided dice with him. We were working on the theory that the killer was using these to select his victims, or more accurately, so they selected themselves."

"And the girl who survived?"

"That's where he slipped up. She was never supposed to be a victim. She disturbed him while he was abducting Frankie so he had to take her. According to Tucker's note he was so disturbed by what had gone wrong, he didn't want to carry on and didn't want to go back to prison."

"Why did Malcolm lie to me then, why was he so adamant there was no connection?"

Frank shrugged, took a small yellow-leafed notebook out of his back pocket and spent a few moments writing. A waitress in a long pristine racing green apron approached. She cleared the table to their right, smiling at them as she wiped. Laura struggled to smile back. They waited in silence. The waitress walked off, three coffee mugs hooked over the finger of one hand, a cloth in the other.

"Laura, you said he'd been acting strangely in *many* ways?"

She took a deep breath and looked down, rubbing a half-dried coffee ring from the shiny table with the side of her thumb. She spoke to the table.

"Look I'm sure that, with the job you do, what I'm about to tell you will seem pretty tame, but to me it's really embarrassing, so go easy on me, okay?"

Frank reached out to rest his hand on her forearm.

"Come on, you can tell me, I won't judge." Looking at Frank's face for the next few minutes was going to be an impossibility. Laura looked at the froth clinging to the inside of her mug and kept her eyes there.

"His sexual habits have changed. He seems to want to dominate me to the point of hurting me. You see these marks?

Oh God, now I've got to look up.

She raised her chin and pointed to the fading redness on either side of her lips, now dry and cracking.

"He did this to me with a gag." Her gaze dropped back into her mug.

"It's not the only place I was hurting the next morning. I don't want to say anything more than that."

"Are you planning on pressing charges?"

"No, nothing like that and he did apologise it's just ..."

"What?"

Her eyes were on his, she felt like she was pleading, but didn't know what for.

"I don't feel safe around him at the minute and I just need some ... some reassurance ... peace of mind. Can you do some digging to find out if he should have had that picture and check out the encryption - to see if it's used legitimately by the police?"

"Okay Laura, I'll look into it. The second I find anything, I'll call you."

"Thank you Frank. Thank you *so* much. Honestly, it's just a relief having someone to confide in."

After taking her mobile number Frank stood up to leave and offered her some parting words of comfort. "It'll be nothing you know. Everything will be fine."

I wish I could believe you Frank, I really do.

Chapter Sixty-One

As Hilary instinctively swung round, kettle in hand, boiling water leapt in an arc towards Sergeant Jackson who stepped back swiftly to avoid a scalding. Jackson held her hands up in a half defensive, half surrendering gesture. "Whoa ... Miss April, I didn't mean to scare you. I could see the door wasn't shut properly and I wanted to make sure everything was alright."

"You gave me the fright of my life."

"I'm sorry, the door was unlocked. I guess you didn't hear me shouting."

A manila file was pinned between the sleeve and side of Jackson's immaculate uniform. She had a more confident air than when they'd last met.

"Where's Constable Jacobs?"

Guess he's in trouble for not leaving the front door secure.

"Round the back. I asked him to check the garage and shed again. I just can't shake the thought that Mark's going to come back here."

"Well, I do have some news with regards to Mark Adams. I'm reluctant to call it good news under the circumstances, but it *will* put your mind at ease."

"Sergeant, just tell me, what is it?"

"A body has been discovered. We believe it to be Mr Adams's."

"I see." Hilary walked through to the living room and sat, staring absently, trying to digest the news. Sergeant Jackson followed her.

"How do you know it's him?"

"We're checking dental records to be sure but we're pretty confident from the physical similarities. According to our records, he had a tattoo, is that correct?"

"Yes."

"Could you describe it?"

"A star. A pentangle I think he called it, on the inside of his right wrist."

Jackson extracted the file from under her arm. She opened it, angling it to her chest.

Why doesn't she just show me the picture. Probably afraid to upset me, after last time.

She shut the file.

"It's him?"

Jackson nodded gently with a half-smile.

Chapter Sixty-Two

Since returning home with Cassie, Leanne had felt a bond growing between them and a maternal instinct she hadn't felt in years. It was bizarre to think that anything good could have come out of Daniel attacking her, but her own regret at not heeding Cassie's warning, and the subsequent faith she'd placed in Cassie's premonitions, had made Cassie feel believed and belief was the key to rebuilding their relationship. Leanne was convinced of this.

Leanne was emptying the under-sink cupboard, looking for a needle and thread she hadn't used in years, when she heard Cassie call out from her bedroom. Leanne stood up and turned too quickly. She clattered through old tins of polish, and her upper arm brushed the living room doorframe as she hurried to Cassie's room.

The cry must have come in her sleep. Cassie was sound off, taking easy breaths. Still, Leanne chose to crouch by her bedside, gently stroking her hair. When Cassie eventually woke she sat up instantly, looking around her as if she didn't recognise her surroundings.

"Am I late?"

"Sweetheart, why don't you take the day off today? With all you've been through, you deserve it. I'll write a note for the school."

"Mrs Robinson?"

"I've just received a text from her. She's fine."

"Oh. Oh good." Cassie rolled over to face the wall. Leanne detected an undertone in her response and in her body language: *Then people will think I was making it up.*

"Cassie, she's still in danger isn't she? It's alright you know. I believe you." Cassie rolled over again, sat up and hugged her mum, squeezing her neck tightly. "Yes Mummy. She is."

Chapter Sixty-Three

It was seven fifty-five a.m. when Frank Simmons pulled his Impreza into the car park behind the office. He was in a rush. He'd intended to be in by seven-thirty, but some idiot gym member had inadvertently set the fire alarm off, in the middle of Frank's treadmill run. The 'standard procedure' evacuation, with him stood in his shorts next to a fluorescent vested jobsworth, had both pissed him off, and made him late. Most people officially started at nine, but drifted in any time from eight.

As long as I can get in quickly, I might still be okay.

Frank had been allocated three new cases. One attempted murder, a rape and an armed robbery. A real mixed bag, but nothing as high profile as the Eccleston murder. Part of him was relieved. He hated talking to the media. But before he could get to any of them, just the small matter of deciphering Laura's code, which he curled out in his lap, next to his smartphone.

He hated phones with big screens. Almost everyone else loved them. He missed his old Nokia; he missed buttons. He also disliked having to keep them out of the rain. *Great* standard issue choice for English detectives.

Rain silently peppered his windscreen. Frank looked at the car's clock. He couldn't afford the time to have the conversation in the car. He would have to walk and talk. Frank slipped the scrap of paper into his back pocket. He climbed out of the car, finding Marvin's number on his phone. He used his backside to shut the Impreza's door.

Rain speckled the phone's screen. He smeared it with his sleeve then dialled. It rang four times. Marvin, a freelance cryptologist, was usually an early starter and chained to his desk. Frank hoped Marvin wasn't on holiday.

A connecting clunk then a familiar, abrasive voice. "Hello," Sounding more like 'Yello.'

"Marvin, it's Frank, I could do with a favour."

"Could you now? When are these favours going to be returned, young sir? I think I need to reacquaint you with the nature of favours Frank."

"Okay, point taken. Could you take a look at something for me? It's an encryption protocol I think."

"Sure. I hope it's more challenging than the last one, fella."

"Marvin, I'm sure even the KGB can't create a code you couldn't crack in your sleep."

"False flattery doesn't become you Frank my dear boy. Is it on a file?"

"It's a hand written note."

"Always low tech with you Frank. Send it through."

I'm just getting into the office now, give me five minutes. Someone held the front door of the building open for him and Frank said, "Thank you."

"What for?"

"Not you, I was talking to someone else."

"Oh ... was I boring you?"

Frank ignored Marvin's question.

"I need it back quickly, when I get to my desk I'll scan it and email it to you."

"Oh Frank, you're priceless."

"What?"

"You need it quickly, so you're going to boot up your computer, which I'm guessing takes fifteen to twenty minutes, then you're going to scan it, which takes another five then-"

"Okay Marvin, what do *you* suggest?"

"Well you know that thing you have pressed to your ear. My bet is it feels shiny, smooth against your ear. And that surface is designed to show things we call photographs."

Marvin you can be a great guy, but for once take a day, or maybe even just an hour, off taking the piss.

"Alright Marvin," he resisted substituting *Marvin* with *Smartarse*. "I'll take a picture and email it."

"Where from?"

"My phone."

"That's my boy."

"Stay on the line."

Frank, standing midway along a corridor, rolled out the scrap of paper against a cork notice board, finding a space between pinned, ineffectual laminated notices. Another thing he hated about smart phones was how steady they had to be to take pictures. His hand had a perpetual, if barely discernible, quiver, making photography a challenge. The first picture he took was out of focus but still legible.

"You still there?"

"Yep."

"When can you get back to me?"

"Well that depends on how simple it is. If I've seen it before, you can have it back in ten minutes. If it's new, it might take a while."

"Okay, and Marvin, could we keep this one between you and I?"

"Can't promise that Frank. It's good form for cryptologist to share new codes."

"That's fine, just don't talk to anyone else from the Met about it."

"Whatever you say."

"It's on its way." Frank emailed the picture from his phone and hung up.

Three minutes later the phone rang. "Frank, it's Marvin."

Frank had his phone wedged between his chin and his shoulder. He was pumping change into a vending machine.

The coffee was poor as it always is when made with powdered milk and water, which has sat all night in ageing pipes. The vending machine was on the way though, and contained caffeine. Good enough.

"That was quick. Less than five minutes."

"Actually I was brewing up when it came through. It took me approximately twenty seconds."

"So you've seen it before?"

"Yes, only the once though and a good job I had. If I hadn't, I'd have needed multiple file names to establish the pattern. It's a crude password encryption I saw used in a case a few years ago. Do you remember the Justice Stephens case?"

"Vaguely, Lord Justice Stephens?"

"That's the fella, just not a *Lord* anymore. He had that privilege taken away. As it transpired, Justice Stephens had a taste for nasty porno. He, and a number of others, were using this method to mask file names of illegal images they were creating and sharing. Don't you remember it? It was all over the papers."

"I don't read the papers."

Frank, having made his way through sterile magnolia corridors, placed the beige plastic coffee cup on his desk and settled into his squeaky leather chair. He swivelled the chair, scanning the office, before speaking. Most desks were empty, with blank computer screens. One monitor was on, displaying rows of photofits; a sinister game of Guess Who. Frank smiled at the thought. Next to the faces, parked on the base station, was a steaming mug. Its owner was nowhere in sight. Still, Frank spoke quietly as a precaution.

"Can you translate what it says?"

"Of course, but it's quite straight forward to read. Especially for someone in the police or armed services."

"How come?"

"The letters and numbers are in pairs. The letter refers to the corresponding word from the phonetic alphabet. A means alpha, etcetera."

"And the numbers?"

"I was just getting to that."

"Sorry."

"Forgiven. The numbers reference a letter in the phonetic word."

"I'm not sure I follow you."

"2i means the second letter of India.... N. 40 means the fourth letter of Oscar. A. Get the logic?"

"Yep. So what's *this* file name?"

"Don't know, I haven't worked it out yet, but I'm sure it'll only take you a minute."

Marvin hung on the line whilst Frank extracted a notepad from his desk drawer. He turned over the top page, and used the second to write his decryption. Marvin sounded like he was chewing something.

N ... A ... K ... E ... D ... B ... L

"Wait up, there are now two numbers together."

"Don't let that throw you." He mumbled through food. "They're still pairs, the n with the two, the t with the five"

... O ... N ... D ... E.

"Naked Blonde."

"Bingo, Frank you've got the hang of it."

"Great, thanks for your help, if I get a load of these file names, have you got something you could run this through or do I have to work it all out manually?"

"I'll send you a spreadsheet we put together for the Stephen's case. All you have to do is type them in and it will give you the answer."

"Marvin you're a legend. I-"

"Owe me one, yes I know. Later Frank. Oh, and don't forget to send me a job number to charge against ... kids to feed and all that."

Chapter Sixty-Four

"Cassie, why don't you try this top with those jeans?" Leanne laid out clothes on Cassie's bed. She couldn't remember the last time her mum had helped her choose clothes. Cassie was in a fine mood, full of smiles. She even had snatches of time (perhaps as long as twenty minutes) without thoughts of Mrs Robinson.

"Okay Mummy." Leanne watched her getting changed.

How did she get so grown up? Oh God, look at the legs of those jeans. Next dole cheque - all on Cassie. I'll go without food for a few days if I have to. Definitely no booze.

There was a time, not *that* long ago, when Cassie needed help with every button and every lace. So many self-interested, self indulgent years had slipped by, with Cassie rarely noticed. Leanne winced at the painful truth and shook her head.

"You okay Mummy?"

"Yes sweetheart. I am *now*."

Cassie had almost threaded her arms through her sleeves when Leanne hugged her shoulders.

"Not too tight on my shoulder Mum."

"Oh, sorry ... I forgot."

"It's okay, it doesn't hurt that much now."

"Listen Cassie, I've been thinking about what you said about Mrs Robinson. If she is in danger-"

"She is."

"Since she *is*, I think we should go to the police." Cassie's smile disappeared.

"Mrs Robinson didn't believe me. The police won't believe me."

"Cassie..," Leanne took hold of her hands encouraging her to sit on the bed. Their eyes were at the same level.

"The difference is that now *I* understand. I can help you figure out what to say to them. They might believe you. And if they don't, then at least we've tried."

"If they don't believe me, won't someone take me away?"

Leanne's pencilled-on eyebrows squished together, her eyes narrowing, "Like who?"

"Those men. They used to say they had white coats but I heard they don't wear coats like that any more."

"No honey. No. That would never happen. Nobody's going to think you're crazy. They might think that you have a strong imagination, but that's all."

"You don't think it's my imagination, do you Mummy?"

"No Cassie, I don't. Do you feel brave enough to tell me what you would say to the police, if we spoke to them?"

"I think so. And I promise I won't get angry again Mummy, like I did with Mrs Robinson."

"I know you won't sweetheart."

"I think I should start from the beginning."

Two hours later, Leanne was in the kitchen, on the phone to the police. She had further information regarding the murder of Peter Eccleston and wanted to report it. She was asked to hold.

As some symphony she couldn't name crackled down the line, Leanne wondered if the composer ever envisaged the invention of the telephone and their work being used to grate on waiting callers. For the first time in a long time, she smiled in amusement.

Eventually, a different woman's voice mechanically thanked her for holding, and instructed her to come immediately, with Cassie, to Scotland Yard, Broadway and make themselves known to the reception. She sounded bored or disinterested.

They've closed the case. Moved on.

Leanne considered whether she should put her daughter through this experience. She convinced herself that, given Cassie truly *did* have some type of precognitive ability, she was already *going through it*, seeing and feeling things no nine-year-old should. The least Leanne could do was help Cassie feel as though something positive might come out of this.

As Leanne came off the phone, Cassie was walking through from her bedroom. She held Katie by her one, well-secured arm. Leanne hadn't seen her with Katie in ... she wasn't sure - a long time. She wished she'd thrown the creepy thing out years ago.

"Can, I take her with us?"

"Of course you can."

Scotland yard was over an hour's ride away, with two changes. As they sat on the tube, Cassie was overly quiet and spent much of the journey looking at the map of interconnecting stations running the length of each carriage. When she wasn't studying tube stops, she was thinking.

She'd finally forgiven her mum for lying to her about coming to school that day. She understood that her mum felt ashamed of staying home and getting drunk when Cassie needed her. Cassie's physical pain had all but subsided too and, with it, any lingering sense of resentment. Her mum had told a small lie so that Cassie wouldn't hate her. Surely this meant Mummy wanted Cassie to like her, to love her too.

Then her thoughts turned to what would happen when they got to Scotland yard. She asked only one question during the whole journey: "The policemen will be nice, won't they?"

They sat upright on flat leather sofas near the entrance. Leanne watched the receptionist deal with other visitors, guessing the woman was in her mid twenties. She wore a neatly pressed suit, and wide dark-rimmed glasses that would have looked nerdy on a spotty teenager, but made this woman, with her neatly straightened hair, look like a secretary you wouldn't want to leave your husband with.

The receptionist glanced over her shoulder and must have received some sort of signal because she walked around the desk, leaving colleagues to pick up the slack. She bent over, placing her ID badge against a glass plate on top of the security barrier. The waist high glass panels parted like curtains, and she waved Leanne and Cassie through. Leanne was called to one side for a search.

The receptionist smiled in apology. The overly dour security guard, doing the frisking, did not.

"Sorry, it's nothing personal, purely random." Leanne imagined the receptionist was probably sick of saying that.

Cassie stood, clutching Katie, confused about Mummy being treated like a criminal. The receptionist looked down at her and beamed. It was a broad - *I've never needed to have my perfectly straight teeth whitened* - kind of a grin. Cassie returned it, her smile less assured.

The room they were escorted to was barren and formal. It reminded her of rooms she'd seen on police shows, where tough cops interrogate distraught suspects. They were asked to sit down at a solitary table against the far wall.

A square black plate was secured to the wall, to Leanne's left. A wire hung from it.

Perhaps its some sort of microphone.

A box sat on the desk to her left, flush against the wall. On its side was a red Perspex cube the size of a sugar lump. Leanne imagined the cube lit up when the tape was running.

On the far wall, opposite them, a piece of dark glass stretched from just below the ceiling to waist height. It looked like the screen of one of those enormous projection televisions (the type you have to be a distance from to watch.) Leanne imagined people behind the screen, watching them.

"Someone will be here to speak with you shortly. In the meantime, can I get you a drink? What about you?" The receptionist looked at Cassie, bending at the hip, hands on her thighs. "Would you like some juice?" Cassie nodded. As they waited, Leanne questioned whether she'd made the right call in bringing Cassie here. The room had a vibe she didn't like. She tried to hide her nervousness.

"It'll all be okay, Cassie, you'll see. We'll just tell them what we discussed and then we'll be on our way."

Cassie's juice arrived quickly, "There you go honey, someone will be with you in just a couple of minutes. Are you sure I can't get you anything Miss Janus?"

"No. But thank you." They were alone again.

Chapter Sixty-Five

Constable Alistair Clough approached Robinson, who stood, arms folded with his face a few inches from the one-way glass. They'd worked together for two weeks, but work had, if Alistair was honest, been more like shadowing. You don't let a constable with his limited experience loose on anything significant, and significant it had been, until their discovery of Tucker. Now it was admin, tidying up and so Robinson had slackened the reins, so to speak.

"Sergeant, are you sure you're happy for me to conduct this alone? ... Sergeant?"

"What do you see, Clough?"

Alistair looked to his left to the girl and her mother who occasionally glanced at each other, but mainly regarded the room, the way you do any new intimidating space.

"A frightened kid - to be expected I guess - and her mum."

Malcolm expelled air through his nose, misting the glass, and smiled, turning to face Clough.

"I guessed as much, that's what young, inexperienced eyes see. Do you know what *I* see?" He turned back to the glass.

"No sergeant."

"Paperwork. An hour or two perhaps, if it's handled tightly. Three days, maybe more, if it's not"

"Sir?"

"Do you know what, in time, you'll get used to spotting?"

"No sergeant, what?"

"Wild goose chases. And children are a major source of them. Have you read the Wilcox study?"

This sense of being tested smacked of his gruelling assessment, eighteen months in the past; a lingering ordeal. He barely remembered the name Wilcox and inwardly cursed his powers of recall. Nothing came and he was grateful when Robinson filled the silence.

"Well, it's an important study on the reliability of child witnesses. Did you know that seventy-two per cent of evidence given by those under ten is later contradicted? And of that seventy-two, thirty-seven is later retracted, as the child confesses to either making up or exaggerating their account?"

"Now you've said that, yes, I do remember."

"Be mindful of that, when you conduct the interview. Let's not waste resource. God knows, we've got enough cases demanding our attention, without re-opening this one."

Alastair looked through the glass at Cassie Janus, clutching her doll in one arm, and sipping juice with her other. He felt sorry for her, presumed a liar before she'd even spoken. Still, he had to proceed with caution, he was being judged.

"I'll bear that in mind. Will you be overseeing the interview?"

"Of course."

Chapter Sixty-Six

Frank sat at his desk. It was mid afternoon and, after the conversation with Marvin plus a few gentle but successful enquiries with colleagues, Frank was ready to call Laura. He leant against the back of his chair, (too springy for most, but for some reason Frank loved swinging back on it) took his mobile off charge, and called Laura.

As he waited for her to pick up, he reminisced about the days when his phone wasn't semi permanently tethered to a plug.

"Oh thank God it's you. I've been at home, stewing over what we discussed. It won't be long before he's back and I really can't bear to face the evening and another sleepless night, worrying about all this. I'm not sure how much longer I can stand living here."

The sound of her rapid breaths on the phone's mouthpiece reminded Frank of wind blowing across a microphone.

"Laura, listen to me, take a deep breath and calm down. I have good news."

"Really? What?"

"I made some subtle enquiries with a couple of people who worked closely with Malcolm on the Archer/Mendoza case. I asked whether they had any other evidence relating to the attack on the girl, other than her statement and her physical condition. They said Alfred Tucker had taken photographs and left copies at the bank where he was keeping those kids. They were described as 'pretty grim.'

"Oh thank God for that. I'm sorry I don't mean ... you know what happened was awful but-"

"It's okay, I know what you mean. Malcolm was probably just sorting out the case file as he said. He shouldn't have brought them home, but I know others who do the same. They just can't keep on top of the paperwork sometimes, with all the distractions in the office, you know." Laura's breathing eased until she remembered the encrypted files.

"But Frank, what about the file name, did you managed to make any sense of it?" Frank looked around to make sure he was still out of the earshot of colleagues.

"Yep. I don't think you're going to be best pleased but it's something I'm sure a million men are doing as we speak."

"What have you found?"

"I think he's storing pornography." Frank left a pause for it to sink in.

"Oh."

"Laura, can I ask, has he shared any of this with you? Ever wanted to show you pictures?"

"Of course not." She hesitated.

"Actually, a few years ago we did start to watch a programme about 'pornography on the internet.' It was just that there was nothing else on and ... oh anyway... he started asking whether it interested me. He suggested watching a film together. He claimed to know loads of couples who did it. I told him it did nothing for me and changed the channel. Nothing's been mentioned since."

"The file name you gave me was crudely encrypted to cover up its meaning. It's an encryption known to those who worked on another case - I can't go into details. I guess he knew you wouldn't approve and that's why he's been covering it up."

"What did that file name mean Frank?"

"Naked Blonde."

"Oh."

In the silence, Frank pictured Laura looking at her feet, the colour rising to her cheeks. He felt sorry for her.

"Look Laura, to put your mind at rest, why don't you send me through the rest of the filenames. I'll check them and get back to you."

"Okay. Frank, should I ask him about this, this liking he has ... for porn?"

Frank breathed in sharply. "Laura, *I* can't answer that. I don't know. Perhaps think of a strategy to get him to open up. In the meantime, send those file names through."

"I don't think they'll copy and paste. Can I get them off the screen somehow?"

Frank wasn't the best person to ask, but they talked it through, figuring it out together.

"Does he carry a mobile device on which he can pick up emails?"

"Yes"

"Can he get access to your emails?"

"I think so."

"Best send them as a scanned fax then."

She followed Frank's instructions carefully, anxious not to mess up. Malcolm had recently been home by five and it was already ten past four.

"Laura, okay, it's come through. Give me fifteen minutes to decode them and I'll call you back. Okay?"

"Okay, thanks Frank."

Chapter Sixty-Seven

Silence lingered so long that Leanne flinched at Constable Alistair Clough's boisterous entrance. He nodded at them and took his cap off, gripping it under his arm alongside a thick file. He dragged out his chair, further than necessary, with a scraping that set Leanne's teeth on edge. He undid his jacket's lowest button and dropped the thick tan file on the table, as he sat down opposite them. The file slapped as it landed, bulging pages bound by a stained elastic band.

To Leanne, his entrance had been strangely elaborate. She'd expected something more subdued, more businesslike. He was younger than she'd envisaged too. His cheeks were no longer pitted with spots, but their residual scars had not had chance to weather, to retreat.

"I'm Constable Alistair Clough." He freed the file from its bind and perused the first page, "And you are … Miss Leanne Janus, is that correct?"

"That's right. This is my daughter Cassie." He turned to Cassie and smiled, but she was looking down at Katie.

Did he say 'Constable?' Isn't that rank a bit junior, for a murder investigation?

He left the file open, at a mostly blank page, and sat with perfect posture, elbows resting either side of the file, his fingers steepled over the pages.

"I understand you have information relating to the Alfred Tucker case?"

"I wasn't sure what you called it. This is a case involving three murders: Dacia Cartwright, Peter Eccleston and Frankie Archer."

"Four murders," Cassie corrected her.

"Yes Cassie, but we'll get to that."

Clough's eyes left Leanne's and took a brief darting detour towards Cassie, then returned.

"Okay Miss Janus, it sounds like we're talking about the same investigation. What is it you wish to report?"

"What Cassie's alluding to is that whilst you may be sure that Alfred Tucker is solely responsible, others may be involved."

"Miss Janus, we have a written confession confirming he acted alone."

"Didn't write it," Cassie muttered inaudibly. Clough turned his ear towards Cassie, "What was that?"

"Was it a signed confession?" Leanne's enquiry sounded like a challenge.

"You have to understand there's only a certain level of detail I'm permitted to divulge."

"Constable, there are things you need to know."

"Such as?"

Leanne looked at the box, at its dormant red 'on' light. "Shouldn't you be recording this?"

"I am." He pulled a silver parker pen from his inside pocket and smiled as he clicked its end with his thumb.

"I guess you're not going to confirm this, but I heard the teenagers were held in a vault inside a disused bank branch." She looked for signs of agreement or denial. She got neither.

"Go on."

"I worked briefly for a high street bank as a records manager - a grand title for a filing clerk, I know. Whilst I wasn't authorised to access it, we *also* had a vault on the basement level." Her lie was well practiced, in her head at least, and she was pleasantly surprised by how smoothly it flowed. "It had a double locking mechanism. Two people had to unlock and lock the vault simultaneously. If those kids were locked up in there, a person acting alone wouldn't have been capable of doing it."

"Excuse me for being so candid, in front of your child, Miss Janus, but the teenagers were chained inside the vault, there would have been no need to lock it."

"It *was* locked." Cassie raised her eyes to the constable's chest, "Annie was afraid they'd run out of air."

Clough swivelled to face Cassie, leaning in. Leanne shuffled in her chair.

"Okay Cassie ... what makes you think that?" Cassie clammed up, remembering what her mother had advised her.

"The way social media is you can't stop kids hearing things, like you used to be able to, can you? Cassie, honey, let's just tell the constable what we know."

Leanne looked at Cassie, desperate for her to know she still believed her, despite her words. Cassie had a look of indifference, of trust.

Leanne's attention turned back to Clough. "It would be easy enough to check with this girl, Annie, wouldn't it? All you would have to do is to ask if she heard the door locking."

"Miss Janus. *We'll* decide whether there's merit in speaking with the victim again. I'm sure you'll appreciate that she's been through enough already."

"Constable ... Alistair, that's your name isn't it?" He nodded. "We're trying to help here. It's possible there's someone, not in custody, who's a danger to the public."

"Alfred Tucker's DNA was at each crime scene. All other DNA has been accounted for." Clough opened his mouth, then closed it again, as if he'd already revealed more than he'd planned to.

Leanne considered going on, telling him about what Cassie had said about the samples collected from Alfred, but thought better of it. How could they legitimately know that?

The police wanted the case to remain closed and the last thing they wanted was to open up a whole new investigation.

Won't help your statistics, will it, if you have to reopen the case.

Just one more chance, one more roll of the dice, to make them listen.

"I heard that Annie saw an identifying mark, a tattoo, on the wrist of the person who did this. Just check Alfred Tucker, did he have a tattoo?"

"Heard from who, Miss Janus?" For the first time, he looked genuinely interested, scrawling a bullet point on the bottom of the file's cover sheet.

"These things spread quickly, Constable."

He shook his head and clicked off his pen, slipping it inside his jacket. Leanne expected an interrogation about precisely who had told her about the tattoo. She had a convincingly vague story prepared about overhearing mums talking at school. But she didn't have to use it. He closed the file, and repositioned its band. They were done.

"Look … We'll check out what you said. I may have come across as ungrateful for the information and if so, I apologise. It's just that the evidence against Tucker is overwhelming. But leave it with me and thank you for coming in."

Clough left them alone. For a moment, Cassie, Leanne and Katie stared at the black glass opposite them.

"Come on Cassie, let's go."

Chapter Sixty-Eight

Frank worked surreptitiously and at pace. On the desk he had a print out of the faxed screen shot that Laura had taken. A file was placed over it, between glances. On his computer he had Marvin's spreadsheet open. He started typing the first line then recognised it as the one he'd already decoded. He moved onto the second. It was such a simple task, in theory.

His eyes weren't used to reading number and letter combinations. The print quality was poor; a dying ink toner meant vertical lines ran down the page. The characters merged together as he stared at them. He typed methodically, with two fingers.

"y2q4j2o2w6I3o2w6v1w6t3j6w6w6t3
6ft5t5w6I3g4y2v3h4I3I3t5w1t3
t5f6t5w6I3g4y2v36wj2p3
a4j2t3t5y2t3I3w1a4u3pp33h4I3
u7h5w6c4y2p36w
u7j2c4I3w6c4v1t5w7w6j2c4"

He had finished typing the seventh, realising that a quarter of an hour had gone by since he'd spoken to Laura. He decided to run the report, showing the file list so far. The others would have to wait. He pressed the "decrypt" button and another spreadsheet opened up with a list of results. He scanned his eyes down it:

"nakedblonde

abusedseventeen
gaggedfaceddown
gaggedfaceup
hungandwhipped
malerape
murdervoyeur"

He picked up the phone to call Laura, looking around to make sure they could talk discreetly. The phone rang and rang. "Come on Laura pick up the damn phone." Conscious of the content on display, he locked his screen, turning it black. He hung up and tried Laura again. Nothing.

Chapter Sixty-Nine

Laura logged out of Malcolm's account and closed the computer down, convinced that she'd left no trace of her snooping. She paced back and forth across the carpeted study, awaiting Frank's call and repeatedly looking out of the window to catch a glimpse of Malcolm's car, should it come briefly into sight before pulling into the drive. "Come on Frank."

Just remember, like he said, probably nothing. I really don't get men, I really don't. I thought it was just some of the fathers I have to deal with, that it was the nature of my job. But a man like Malcolm, a detective sergeant in the Met, for Christ's sake. What's he doing keeping pictures of women and, worse, hiding them away like some dirty secret. Aren't I enough for him? I always thought, mostly thought (she corrected) that we had a healthy sex life. Why the hell would he need anything else? Oh come on Frank.

Oh shit, the printout!

Realising she hadn't shredded the screen shot, she bent down and began scrabbling clumsily underneath the lid of the scanner. Because of its location on the desk, the lid only lifted a few inches before hitting the shelf above. She slotted her fingers in the thin, wedge-shaped gap under the lid. The screen's static stubbornly clung to the paper, frustrating her fiddling fingers. She tried to get her nails under it.

For God sake Laura, you're making hard work of this. Nearly ... got it.

She moved quickly. The shredder sat on their hip-height filing cabinet, opposite the desk, near the window. She tried to force-feed the paper into the shredder's metal jaws, but it was refusing to eat. Realising it was turned off at the wall, she shook her head, bent over, and flicked the switch.

Slow down and calm down, you're not thinking straight. If he comes back now, he's going to know something's up unless you calm down.

As Laura stood upright she glanced out of the window. Despite the weak light and her limited view, she could see Malcolm's car on the driveway. The orange glow of burgeoning streetlights reflected off beaded raindrops on the car's roof.

The noise of the shredder masked the squeak of the study door's hinges. Half the encrypted file names were still visible as she felt a large gloved hand rest over her mouth and nose. Her head was clamped between this and another hand, which surrounded the back of her skull. Laura heard the squeak of his leather fingers rubbing together as his grip tightened. She tried to scream but the muffled sounds sank into her, filling her lungs with an air that made them ache. She tried to lash out behind, her elbows landing impotent blows. Her arms soon weakened.

In her feeble state she couldn't prevent the painful strike of his shoe's heel on the back of her knees, which brought her to the ground. As she landed on her side, he kept tight hold of her face.

His body mirrored hers as they lay on the carpet like lovers positioning to sleep. As consciousness slipped away her fear was mixed with a sense of familiarity.

"I nearly let you go, you know." In her semi-conscious state, she could decipher neither his words nor their meaning. She became slowly aware of her surroundings. The room was dark and she imagined that the curtains behind her were drawn.

A buzz came from the pocket of Laura's jeans - jeans she was no longer wearing. Her clothes were laid under their desk, in a neatly folded pile.

"Oh ... Laura!" His pitch was high as if mimicking a mother calling her children in for their dinner. "Look at me. Your eyes are wandering all over the place. You're a complete mess. That's better. Focus." And as she did, her muscles strained to escape. Panic had a veracious appetite, devouring sense and rational thought.

In front of her, Malcolm sat in their office chair. He was sitting on it the wrong way, elbows resting on the seat back. He swivelled the chair, one way then the other, playfully. He was wearing his navy uniform and black leather gloves, looking at her intently, displaying a smile she didn't recognise.

Laura was strapped to a dressing table chair he must have dragged through from their bedroom. Her shins were tied independently and tightly with an abundance of silver Duck tape. The wooden struts, designed to maintain the integrity of the chair, each had a belt wrapped round them forming a loop around her naked thighs, keeping them parted. He slid his chair forwards so that it touched hers and reached over, tightening each belt and, in doing so, parted her legs further. Numerous pairs of nylon tights, tied tightly, wedged her mouth wide open. Her head thrashed back and forth in desperate protest.

As his chair twisted, she saw a large transparent bag sitting in his lap. He picked it up, stroking out its creases. Her legs and arms twitched as she strained in a futile attempt to break free.

"It would have been easier to let you go, but that didn't seem like an appropriate end for you. For a minute I thought my first aid skills were escaping me. But then, your lungs kicked in. Amazing really, the body's instinct; entirely lacking logic. Do you think they would have burst back into life, if they'd known? Hmm?" Tears rolled down Laura's cheeks, soaking the nylon which muffled her throaty, squealing screams.

"Don't fret. I'm going to leave you now. But I'll be back soon. You won't see me though, you'll be dead. It's such a shame, you know, that you had to go round asking questions. Always the questions with you. Anyway, I'll be back to dispose of your body and file a missing persons report. Bet you're wondering where I'm going, aren't you? Just tying up another little loose end who couldn't keep her nose out."

He looked down at the bag in his lap. "These are my favourites, the biggest you can get, you know. A person can last about five minutes in these, if they keep calm. You don't seem so calm though. Oh well, the slide show lasts five minutes. You might not see all of it."

He swivelled in the chair and hit the space key on the keyboard. The computer screen was split in two. On the left, the web cam showed a live video image of Laura, bound and naked. On the right, one image dissolved into another, accompanied by the faint music: "You've got a friend in me." The slideshow transitioned with grim flair from one photo to the next: first Annie, then Peter, then Dacia, then others she didn't recognise.

As he loosened the tights that kept her from screaming, Laura closed her eyes and tried to slow her breathing, knowing that the bag would soon be over her head and tied around her throat, exactly as Cassie had warned.

Chapter Seventy

No takeout tonight. Not for us Cassie my love. We're going to be eating mushroom risotto with rocket salad.

Christine had recommended the recipe, saying it was 'delicious and inexpensive.' Leanne had tried not to take offence (*does she think I can't afford to feed my own kid?*) She became grateful that Mrs Hall had gifted her the porcini mushrooms; when she'd shopped for the remaining ingredients, she'd seen how expensive they were.

Leanne stood in the kitchen wearing the plastic apron Cassie used to wear when finger painting. It provided scant protection but she reckoned it was better than nothing. She was following the recipe by the letter, which meant she'd spent much of the afternoon staring at ingredients she'd never used before, all of which were lined up neatly on the work surface.

Leanne's sight had returned, the swelling around her eye having reduced to the size of a marble. She studied the packet of porcini mushrooms, wondering whether she'd read the recipe correctly: *soaking mushrooms in water?!* She was interrupted by a knock at the front door. She put the packet on the side and dipped her hands in the sink's soapy water before shouting out, "Wait a minute."

She dried her hands on the move, with the first tea towel she could find, and opened the door in a fluster. She hadn't followed her usual habit of looking through the living room window to see who it was before answering the door.

That's a good sign, Leanne; you're getting less suspicious, more trusting. You'll make a good mum yet.

Leanne opened the door to a policeman she didn't recognise.

"Miss Leanne Janus?"

"Yes officer?"

"Sergeant. Sergeant Malcolm Robinson. This afternoon you spoke to one of my team, Constable Clough."

"What can I do for you?"

He stood on a cracked concrete step, four inches lower than the hall carpet. Despite this, Leanne craned her neck to look up at him.

"Can I come in?"

"Well," she made a half turn, glancing down the hall, discarding the tea towel on the radiator behind her.

"I'm in the middle of making dinner and-" He moved forward, filling the gap between Leanne and the doorframe. As he brushed past her, she stepped away from the door. She wondered if he felt her glare burn into the back of his head. His pushiness had riled her.

"This is important Miss Janus and concerns the case you and Cassie kindly came to see us about. Is this the living room?" He was already opening the door as he asked the question. He sat down on the sofa bed, uninvited.

Leanne closed the living room door behind them. Cassie had endured enough today without overhearing this.

"Sergeant, we've told the police all we know. Is this going to take long?" He appeared either preoccupied or was deliberately ignoring Leanne's question.

"Is Cassie home? I really need to speak with both of you."

"She is but-" Cassie opened the living room door. Her face was pale and Leanne noticed something she imagined a thousand others would have missed entirely: a small flake of dried blood clung to the corner of her lip.

She's had a seizure and cleaned it up herself.

"Miss Janus, I spoke with Constable Clough after your interview. I'm sorry if my colleague came across as dismissive.

We get a lot of bogus information in such well-publicised cases, as I'm sure you'll appreciate. You'll be pleased to know we're following up on what you told us.

It looks as though someone else *may* have been involved and we need to ask you further questions about the source of your information. We also have some evidence we'd like you to look at. I'd finished for the evening but since I live nearby, I offered to bring the both of you in."

"I understand the importance of this Sergeant, but you could have called me to make sure it was convenient." Folded arms bunched her inadequate apron, below her breasts.

"Miss Janus, I apologise if it's *inconvenient*, but this morning you clearly believed that a murdering rapist was at large."

"Please, Sergeant." She gestured towards Cassie but he completely ignored her hint to be mindful of his words.

"I'm offering you safe escort and it's possible that protection may have to be ongoing. Forgive me if I don't see a delay to your meal as a major concern." Leanne felt anger rising in the pit of her stomach and she was about to instruct Sergeant Robinson to get the hell out of her flat when her thoughts were interrupted by Cassie's voice behind her.

"Mummy, can you get me a drink please?"

That's strange, Cassie always get's her own drinks. Perhaps she's enjoying me being a bit more like Mrs Hall, more attentive.

"Oh sure sweetie. Sergeant, you're going to have to excuse me a minute."

Leanne lifted the Apron off, over her head, as she walked from the living room into the kitchen. Cassie followed, closing the door behind them.

"What can I get you Cassie?"

"I don't want anything, I need to tell you something." Her voice was soft, conspiratorial.

"What is it?"

"I need to whisper." Leanne bent her knees until Cassie could place her mouth right next to her mum's ear. Cassie's hands formed a shallow tunnel to prevent sounds from escaping. "We need to go with him."

"Why Cassie?" was Leanne's hushed response.

"If we refuse and try to escape, he'll trap us in the living room. He'll hold his gloves over your face until you stop breathing. I'll try to pull him off you, but he will be too strong. When you're dead, he'll do the same to me, then pile our bodies on the floor, against the kitchen door, thinking what to do with us next and hoping the neighbours didn't hear me screaming."

The cold, matter of fact, tuneless statement made Leanne think that Cassie was detaching words from their meaning, unable or unwilling to absorb the picture she painted.

Still crouched, Leanne turned to face Cassie, holding onto her shoulders. "Cassie, ... I *do* believe you have a gift ... that you *know* things which are impossible to know. *You* believe that *I* believe, right?"

"Yes, I do."

"Then forgive me for asking this because I have to be certain. How sure are you about this Cassie?"

"More sure than I've ever been." Leanne hung her head. A grave thought jumped at her from nowhere.

"Has he been involved in the murders?"

"I'm really not sure ... maybe."

"Good enough honey. We're going to get through this."

Leanne looked round towards the kitchen window. The left hand pane opened but the gap wouldn't be big enough for them to climb through. Two doors down, the owners of the ground floor flat had installed a back door in their kitchen. Leanne remembered being jealous at the time. She was more jealous now. There was no way out.

Leanne swept her hands over her jean's pockets, not sure what she would do with her phone, but feeling like it was somehow important. Her sweeping stopped; she'd left it on charge in the living room.

Chapter Seventy-One

The bag over Laura's head had misted up, obscuring the instant replay of her own writhing body and the seemingly endless pictures of abuse. Diminishing levels of oxygen increased the tempo of her gasps and induced a state of mind that brought with it a clarity, which surprised her.

You've got one shot at this Laura, if you mess it up, you'll be dead. If he has his way, your body will probably never be found - either that or it'll be washed up on a shore somewhere in months to come. Yes, one chance, that's all. As the air depletes further, the bag will deflate. If you pick the right moment, the right breath, and suck hard enough ... one, two (not this one, the next one) three, go.

Laura sucked so hard that she almost coughed the air straight back up (*hold it, hold it*). She bit down. Her intention had been to trap the plastic between her molars but the bag refused to enter her mouth as far as she wanted and was snared by the canines on the right side of her mouth. She ground her teeth together, refusing to let the plastic go, like a police dog gripping the arm of a suspect. The squeaking of teeth on plastic rung through her head, drowning out the eerie irony of, "You've got a friend in me," which accompanied the macabre slideshow.

It's hard, too thick, you won't get through it.
Don't give up, don't give up.

She widened her jaw's motion, her teeth circling each other with the plastic stubbornly keeping them a fraction of a millimetre apart. Her teeth had always been weak (years of sugary Lattes had caught up with her) and shooting pains ripped up the root of each tooth.

Then the sound changed, from one of squeaking to grinding. *I'm through. Please god, make the hole big enough to get enough air in.* Her teeth released their grip on the bag. Her lungs demanded more oxygen than they were receiving to help her recover from the exertion and she gasped. The bag collapsed, clinging to every part of her head. The small hole she'd created helped only incrementally. She needed a river of air. She was getting a trickle.

If she could have seen past the mist of the bag, Laura would have noticed the patches of blue and purple appearing amongst goosebumps on her thighs. As she drifted into unconsciousness, strange thoughts invaded, the strongest was also the most trivial: I hope my mum doesn't find me like this. Then for the second time that day, she stopped breathing.

Frank was half driving, half staring at Laura's address scribbled on a yellow Post-it note resting on the passenger's seat. He'd been infuriated by the Met's HR department's refusal to release Malcolm's home address. Children's services had been far more accommodating but all the while, he'd been losing time. He started to regret his decision to keep this to himself. Perhaps he could have persuaded the local police to check it out, that might have been quicker.

Would you have persuaded them to break into the house of a detective sergeant, on the back of unanswered phone calls and a list of file names that could have been printed off anyone's computer? Get real, Frank. You made the right call.

For Christ's sake, it must be round here somewhere.

After five minutes of circling, he decided the extra minute it would take to enter the address into his sat nav was a worthwhile investment. He couldn't recall having felt so frantic, dreading that his worst-case scenario would be proved right; Laura was dead or dying. His thick fingers laboured on the touch screen, frequently hitting wrong keys. He took a deep breath.

Go slower to go faster.

It took so long for the route to calculate that he started to think he was in the wrong area of London.

But I was sure it was somewhere near here.

An unfeasibly short suggested route came up. He pressed 'Done.' A voice clearly announced, with Received Pronunciation, 'you have reached your destination on your left'.

He looked up, estimating that the house was about fifty yards away. He snatched at the handle of the car door. He slammed it shut and broke into a sprint, wishing that he'd brought a firearm.

His boots displaced puddles, flicking water up behind him as he ran. In moments like these, he was grateful he'd continued to spend an hour a day on the treadmill. He reached the house quickly and noticed that, in an upstairs window, the curtains were drawn. All the lights were out at the front of the house.

Frank ran down the drive to the back, looking for signs of life. He peered through the kitchen window. The house was in darkness. He banged on the pane. Convinced there would be no response, he looked around for something to help him break in.

Frank noticed a shed, flush to the fence, in the far corner of the garden. A plastic capped outdoor light was screwed to its wall, inches below the pitched felt roof. The weak light helped Frank spot a loose concrete block, upended on the shed's standing, appearing redundant. He ran to it. It was wedged between the shed and a short fence which separated the concrete standing from the lawn. It took all his strength but he managed to dislodge it. He ran with the slab tight to his chest, grunting with the exertion. The double-glazing looked tough, he knew it would take all his effort to break it.

You'll have some explaining to do, if she's okay.

With a throaty, "Aarggh," he thrust the block towards the kitchen window. The concrete shattered the first pane and cracked the second. He had to sidestep the block as it bounced back at him. The boom, which accompanied the sound of breaking glass, was so loud it induced an excruciating, high pitched ringing in his ears. The slab settled on the lawn, like a spinning coin coming to rest. Through the ringing, he could barely hear the disturbed barking of neighbourhood dogs.

He had to regain strength, bending forward with his hands on his knees and breathing hard. He felt a trickle of sweat running down his spine.

Frank lifted the concrete from the damp grass. It was slippery, but he managed to keep hold. He backed up over ten yards and ran again. This time the block shattered the second pane and landed on the kitchen floor.

Triangular juts of broken glass protruded from the seal along the bottom of the frame like shark's teeth and he used his elbow to knock most of them out before climbing through and jumping down from the work surface.

"Laura? LAURA?!" The house was silent, other than the click click click of him turning on light switches and the muffled final bars of: "You've got a friend in me." The whining in his ears quickly diminished and he realised the music was coming from upstairs. The stairs, rising from the living room, had a ninety-degree bend, three steps up. He reached up to the bannister, taking the first three steps in one stride, pulling so hard that a creaking crunch accompanied the structure's flinch. The bannister held, just. An eight-foot crack stretched through white gloss at its base. With five long strides, he was up the stairs, across the landing and outside the study door. Music was fading away behind the door as he swung it open.

No time to assess the situation. Instinct took over. The quickest way to get oxygen to her was to rip open the barely visible puncture in the front of the bag. His hands, though weak from lifting concrete, managed to split and rip the bag enough to lift it over her head. The plastic now surrounded its securing cord, forming a thick collar around her neck. He couldn't afford to lose the time it would take to unstrap her; her skin tone was mostly purple, her lips turning blue.

How long has she been like this? A couple of minutes, maybe more? Have I lost her?

Frank held her nose with his left hand, his palm covering her eyes, and pulled her head back to open her airways. He placed his free hand on the top of her left breast. It was cold, but he detected the faintest of heartbeats. He brought his hand back, under her chin and blew air into her lungs, letting them inflate and deflate half a dozen times.

Can I risk the time it takes to get her out of the chair to give her chest compressions? No. She's strapped with too much Duck tape. He felt her pulse again, it was there but weak. Fading.

He pressed his lips against her mouth and blew. This time, she coughed back a lung-full of air into his face and then gasped another breath. The joy that accompanied seeing her breathe again was quickly outweighed by fear.

Please God, don't let her be brain damaged. If I'd been quicker in finding the house. Please, please God.

Laura's eyes were wide as though her nightmare had been paused and Frank had pressed the play button. She screamed.

"Get me out of here. Get me out of here!"

"It's okay, it's okay," He unbuckled the belts first, trying to make it clear he was looking away as he did so. Laura didn't care whether he was looking or not. Staring death in the face had left her with a radically altered perspective; modesty now wholly irrelevant.

Frank freed her arms. Then they got to work on the thick silver tape restraining her legs. Each time he yanked a length of tape, he looked for a pained grimace on Laura's face. Fine hairs were stripped away as they pulled. Laura didn't react at all; freedom and survival anaesthetised her.

Once she was free, her body fell forward and he laid her down on the floor. She was shivering. The purple, which had virtually covered her, retreated quickly into patches. He ran out of the room, looking for something warm to cover her.

A panicked question, "Where are you going?" crept out of her lips. He was back quickly, with her thick plum towels. He laid them over her legs, middle and chest, a sloppy mummification. Frank sat on the floor next to her, his back against the wall. He breathed rapidly, like an athlete preparing for a post-race interview. His forehead glistened. He wiped across it with the back of his wrist.

Eventually a "Thank you," came from Laura. Frank felt the depth of her appreciation. "You're welcome."

"I need to get you to a hospital. I left my phone in the car, where's yours?"

Laura's look of relief and deep exhaustion gave way to a wide-eyed urgency. She tossed her head one-way and then the other, as though the floor was suddenly covered in scurrying rats. "My phone, Frank. It's in my jeans pocket. There, under the desk. Get it, quickly, please." Frank rooted through the pile and passed Laura her mobile.

"Laura, whatever it is will have to wait. You're in no fit state to-"

She cut across him, not really listening, "I know." She sat upright, propped against her filing cabinet, holding a towel to her front - the others had fallen away. She dialled Leanne's number, "I think I know where he might be." As she waited, listening to the phone ring, she looked up at the computer screen. "Frank, please turn that off." He hadn't even noticed the slide show. "Malcolm?" was all he needed to say.

Laura nodded.

Chapter Seventy-Two

Leanne copied Cassie's hand tunnel, whispering into her ear. "Let's get that drink, we need to act normally."

There was no time to mess on with cordial and water. How long could they take to get a drink, before Robinson became nervous, suspicious? Leanne took out an almost empty bottle of coke from the fridge, and poured it, without ice, into a glass which had only partially drip-dried on the draining board. As she passed the glass to Cassie, she caught sight of the mushrooms on the worktop and an unwelcome question snuck up on her: *will I ever get to find out how they taste?*

"Come on, let's go and speak to the nice Sergeant." Her voice was louder now, perhaps too loud.

She'd left the plastic coke bottle on the work surface. Its middle was squeezed and, as they opened the living room door, the bottle popped out. The '*thonk*' was dull but loud, and Cassie's drink-carrying hand wobbled in fright. Coke sloshed in the glass, but she managed to prevent a spill.

"Sergeant, if you can give me a minute to get my coat, Cassie and I will come with you." Her eyes moved from him, to the electrical socket towards the bottom of the wall, to Robinson's left. Her black bulbous USB charger was in the wall. Its concertinaed cable snaked out across the carpet. Her phone should have been attached to the cable, but wasn't. Instead, the silver male circular charging end looked up at her with its tiny black eye. She couldn't afford to let her gaze linger there.

The landline rang from the hall. Leanne looked at Robinson who looked back, blankly.

Is he going to risk me answering that call? I could ask for help and give them my address before he could stop me, I'm sure.

But that's a big risk Leanne. It wouldn't take long for him to kill us both. I bet he could do it quicker than the police could get there. It would take time for them to dial nine nine nine, give all the details and for someone to be dispatched. And even if he didn't kill us, just acted naive, perplexed by my actions, what evidence do we have that we were ever in danger?

The phone rang for a second time.

Then there's my mobile. I'm certain I left it there on charge.

Certain? Really?

Almost. Shall I confront him, or at least innocently comment, 'I'm sure I left my phone on charge' and gauge his reaction. No ... say the fewest words you can get away with. And answer that damn phone. He's going to wonder why you're hesitating-

"Aren't you going to answer that?"

"Sure."

She walked through to the hall, Cassie followed, Coke in hand. She was sipping, not really drinking. Leanne heard Cassie's soft slurp and another sound, a creak she recognised well: the sound of getting up from her sagging sofa bed. Robinson was following her.

Leanne reached for the ringing phone, which stood proudly in its cradle. The green display showed a number she recognised. As she picked up, she half heard Cassie say she was going to her room to fetch Katie and would be right back. Robinson swayed behind Leanne and she sensed his attention splitting between her and Cassie. She moved the phone to her ear, hiding the display, as Robinson's prying eyes looked over her shoulder.

She capped the receiver's mouthpiece, turning in the direction of Cassie's room, "Sure honey ... "

Chapter Seventy-Three

"Sure honey ... Hello?"

"Leanne, thank God. Is Cassie with you?"

"Uh-huh." Something in Leanne's tone didn't sound natural.

"Is everything alright?"

"Oh, no. Honestly. No, honestly."

Is someone there? Someone she wants to hide this conversation from.

"Leanne, is there a detective sergeant Malcolm Robinson with you?"

"Oh yes, of course, no worries. We'll see you soon. Take care." There was a click and then the sound of the dial tone. Leanne was gone.

"Frank, we've got to get round to Leanne Janus's house, now. Malcolm's there."

"Laura, you're in no fit state. We'll call the police."

"Sorry Frank. Trusting a policeman got me into this mess." She saw the hurt on his face. "I didn't mean it like that. If you dialled nine nine nine now, how quickly would they get there?" Laura sprung naked to her feet, found her panties in the clothes pile and pulled them on. As she dressed, she held onto the desk for balance.

"Laura, slow down, there will probably be complications."

"How long Frank?"

"Where are they?"

"Harrison's Rise."

"By the time they log the call and dispatch. Eight maybe nine minutes."

"I can do it in less than five. You have a fast, unmarked car?"

"Of course."

"We'll do it in four, come on. We'll call your colleagues from the car." His concern for her remained, she could see it in his face.

"Thanks to you, I've got the rest of my life to recover. If we don't get there soon ... well, you know how you found me." He relented and they rushed along the landing in single file. They hurried downstairs, Laura with her arm on his shoulder to maintain balance.

Chapter Seventy-Four

Katie was on Cassie's bed, propped against the pillow next to her folded pyjamas. She grabbed her, squeezing her tightly under her arm. She yanked her bedside drawer open. Aaron's old iPhone was in there somewhere. How could she have been so stupid as to bury it? She pushed aside packs of Loom Bands and lifted up a tray of Hama Beads. The phone had slipped underneath the tray, next to the pack of splayed playing cards, which fanned out of their packet.

Cassie hadn't sent a text before. 'Messages,' that must be it. Then, a pen symbol. Texting was easy, but still not fast enough. She heard his heavy boot-steps nearing, as her finger connected with 'send.' She wished the phone was smaller and thinner like Aaron's new one.

He's sure to notice it in my pocket.

She shoved the phone under the cream sewn-in belt of her jeans. The waist was already pinching, and the cold phone pressed into the scarce flesh of her stomach. He opened the door as Cassie stretched her t-shirt down over her jeans.

"I've got her," she said, holding up Katie, smiling.

Malcolm looked down at her as she pushed past him in the doorway. She didn't look up.

Malcolm's car was an unmarked silver IS200. Leanne knew this, because that's what it said on the back. She didn't know what the L in the silver oval stood for.

"You'll need to get in the back. Here, I'll get the door for you."

His car was parked with two wheels on the curb, Leanne's side of the street. She walked around the far side, so Cassie didn't have to stand on the road to get in. Cassie curled her fingers into the handle's recess, and pulled. The handle snapped back.

"Cassie, it's locked, wait while I get your mum in, and I'll come round and get you in."

Cassie didn't like that. Not one bit.

What if he goes off now, with Mummy, leaving me on the pavement?

Malcolm, standing beside Leanne in the street, bleeped the car to open her door, then bleeped again. Cassie grabbed for the handle. The car had only been unlocked for a fraction of a second. It was too late.

Leanne got in. She felt Malcolm's hand above her head, like she was some cuffed drug dealer. She sat back and reached above her left shoulder for her belt. Malcolm stopped her, gently but assertively, holding her wrist.

"Wait, it's a weird mechanism, everyone struggles with it. I'll get if for you."

Thoughts of how stupidly chivalrous a deranged murderer could be, melted away as he leant across her. His shoulder brushed her chin and she felt every nerve in her skin retreat. The pores across her abdomen tightened to the point of aching.

He walked round the back, and to the curb where Cassie stood. The combination of being strapped, and seeing him move towards her daughter, made Leanne want to run round the car and pull his thick hair out in clumps. Cassie's face, through the car's window, reminded Leanne's of a doll's; eyes wide and glossy, sullen, lost. Cassie placed a hand on the window, faded green and red felt pen lines hashed across her palm from last night's colouring. Katie was in an affectionate headlock under her other arm.

Malcolm let Cassie in. She placed Katie on the floor at her feet. Malcolm went through the same routine with the seatbelt, insisting on strapping it. Cassie pushed her back so far into the upholstery, as Malcolm leant across her, that for a brief moment Leanne couldn't see Cassie's chest beyond the mould of the seat. Malcolm's broad shoulders hid Cassie's face.

The touch of his hand on Cassie's wrist connected a thousand dormant circuits at once. Her eyes drowned in white, before the light drew away, leaving her seeing through Malcolm's eyes. It was a vision so clear that she *was* him, could feel his anger, his passion for the game. For a fraction of a second, feeling like minutes, she was drowned in his being. The memory was so strong, so clear.

There's barely any light - only the glow from his cigarette tip. We're on a track, in a field. He's smoking in front of me, leaning against the car's bonnet. I don't trust him. He said he wanted to help, but there's something he's not telling me.

I'm angry. "Still alive? What do you mean she's, 'still alive,' I thought I told you to clear up?" I snatch the cigarette and stamp it into the ground with the toe of my boot. The ground's wet squelching under my steel toecap. We're in total darkness.

"Hey. That was my last one. Anyway, we've got to let her go. We're not supposed to kill them."

"You useless fuck. They can pinpoint the time of death within plus or minus two hours. We're already outside of that. How the hell are we going to make it look like he killed them, when he's already been dead for hours?"

"Look, they never saw us together, we always covered our faces. They'll still pin it on him. There's no harm in letting her go."

"It would have been cleaner my way. The dead don't talk." The untrusted one looks down and shakes his head. I think he's an idiot, incompetent.

"You know I'm right. Anyway, I guess we don't have much choice now, given that you royally fucked up. One simple task, that's all it was."

I'm reaching down, lifting my overall's leg. The leather sheath is strapped over my thick, hiking sock. A hunting knife. I pull it out and run it over his neck, right to left. The blade should glisten, but the moon is smothered by clouds. His fingers are clutching at his throat, his eyes bulging. His knees hit the mud. He tries to speak - faint gurgling.

He reaches out at me in desperation. I step back, avoiding bloody handprints.

"'We're not supposed to kill them,'" I'm mocking him. "Friggin' foot soldier."

I'm now above a ditch. My boot's pressing against his arm. I'm shaking my head as I watch the body roll. It slaps against the water and semi-submerges.

I shouldn't have let the foot soldier get involved. That was a mistake. I brush dirt from my gloves. Not much time. I have to call the police.

The white light was back and, for a moment, it looked like heaven approaching.

"There you go sweetie, all strapped in."

It was like coming round from seeing Laura being attacked, but worse. Cassie kept her eyes down and to her right, not wanting Mummy or Robinson to see her face.

Malcolm got in the driver's seat and gave Leanne a too-big-to-be-friendly smile through his rear-view mirror. She tried to smile back, her lips clinging to her teeth. He fired up the ignition.

The IS200 lurched lazily off the curve. Katie fell onto her side, Cassie's head rocked gently. She reached down to the well, blindly grasping Katie's head like a claw at a seaside amusement arcade, still averting her eyes. Cassie wedged Katie between her arm and the door, squeezing Katie's hand so tightly, her plastic palm squished flat in Cassie's fist.

Chapter Seventy-Five

Mrs Hall was leaning against her work surface, thumbing through the local paper, when the sound of Aaron's voice and thudding footsteps drew her attention.

"Mum, Mum!" Aaron burst into the kitchen, holding his phone. The door squashed the rubber doorstop and rebounded against his arm. She felt his pain, "Oooh Aaron are you okay? I've told you not to run thr-"

"I've just had the weirdest message from Cassie." He thrust his phone's screen towards her. She held his hand still, looked down and read out loud.

"'In trouble ... track us ... call for help, but not the police'. Aaron, what does she mean, 'Track us?'"

"She must have her phone with her." If that was an attempt at an explanation, it had entirely gone over his mother's head.

"Aaron, you're not making sense."

"Quick, I'll show you." Aaron raced upstairs and Christine followed. He ran into his bedroom and turned his computer on. He hoped he was still logged onto the website. He scrolled through open tab after open tab on his Internet browser. "Yes, it's still open."

"What's still open?"

"The website the phone's linked to. There, look."

He pointed to a green dot about to disappear off the corner of the map.

"That's Cassie."

"But it says Aaron's iPhone"

"I know, I gave my old phone to Cassie."

"You did what? Oh, never mind that n-"

"From her message, she must have it with her. That blue dot, the still one, that's mine." He pointed to the dot which was labelled: 'Aaron's iPhone 5C.'"

"Aaron, I hope this isn't some sort of joke on Cassie's part, because I'm calling the police." She moved towards the door.

"NO," Aaron shouted. He hadn't raised his voice to his mother since he was a toddler. He knew better. She was startled.

"Aaron, if she truly is in trouble, we have to call them."

"NO, NO, NO Mum, if she says not to call them, there'll be a good reason *not to call them*. Trust me, I know Cassie."

"Aaron, I'm going to call Miss Janus and if she's not in, I'll try Mrs Robinson. *They* can decide. If they agree with you Aaron, then fair enough, but if I can't get through to one of them or they agree with me, I'm calling the police and that's all there is to it".

Christine left Aaron, making her way to the living room. She tried Leanne. The phone rang and rang until eventually she gave up.

If Mrs Robinson's phone goes to voicemail, I'm calling the police. Aaron will just have to live with it.

Chapter Seventy-Six

Cassie and her mum tightly held hands in the back seat, both guessing each other's thoughts.

Where is he taking us? Will we both survive?

Leanne clocked how slowly, cautiously he was driving.

He doesn't want his car to be noticed, he's not supposed to be on duty.

As Leanne attempted to memorise their route, she noted their turn, Westbound on the A232 rather than Eastbound towards the A236, which would have been the last semi-direct route into London.

We're heading out of the city, best show some surprise. He'll be expecting that.

"Aren't we heading in the wrong direction, for Scotland yard?"

"The evidence I'm taking you to verify isn't at Scotland yard. It's at the location where Tucker was holding Miss Mendoza."

"Oh."

With everything I bet you've done, I expected a more convincing lie than that, you sick bastard!

Six foot three and, what, eighteen stone? I don't give a damn how big you are. God help me I'll gouge your eyeballs from their sockets before you can lay one finger on Cassie.

I'm not going down without a fight.

Can't let him take us out of the city.

Frank got to Leanne's front door moments before Laura. It was unlocked. They let themselves inside, moving along the hall. Frank checked Cassie's bedroom as Laura searched the living room. Their overlapping cries echoed through the flat, "Miss Janus! Cassie!" No response.

"Frank, we're too late. Shit. What now?"

"We radio this in and see if we can get a helicopter to sweep the area."

"That's *it*, isn't it? They're gone. If I'd just listened to Cassie. I *knew* she was right and I killed every instinct to believe in my marriage. Idiot. Now it's too late." Frank turned to face her and took hold of her shoulders. "Laura, for God's sake, let's not waste time beating ourselves up." He ran out to the car. She followed.

Laura almost sat on her phone; it was buzzing away on the passenger seat of Frank's car.

Must have fallen out of my pocket.

Laura answered the call whilst Frank unclipped the radio receiver from the dashboard. She pressed her spare hand against her right ear to block out the noise of Frank's urgent voice which dominated the confined space.

"Hello."

"It's Christine Hall. Thank God you answered. I really don't know what to do."

"Christine, slow down. What is it?"

"I wondered whether it was a joke, but Aaron's adamant. We think Cassie's in trouble."

"What, how, how do you know?"

"She sent Aaron a really short text asking for us to track her, using her phone. Aaron's doing it, I don't really understand how, but she also said not to call the police and I was about to. But I wanted to speak to you. Should I call them?"

"No, Christine, it's alright, we already have. We're at Leanne's. No one's here."

"That's because they're on the move."

"Can you locate them?"

"I think so … "

Christine ran upstairs with the phone to her ear. She was out of breath by the time she got to Aaron's room and found it hard to speak.

"… they're on … on the A237 …. heading north."

"Stay on the line."

"Mum, put it on speaker phone so I can talk to them as well."

"How do-" He grabbed the phone from her, "Aaron!"

"There." He placed it on the table and they could hear Frank in the background talking to the police and Laura trying to get his attention.

"Frank, I know where they are, put down the radio and drive."

Chapter Seventy-Seven

Cassie was trying to be brave. The worst now was not knowing what would happen.

Should I try to go under again? No.

The situation was volatile, she couldn't risk slipping into unconsciousness, not now, her mother needed her.

Cassie had never felt fear like it, not when Rachel had chased her, not when she'd been run over. Even the visions of what this man *(men?)* did to those people could not compare to this cold, gripping terror. She squeezed her mother's hand even tighter.

Leanne saw the fear in Cassie's face and leant over to put an arm around her shoulders. She expected her seatbelt to stretch as she did so but instead it came loose. The belt's housing had completely come away, both from under her seat and from behind her left shoulder. Leanne looked down at it, draped over her arms like a dead snake.

"What the ... ?" She saw a glimpse of his cold smile in the rear-view mirror.

"So I guess the cat's out of the bag, now you've found my insurance."

Leanne examined the seatbelt. The bolts were missing from the housing. She thought back to the way he had insisted on helping them get strapped in. Leanne reached over to Cassie's seatbelt. Hers was the same, the tension holding for now but liable to come loose in an instant.

"You bastard. Stop the car. It's not safe."

"Actually, it's perfectly safe, because we're not going to crash. If I get a hint that either of you are trying to escape, I'll slam on the brakes and, presuming her little body travels faster than yours, the last thing you'll see is your daughter slamming into the back of my seat, or as likely, through the front windscreen. So my advice would be to sit tight and behave yourselves. Oh, and if we have to stop, don't bother trying the doors. The child locks are on."

Leanne pressed her back into her seat. As much as she fought them, graphic scenarios of what he might do to them crowded out constructive thought.

Yet predicting their fate wasn't the worst part. What ate at Leanne the most, what caused that nauseous uncontrollable scraping at the pit of her stomach, was the control he had over them; their fate entirely his to decide. The taut fingers of her free hand gripped her scrawny thigh, above the knee. The tendons on her lower arm tightened.

Think. Christ Leanne think! Never mind what he might do, what are you *going to do to get both of you out of this*?

No plan came to her. She leant over and whispered to Cassie, "Have you any idea what will happen now?"

"Sorry Mummy. I don't."

Chapter Seventy-Eight

The siren of Frank's car wailed as they screeched through suburbia, swerving past cars whose windows reflected blue flashing lights.

Laura conveyed Cassie's location to Frank, from the description Mrs Hall phoned through. Frank relayed these over the radio to the controller who was coordinating the police response. They repeated this pattern as they drove. Laura eventually put Mrs Hall on speaker, holding the phone up to the radio, allowing Frank to focus on driving.

He broke every speed limit, manoeuvring through red lights, desperate to gain ground. Laura covered her eyes as Frank swerved towards oncoming traffic, to avoid clipping an open-backed lorry in front of them.

They had started out six miles behind. Within eight minutes they'd closed the gap to less than two miles.

Malcolm slowed towards a red light at a major crossroads: the A237 was crossing the B271. Leanne looked out front, at cars passing along the well-lit B-road. They were briefly illuminated; blurred impressions of normal people, heading home from work no doubt.

Perhaps I can get someone's attention, whilst we're under these lights.

Once through the crossroads, the streetlights would become sporadic. Leanne imagined roads becoming increasingly rural as they drove - they would finally hit one that was pitch black.

She envisaged the glaring reflection of cat's eyes in the darkness of the night, of being barely able to see Cassie beside her.

I've got to act now, whilst we're in the light. I must be able to signal to someone that we're in trouble.

A white van approached from behind. She could make out discarded newspapers in its window, wedged behind the dashboard. She let go of Cassie's hand and placed her palms on the back windscreen, getting ready to mouth, "Help." But the driver appeared to be looking at his knees or, more likely, his phone and didn't see her.

She heard Malcolm chuckling. The lights had turned green. She sat facing forwards again, catching his gaze in the rear view mirror. She fixed her eyes on his, raised a fist and flicked out her middle finger. He looked away, eyes back on the road.

Leanne thought about Cassie's premonition of him suffocating them. Anger rose in her again, uncontrollably.

Not going to be a victim anymore, not going to, not going to, NOT going to.

Leanne felt around her to see if the lap-belt in the middle of the back seat had been tampered with. She tugged at it, eyes fixed forward to avoid suspicion.

This is my chance. He's not *going to take us. I would sooner die here than have him kill the both of us, dumping our bodies in a ditch somewhere.*

She reached over Cassie's legs and in a single, well-timed movement, leaned forward, sliding Cassie's light frame underneath hers and clicking the seatbelt into place.

"What are you d-"

Malcolm didn't get the chance to finish his sentence. By the time he realised what was happening, Leanne was standing almost upright in the back seat. Her neck was bent, the side of her head pressed against the clear plastic of the car's interior light. She'd folded her long spindly arms around both his head and the headrest, clamping them together. Not leaving enough time to contemplate how disgusting it would feel, she pushed her thumbnails into his eyes, bisecting his corneas.

"Mummy, nooooo!"

Malcolm let out a guttural, ear-splitting scream, the sound of battlefield surgery. He had a reflexive reaction, a visceral spasm down his side, making his leg extend against the accelerator.

No matter what happens to this car or what he does to hurt me I'm going to squeeze tighter and tighter. I'm going to hold on, no matter what. I won't be happy until I sink my nails through the back of his skull. You won't touch my daughter, you won't touch her.

The safe distance Malcolm had maintained, between his car and the Ford Mondeo ahead, shrank rapidly. Cassie was the only one to notice, she closed her eyes, gripping the lap belt with tight fists.

Malcolm reached up, trying to pull Leanne's thumbs from his eye sockets. They were too embedded so he grabbed her smallest fingers, one with each hand. His powerful arms and wrists made quick work of snapping them from their sockets. The pain tore through Leanne's forearms but she held tight and screamed in his ear.

"Aaaargh, you sick son of a bitch. Break everyone of them and I'll still have hold." His foot was now off the accelerator, but the road in front had a gradual downward incline, maintaining their speed. They were travelling at fifty miles-per-hour.

The unmanned steering turned fractionally, to and fro, as though a ghost was holding the car on a straight course, until a manhole cover interfered with the alignment of the wheels and a small turn quickly grew into a spin. The back of the car slid round, overtaking the front, narrowly missing the back of the Mondeo. They bounced through the central reservation into two lanes of oncoming traffic. The wave of cars parted, peeling to the side, one after the other. Cassie let go of the belt and put her hands over her ears, wishing she could block out the noise of squealing, juddering tyres.

Cassie whispered a frantic prayer. "Please God, save us, please God, please God."

It was the back of Malcolm's car hitting the grill of an oncoming lorry, which finally released Leanne's arms from around Malcolm's head.

She hit the rear windscreen, shattering sufficient glass, and pushing enough of the rubber seal away from the metal frame, for momentum to carry her body through the window. Leanne briefly came to rest on the boot, before the car's final motion caused her to slip from the metallic surface. She landed face down on the concrete of the narrow hard shoulder.

The sound of approaching police sirens accompanied distant shouting. The impact had jarred Cassie's head and neck and she briefly lost touch with the world before regaining consciousness. A strong smell flooded the car. It was a smell Cassie didn't recognise, the smell of diesel.

Through the gap in the headrest, she saw his neck moving. She heard wiry hairs bristle against the headrest's upholstery. *His seatbelt saved him too.*

I've got time before he comes round. I can hear people coming. I'll be safe. What if the other policemen are like him?

Don't be stupid Cassie, just get out of the car.

In that instant it came back to her - Mummy had been thrown from the car. She turned and knelt on the seat. She looked towards the parcel shelf, covered in fragments of glass, and a few feet beyond, to the enormous steaming chrome grill of the stationary lorry.

Where's Mummy now? Is she alive? Got to get out.

Cassie unclipped her seatbelt, pushing past Katie's head to try the door. Robinson hadn't lied - it was locked. She shuffled over to the other side, becoming aware that he was making weak, 'Uhhhh,' noises.

He's waking up.

She tugged on the other door handle, locked as well.

If I sit tight the police are sure to get to me in time, aren't they?

"Cassie? You there Cassie?"

She sat in silence, frozen in fear, trying to breathe quietly.

Malcolm reached to his left, unclipped his belt and turned, looking into the back seat with unseeing eyes. His body was wedged sideways between the front seats. He groped out blindly towards Cassie.

"Look what your bitch-mother did to me."

She tried to be quiet, tried to contain it, "Leave me and Mummy alone."

Wait, if Mummy was forced through the back window, I must be able to climb through. It's my only way out.

Cassie scrambled up the back seat, reaching out to the frame of the rear window. Fragments of glass, still stuck in the window's seal, cut into her hands and she cried out but preserved her grip. He got lucky and took hold of her left ankle. He was so focussed on getting to Cassie, he was unaware of the driver's door opening.

"Let me go, let me go." Her thin legs lashed out but his grip was too tight. She felt her left Reebok, sliding off her heel.

"Can't do that kid. You know too much."

"As do *you*." The words came from behind her, in a voice she didn't recognise and, as if to offer a full stop to his sentence, a shot rang out. A deafening crack reverberated around the car and Cassie saw something red, spraying to her right. The blood and sinew clung, then slid down the window the way red wine grips the inside of a glass.

Cassie felt Malcolm's grip on her ankle disappear. Without hesitation, she continued her scrambled climb, leaving her trainer behind, in Malcolm's lifeless hand. She glanced over her shoulder towards Katie, who lay in the footwell. Perhaps it had been the impact of the crash - both Katie's eyes were fully open. Blood speckled her face.

Fleeting thoughts of turning round, to collect Katie, were broken by a man's voice. Her instant reaction was to recoil.

"Cassie, it's okay. It's me, Frank, remember? I'm with Laura."

A man in a navy uniform took her by her wrist. Cassie recognised him and decided to trust him. He pulled her sideways from the car boot's polished surface. The toe of her Reebok became caught in the grill of the lorry. Frank grabbed it, pulling her foot free and helping her to the ground.

Frank watched the officer who'd fired, ushering people away from the scene. He was shouting, "If you're not with the fire service you have to get back, GET BACK!" Frank tried to lead Cassie safely away from the pileup but she turned round, looking for her mother.

Leanne lay facedown on the ground, her arms angled awkwardly behind her back. Her jeans had been half torn off by the impact; empty denim belt loops lined the tops of her thighs. Her head rested, motionless, in a growing pool of blood. Beyond her, a policeman walked quickly away, urging people to retreat in the same direction. Drivers with various injuries, incurred from veering off the road, had managed to get free from their cars and were following his instructions, some stumbling, some running from the scene.

"Mummy!" She changed direction, trying to pull away from Frank, but he had good hold of her arm. "Cassie!" She appeared not to hear him, so he shouted, "Cassie, firefighters need to stabilise the car so paramedics can help your mum. We need to get a safe distance." He placed one arm around her shoulders, the other gripping Cassie's upper arm. With effort, he dragged her further away.

She yelled back, seeming to have no control or understanding of her own volume, "Why?"

"We just do." They weren't making fast enough progress. Frank stopped, swooped to bear hug her thighs, executing a fireman's lift. With Cassie over his shoulder, he ran towards Laura. She was standing next to Frank's car, rocking as if itching to move towards them.

Frank and Cassie were thirty yards or so from Laura when the explosion came. It started at the front of the lorry,

313

triggering a second fireball in the underbelly of the car, spinning it like a tossed coin into the air. The crunch as the car landed on its roof was mostly drowned out by shrieks and a symphony of scattering glass. Cassie, dangling limply over Frank's shoulders, couldn't see the explosion. Her partial deafness made the series of thunderous booms sound distant.

And yet she knew in that moment - her mother was gone.

Chapter Seventy-Nine

One week later.

"Cassie, it'll be okay." Laura took hold of Cassie's hand but it was a while before she felt her squeeze returned.

Cassie couldn't help but repeatedly lean towards the centre of the back seat, getting a better view of the hearse in front. On her mother's walnut coffin sat one small white, circular wreath of calla lilies. Cassie kept thinking, for what she did, it's not enough. Nowhere near enough.

Laura was unsure whether to encourage Cassie to talk about her feelings or to raise a different subject, to distract her. She couldn't imagine how hard this must be for Cassie. It was different for Laura; Laura's mother was still alive. She was old, cantankerous, infuriating at times but still alive.

I've got to appreciate her whilst she's here.

"Cassie, how has it been at Aaron's?"

"Fine. I don't think his mum quite knows what to say. But you know Aaron, he never shuts up." Cassie turned and feigned a smile at Laura, squeezing her hand again.

Oh my God, she's so brave, so ... so brave. Miss April was right, 'a special kid.' She tried to save my life and I didn't even listen. I'm going to protect this child for the rest of my life.

Cassie kept tight hold of Laura's hand for the entire service. As the minister spoke, Laura glanced around the room. She counted eight people there: herself, Cassie, Frank, Aaron,

Aaron's parents, Leanne's mother and father (who, for now, were speaking again - to each other, they'd barely said a word to Cassie). The thought of how Leanne's life had ended and how undervalued she'd been, tugged at Laura's heart. Hesitant tears pooled in the corner of her eyes, then spilled as she searched her bag for tissues.

Stop it Laura, be strong for Cassie.

She couldn't help it. In that moment Laura made a decision that would shape the rest of her life.

I'm going to quit my job. With my widow's pension and savings I'll have enough. I'll move to a smaller place if I have to. I'll only need two bedrooms. One for me and one for Cassie.

Chapter Eighty

He sat back in his leather chair, swivelling. There was a stress ball in his right hand and he kneaded it absentmindedly, waiting for the call.

He said he would call at two p.m.. He better not start with me, we did everything we could.

Eventually the phone rang. It was the man running the switchboard. "Yes Robert?"

"Chief Inspector Regan. I have a call on line one from Governor Pentine."

"Put him through." He heard a connecting click and then a familiar voice.

"David, is the line secure?"

"Yes, we can talk freely."

"Good. I wanted us to have a conversation about the recent incident."

"Okay ... what do you want to know?"

"My understanding is that Robinson had been an affiliate for years."

"Five years, Governor."

"Then how did it get to this, David? Do we need to look at vetting again?"

"No, I don't think so."

"I wish I shared your optimism. It strikes me that we need to tighten the circle for a while as we weed out those who can't follow the rules."

"I don't think that's necessary,"

"Well let's examine this. Remind me, what *are* the three rules?"

"You know, I know them Governor."

"Rule one?"

"Okay." He attempted to keep his agitation in check, "We don't kill them."

"Correct. I would say he failed miserably in that regard, wouldn't you?"

"Yes, but we dealt with it."

"Rule two?"

It was senseless protesting anymore, "Anonymity always."

"Precisely. I heard he even targeted his wife."

"That's true. But nobody could have foreseen-"

"His WIFE David."

"I know. We had to take action and we did: decisive action."

"Well, we'll examine that in a moment. Rule three?"

"Keep files secure."

"Meaning?"

"Not stored on laptops, desktops and above all, never shared via the internet."

"So did he manage to stick to that rule?"

"We believe so, apart from leaving a hard drive attached to the computer at the house, but we took care of that. We destroyed it and corrupted the drive of his desktop, beyond repair."

"Okay. Look, I'll be straight with you David. Some of the other cell leaders are starting to doubt you have sufficient control over your people. Several of them went to great lengths to get Adams out, to help you tighten the reins on Robinson. He was one of their best affiliates, a man who took precautions-"

"Must have slipped up to have got caught."

"David, never interrupt me. Adams always followed the rules and above all, always stayed loyal and discreet. They're saying you offered him insufficient protection. Should I disagree with them?"

"Look, until three months ago, Robinson was a model affiliate, he supplied more than his fair share of images and was entirely discreet and yes he *did* stick to the rules. Something changed within him. Perhaps it just wasn't enough for him anymore. I really don't know. But I raised a flag the second I realised he was a loose cannon. I was assured that Adams was the man to rectify the situation, but when that didn't work out-"

"Work out? Robinson killed him!"

"Precisely. When Adams failed to control the situation I mobilised the cell and they took care of it. So do thank the other leaders for their support but, whilst I admit we lost control for a while, ultimately I resolved the situation"

"Convince me."

"The case has remained closed. As far as Robinson's wife's concerned, he acted alone and has paid with his life. She doesn't want to open all this up again, to save the reputation of an ex-convict. Tucker is still guilty in the media's eye. The only surviving witness is Annie Mendoza and Robinson altered her statement before he died, so Adams can't be linked in any way. All images have been recovered or destroyed. As you can see, I've made sure there are no loose ends."

"I can see a very, 'loose end' in what you describe, David. One that certainly needs to be tied up."

"I don't follow."

"Annie Mendoza."

About the Author

Peter Dudgeon started writing short stories at the age of fourteen, inspired Stephen King's early novels. He became an English Language and Literature graduate at the age of twenty-two and has since travelled the length and breadth of the UK (occasionally beyond) as a management consultant. He lives in North East Lincolnshire, with his wife, two daughters and a troublesome Labrador. 'Chance' is his second novel.

The sequel to Chance, 'Circle - The Diary of Stella Moore' is available on Amazon Kindle: http://amzn.to/1RIbALH

Circle - The Diary of Stella Moore

"Is he sharing more than your bed?"

It's 2021. A sadistic criminal web has spread across powerful institutions, filling a void created by society's apathy towards sexual violence.

Cassie Janus has grown up away from London, safely shielded from this malevolent force until Detective Sergeant Frank Simmons visits her in desperate need of her help.

What starts out as a missing persons case quickly morphs into a battle against evil in which Cassie will need to employ more than just her precognitive powers. It will demand all her courage and wisdom if she's to survive a war waged against the Circle.

'Circle' is the sequel to 'Chance', picking up the story of Cassie Janus, seven years later.

Peter would love to hear from you:
Website: peterdudgeon.com
Twitter: @PDudgeonnovels

Other titles by Peter Dudgeon:

Ticket

You're tired, lonely, living a corporate life on the road when you meet a vulnerable young woman in need of your help. She wants to repay your kindness with money and more. When your chance romantic encounter leads to her death, do you stay to face the music, or flee to face your past?

"This book brings together a diverse collection of convincingly crafted characters, in an intriguing race for the truth in a story about dark deeds. I had to keep reading it until I got to the final page just to satisfy my curiosity. Loved it." Amazon Reader.

http://bookShow.me/B00G1Q8N24

16042188R00178

Printed in Great Britain
by Amazon